Chasing the River

Sidney Edgar Giraud

DWITBANG BOOKS

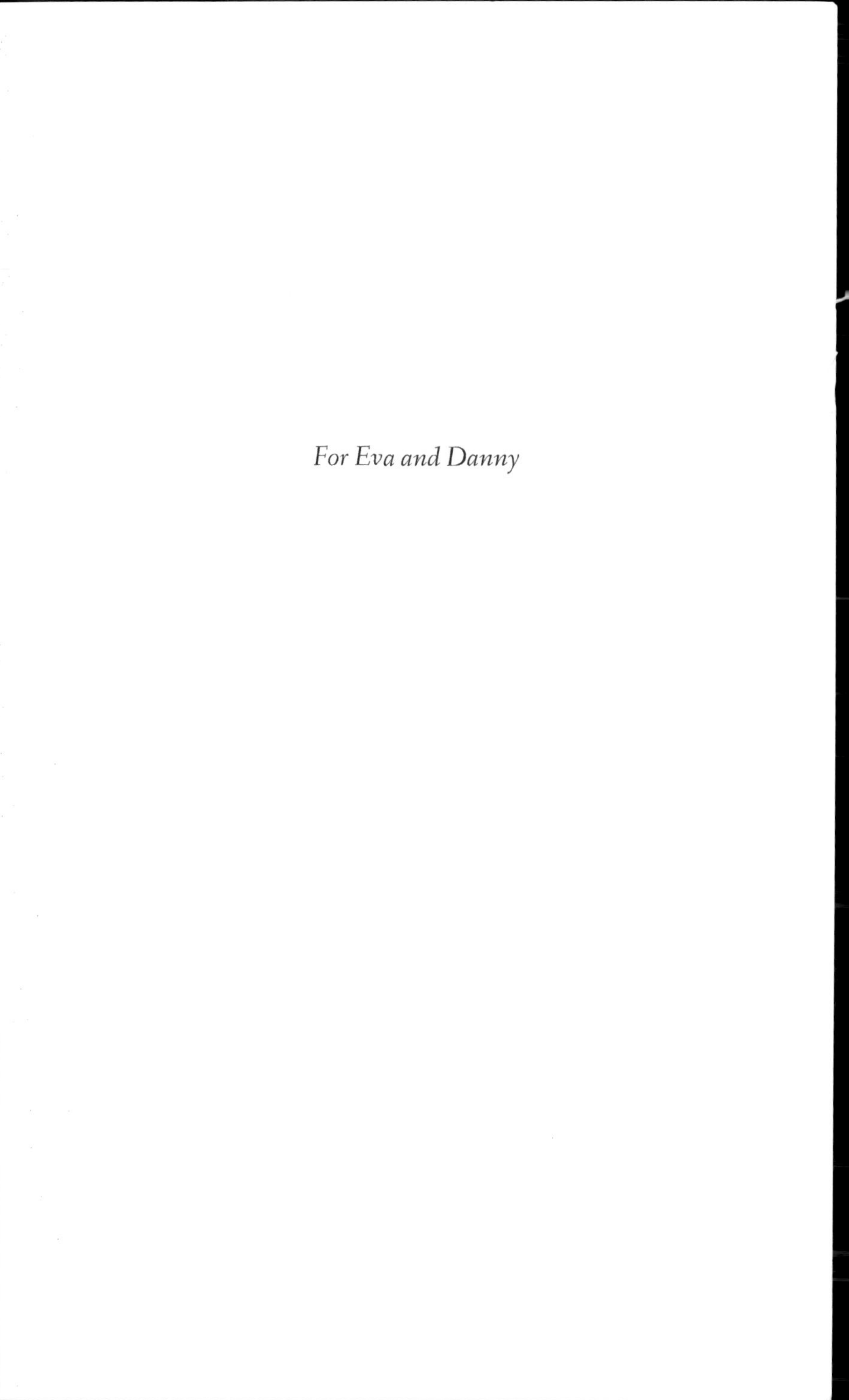

For Eva and Danny

Chapter 1

Danger

"Stay here."

"No!"

"Don't you hear me? Stay here."

"No! I'm going out."

She grabbed his shoulder. Spoke rapidly. "At the market ... they were telling ... militia are moving this way from the north. We have to ..."

"Let me go!"

"Listen to me! We have to move from here ... stay out of trouble."

"No!"

"Yes," she hissed impatiently. "They have many guns. Their trucks can move fast and they're taking hostages."

Oby stared into his mother's face. She patted his cheek and gave a small smile, but he saw it was not real.

Chapter 2

Trek

Oby unknotted his thin sleeping rug from around his middle and spread it on the ground, then gently placed the floppy baby in the middle and folded it. Then he swung the blanket onto his back and trudged along in the middle of the road.

The pup at his side began to limp. It stumbled and its nose hit the ground. Blood trickled from its mouth, so he decided to leave the pup behind. He walked faster.

The pup whimpered.

Oby put his hands over his ears and kept going.

Then glanced back.

The pup tried to get up. Its legs wobbled and gave way.

Oby scratched his ear. Walked back. Picked up the pup and placed it over his shoulder.

The wind had stopped breathing.

The road was baking in eerie silence.

Although the crumbling dirt road that twisted through the rolling hills of Triathia was almost as familiar to Oby as his own hand, it wasn't the same as usual. There was no one on it, except him. There was none of the usual dust rising from the daily tramp of salt workers' feet. There were no songs or jokes filling the air.

Oby glanced around nervously. A sharp crack ripped across the silence. He ducked down. He heard slashing and slicing through the scrub, getting nearer and nearer. He had nothing to defend himself with. Absolutely nothing. His heart thumped as though trying to get out of his chest.

All of a sudden, four spears rose through the air towards him. Oby froze. Two terrified gazelles with towering horns leapt across the path.

Then, stone silence again.

The early morning sun was rising over the peaks of the distant Chagat Hills. Any night moisture on the scrub had already been licked up by lizards. It would take him another hour to reach the Salt Lake.

Already, the sun was trying to drill lasers through his curls. At least he still had them. He had been quick on his feet the day his interfering uncle had stood in the doorway, staring with bloodshot eyes.

"Come here, scruffy boy."

"No!"

A hand came out to grab him, but Oby had seen the rusty, ancient blade snipping and snapping towards him. He ducked and was away, just in time. He liked his tousled hair. He was going to keep it.

The baby and pup were slowing Oby down. He had to leave one of them behind. Which one?

His eyes were already stinging and his thoughts floated and tangled in the rough roadside scrub; his feet dragged like irons and his legs began to shake uncontrollably. Neither foot would move forward. He leant against an acacia tree, his head a thumping war drum.

Oby lowered the baby and pup to the ground, then himself. The pup's tongue was dangling sideways out of its cracked mouth. He pulled the pup towards him and the quaking creature sank its head onto his empty stomach – a stomach which protruded like a football on his skinny frame.

Tears pricked his eyes, but through them he saw a flash. A red flash.

"Maaaa!"

His mother's red dress was disappearing into the bush. At last, he had found her. He leapt up, flipping the pup aside. He ran screaming into the bush. "Maaaaaaaaaaa!" His eyes blurred and he blinked furiously. He chased nothing. His eyes were playing tricks.

Just scrubland.

Oby shuffled back to the acacia and thumped it hard with both fists, but it didn't make his aching chest feel any better. He thumped it again and again, trying to drive his tears to other parts of his body. Slumping to the ground, his fingers drizzled through the dry earth. He clenched his teeth tightly. Each breath squeaked like an old donkey. Oby struggled to his feet again and swung the baby onto his back. The pup tried to get up, but its legs folded.

Oby closed his eyes. Should he kill it?

Yes.

No.

The pup's forlorn eyes fixed on him.

Oby groaned, picked up the pup again and held it next to his chest.

Walking was easier when he kept up a rhythmical pace. He softly sang a counting song the herdsmen used as they moved their animals to fresh pastures. His head rolling from side to side, Oby's thoughts were as stiff as dried leather.

When he next glanced up, a distant white plain was glistening back at him. The Salt Lake. As it danced in the heat, Oby kept his eyes glued on the vision, for fear it wasn't real and might disappear.

Chapter 3

The Wife Of Moussa Khaliffa

The ugly, misshapen hut of Moussa Khaliffa perched like a mouse on a pin, precariously, at the edge of the Salt Lake, on a peninsula of black rock.

Oby left the road and twisted along the path that led straight to the hut. Sitting in the doorway he could see the wife of Moussa Khaliffa. As he drew nearer, he could hear singing and see her rocking her baby back and forth. She didn't look up, but her singing abruptly ended.

Oby didn't go too near. "Where's Moussa Khaliffa?"

"Out on the salt," she bellowed. "Where do you think?"

"When's he back?"

"Why d'you want him?" Moussa Khaliffa's wife half-turned her head and scowled suspiciously.

Oby shuffled on the spot, his head spinning. *Is she going to hit me? I'll go nearer but not too far. She might hit me if I go any nearer ... got to speak to Moussa Khaliffa ... can't go back ... she's bound to hit me if I'm not careful.*

He edged forward.

The wife of Moussa Khaliffa soared to her feet, blocking

the small doorway, raising her arm in a warning for him to stay back.

Oby halted.

Still rocking her baby in one arm, she began wrapping her black scarf more firmly round her head with the other. Her long, loose, black dress battered against her in the stiff breeze and showed up her fat belly. Her attire was blacker than the rocks on which her hut stood.

She bellowed, "Where're all the men from your village this morning? Moussa Khaliffa was fed up with waiting. He's mad. There's no one to load the camels."

"They were all ..."

"Did they spend the night drinking kupti and smoking those foul-smelling pipes? Is that it? I bet it is." She asked and answered all her own questions. "The men from your village are all the same, aren't they? Drunken layabouts!"

Her words flew in a mish-mash around Oby's head. He continued staring blankly ahead.

"Are you listening? Just look at your filthy, skinny self." She flapped her hand dismissively.

Oby turned away. Her noise was getting louder. Every blazing word was ripping his small spirit away.

A weak cry emanated from the bundle on his back.

"Stop, boy! Stop right there! What are you hiding?" The wife of Moussa Khaliffa lumbered forward. Her big shadow completely covered him. She peered inside the bundle. She yanked the sleeping rug away. "What are you doing with this baby? It's sick."

He muttered, "I found ..."

The wife of Moussa Khaliffa held up the unresponsive baby with one hand. "Found?" She sniffed it, tried to detect any breathing, turned it this way and that, then hissed, "Whose baby did you steal?"

His chin was now on his chest. "... this morning ..."

She screeched, "Stop mumbling! I can't hear!"

He took a deep breath. "The baby... and ... and me ... the only ones left ..."

She craned her neck forward to catch his fading words. "Left from what?" The wife of Moussa Khaliffa glowered, with her head tilted sideways, preparing herself to hear an elaborate story, a concoction of excuses, a pack of lies.

"Killers came from the north ..." His voice faded away and the muscles on his face pinched into his nose.

"Killers!" The wife of Moussa Khaliffa stiffened and she ran her eyes over Oby's face, trying to read the story there. "Killers, did you say?"

He nodded. A tear trickled.

"From the north?"

He nodded again.

"Killers!" She hissed in anger. "They came."

Tears flowed down Oby's thin cheeks.

The wife of Moussa Khaliffa rolled back to her hut and placed both the babies inside on a mat.

She returned to Oby, her face softer. She lifted her fat fingers towards his cheeks, then gently picked at the blobs of dried blood that sat there; she spat on her fingers and rubbed at his grubby tear stains. Then steered him towards the hut. She shoved him down firmly onto a soft mat at the entrance, where there was shade.

She was gentle. "What's your name, boy?"

"Oby."

She bustled about and returned with a pail of water, dropped a tin on the ground and poured water into it for the pup; then pushed a plastic bowl into Oby's hands and filled it to the brim. "Drink plenty."

Then she disappeared into the back of her hut, unbuttoned her black dress and fussed and fed the weak baby on her own milk, until it slept.

With her own baby on her shoulder, she then prepared herself to listen. "Speak, Oby," she urged. "You must tell me what happened."

Chapter 4

Raiders

Oby spoke of how he had laid low on the roof of their hut, gripped with fear. He told of crying and screaming that had gone on all night. He said that in the morning everyone had disappeared. There were bodies everywhere. His mother had gone. His brother and sister had gone.

The wife of Moussa Khaliffa had fat lips, but she was pressing them so tightly together as Oby struggled to relay events to her that she seemed to have eaten them. She, too, began to quake and her breath came in short gasps as the story unfolded. "Poor boy. Poor boy," she murmured, stroking his arm.

But she still managed to keep her wits about her and began to bustle about. She gave Oby camel's milk and maize-meal porridge. He couldn't swallow easily, though, and shared it with the pup.

She told him to rest and fashioned a bed for him in the shade outside the hut, on a heap of soft, stinking sheepskins. As he lay there, he could hear her pounding corn and clattering tins. Her noises and the beat of her pestle were steady.

Oby closed his eyes but ugly images spiked his sleep.

* * *

Screeeeeeeeeeeeeeeeeee. Screeeeeeeeeeeeeeeeeeeeeeeeeeeeee.

Oby jerked. His eyes flew open.

He wiped the sweat off his forehead with the ragged corner of his sleeping rug and stayed on his back, staring at the night sky. His heart was faster than a hummingbird's wings. Maybe it was because he was excited about getting ready to travel south tomorrow.

A pebble from his collection rolled away from him, down the sloping corrugated-tin roof. Oby snatched at it but it dribbled faster, out of reach, to the ground. He slumped back onto his sleeping rug, trying to get comfortable. He had to be careful or he would roll off the roof and add to the bruises from two days ago.

Shreeeeeeeeeeeeeeeeeeeeeeeeeeek.

An electric scream cut the air.

Children yelled. Women shrieked. Men roared.

Strange voices.

Oby pressed down flat, trying to mould himself into the corrugated roof so that he would be invisible. He tried to breathe with barely a movement in his chest. He pressed his hands to his ears but some sounds crept in through the gaps in his fingers.

The noises grew nearer.

Then his corrugated roof-top shook as the propped wood that served as a door was yanked away. Thud! Grunt! Squeal! Whimper. A clattering of tins and pots. Oby heard fast padding feet. He heard the whining and yelps of the dogs.

. . .

The only way that Oby could escape the nightmare was to try and stay awake; he pushed open his eyes. He tossed and turned on the stinking sheepskins, fighting his eyes to stay open. Fighting.

* * *

Hiss, hiss, hiss! Towards the end of the day came a new sound. Hiss, hiss, hiss, nearer, hiss, hiss, hiss, as the feet of Moussa Khaliffa came dragging over the Salt Lake.

Oby half sat up in preparation.

Moussa Khaliffa clapped eyes on him. He spat. He snorted. He struck out with his sandaled foot.

Oby shrieked.

The wife of Moussa Khaliffa rushed out from her hut. "God strike you, Khaliffa!" she shrieked like a parrot. "Think before you strike. Haven't I already told you that a man with a quick temper will end up in hell? Do you want to go to hell?"

Moussa Khaliffa eyed his wife from the corner of one eye. The other eye was half closed and oozed puss, an infection that clung to an old injury. He had had the injury for years, caused by flying debris, wind-whipped across the Salt Lake.

Without taking his eyes off Oby, Moussa Khaliffa slowly unwound his white head-wrap and dropped it on the ground outside the hut.

Oby didn't dare move. He was waiting for the foot to strike him again.

"They've been attacked by devils," the parrot voice

continued to shriek. "Some of your workers from this boy's village have been snatched by raiders and marched north. But most of them are dead. Those northern demons are working their way south. They'll be back. It'll be us next. We're next to have our throats slit."

By now Moussa Khaliffa's dusty head was half dunked in a water bucket. For a few seconds he didn't move before lifting out his dripping head and turning it towards Oby. He stared long and hard.

Oby buried his head in the stinking sheepskins.

The wife of Moussa Khaliffa went on. "Only him and the baby..."

"Baby?"

She beckoned her husband into the hut and revealed the sleeping baby.

Moussa Khaliffa stood rigid, breathing heavily. "And what about my brother?"

"He hasn't seen your brother."

Moussa Khaliffa's shoulders sagged as he staggered onto the peninsula of black rock. His eyes cast over the sinking sun, at the vast expanse of the Salt Lake. He scanned the surrounding Chagat Hills, as they blackened into sinister shapes in the fading light. He raised his hands to the sky.

Oby watched as Moussa Khaliffa's mouth opened wide to the sky. Suddenly, a wail ripped across the Salt Lake. Moussa Khaliffa punched his chest with both fists. He screamed into the air. The sounds echoed from hilltop to hilltop. Every hill shouted back.

The pup at Oby's side began to quiver. He picked it up and placed it close to his chest. The pup licked his salty cheeks and swollen eyes.

The wife of Moussa Khaliffa helped her husband into

the hut, and thrust a bowl of camel's milk to his shaking lips, steadying it as he drank, but he struggled to swallow. Dribbles of milk clung to his rough whiskers.

A little later, Moussa Khaliffa came out of his hut and squatted beside Oby. His voice was quiet, wanting to know, yet not wanting to know. "Can you tell me? Can you tell me what happened?"

Oby shifted uncomfortably, and between long silences and tears he recalled the events of that night.

On the rooftop Oby kept still. He was hurting from prickles performing a dance up and down one arm, and one of his legs was so numb it was as if it belonged to someone else. He stayed that way until the night sky began its transformation, gliding into an eerie watery light. He lay there trying to pluck up the courage to climb down. He listened for sounds that might tell him whether there were still strangers there.

As the sky turned pink Oby slipped silently off the roof.

Immediately in front of his eyes was the first body. He felt sick.

The old neighbour – the one who had held his hand as he learnt to walk – was splayed on the hard earth outside her hut, blood trickling from her mouth.

Oby hacked at the dry earth with a wooden hoe. The smells kept rising. Any moment he would be sick. He kept digging. He did his best to bury her. It had to be done quickly, he knew that, because flies had already begun forming black circles above other corpses scattered among the huts. Next, after the flies, would come marauding dogs. He'd never felt so sick.

Some of the dogs lay around, killed in the same mad frenzy as their owners had been. The old bitch of his father's lay dead, her intestines pink beneath her split belly. There was no sign of her pup.

He stood shivering outside his own hut.

Go in? Not go in?

He put one arm through the doorway. Hesitated. Oby took a deep breath and stepped inside. Where was his mother? Where were Bendo and Reeta?

The water jar in the corner was full and he thrust his head into it and gulped. His parents' few possessions lay scattered on the ground.

Oby opened the bundle his mother had prepared the previous evening and searched through it. There was a printed document, some money and a crumpled photograph of his father, smiling up at him.

His father!

Oby dragged his sleeping rug off the roof and knotted these few precious possessions into a corner.

There was one road down to the Salt Lake and one to the north, where last night's raiders came from. There was only one route he could take. South.

As he left the last hut behind, Oby noticed a cloth bundle on the ground. Two dogs lay next to it, whining and pushing their noses into its centre.

He started to walk on, to ignore it, but the hint of movement made him hesitate. He walked over to the bundle, but feared an attack as one of the dogs began to curl its scarred lip. Oby struck out with his leg, then moved the edge of the cloth. He dropped onto his knees, but the two dogs began to return, snarls rolling. Oby hissed in impatience and the dogs skulked away several metres, to where a small pack of nervous dogs *had gathered.*

He lifted the cloth. A baby. It weakly waved an arm. What to do?

He gently picked up the baby.

As Oby moved away, a shaking pup, splashed with blood, slid away from the pack and slithered up nervously, tail tucked under, back arched. Oby put his hand down for the pup to sniff and the pup stayed by his side.

* * *

The wife of Moussa Khaliffa waved her arms above her head as she battled with her flimsy scarf in the wind. "Don't ask the boy any more questions, Khaliffa. Haven't you heard enough? He's suffering enough. His family's missing. God strike you down for your infernal questioning."

"But my father isn't missing."

Moussa Khaliffa and his wife both pushed their faces nearer to Oby.

"Your father? Where is he?"

"He's in El Malla, up in the delta of the Great White River."

"How long's he been there?"

"He went last year after the locusts stripped our fields. He's a guest worker for Madame Betcha, in her fields. I must find him."

"Find him!" Moussa Khaliffa repeated. He and his wife both fidgeted. It was as though they were putting their thoughts in order, as though they had something to say but couldn't arrange the words in a suitable way. Then they both began to talk at once, mincing their words between their teeth and both hoping the other would speak first.

Oby added, "If you could tell me which way to go…"

"Go to El Malla? You mean walk all the way to El Malla?"

"Yes, Moussa Khaliffa."

"It's two thousand kilometres and more." He rubbed both his hands over his knotted, salt-bleached hair. He picked at the dried-up puss at the corner of his eye and scratched his whiskers. He pulled faces and snorted and spat onto the black rock. "It's a long journey to El Malla, boy. It's two countries distant. You'd have to chase the Great White River. It's over on the other side of the mountains. It scrambles down the western drop of the hills and goes on through the Zuda. It's all desert, miles and miles and miles of dunes. There's no shelter from the sun in the Zuda, boy. Only camels and men with experience get through those dunes, not boys alone. Then it doubles back. So, you have to chase west, then north-west then north. Then there's the marsh. It's only damp now, but in two months, when the mountain rivers start to flow, it swallows up the marsh for a hundred kilometres. What then? Swim? Can you swim, boy? No, boy, you cannot go there. No. No."

"Yes … I must." Oby stared directly into Moussa Khaliffa's eyes.

Moussa Khaliffa lowered his gaze, shaking his head.

"What if my father hears about what happened to our village? He'll think everyone's dead. How will he know I'm safe, unless he sees me?"

Oby could only think of what he had to do: chase the Great White River on its journey west, then north-west, then north, but he had no idea where to find it. His grandfather had told him many stories. The river was like a tree. The roots of the tree were spread wide, collecting water from the lands that touched it. The roots fed the trunk, and it fattened and grew strong, forcing its way through the Zuda Desert and breathing life into the lands that sat on its banks. It was green upon green with crops. All the greens in the world.

"I have to find my father," he repeated.

The wife of Moussa Khaliffa started to bustle about and threw two tin plates down in front of her husband and Oby.

Oby scooped up a little rice and chunks of mutton with his fingers, but his stomach was tied in knots. He ate little.

"I have to find my father."

Moussa Khaliffa growled, "Forget it. You're just a kid."

Chapter 5

Gold Teeth

"Be still, Oby." The wife of Moussa Khaliffa pressed his forehead with a cold cloth. He shivered and pushed her hand away. "No, let me. You have a fever and I'm not surprised with everything that has happened. This will help."

He groaned, then raised his eyelids.

Her spongy face was enormous, but her eyes gentle. "Nightmare devils will keep on coming, you know. You have to expect that. But one day they'll fade away. In the end, they will."

He groaned again.

"You've been sleeping a long time ... nearly twenty hours," she said, still pressing the cool cloth. He raised his head a fraction. "Sssh! You need sleep. It's the best thing when you're sick."

He tried to sit up. "I'm not sick. Moussa Khaliffa said we'd talk today."

"Not today. You're not well enough. Anyway, Moussa isn't here ... out on the salt."

An hour later Oby managed to sip camel's milk, but couldn't eat any of her maize porridge. It sat on his tongue like a stone.

"See! You're not eating and it's because you're too sick. Until you can eat you can't go anywhere." She paused. "Today, Moussa went to talk to the camel drovers ... all those planes shrieking over yesterday ... maybe Moussa can get more workers from Tembo Dolo. No workers ... makes life hard." She kept talking, about this, about that, all her thoughts skipping out in short, sharp bursts.

He lay motionless, wanting her to go away. Why couldn't she leave him alone? He had no thoughts, except one – a yearning to get to his father. His father's big-smile face was glued in front of his eyes. The big-smile-alright face. The longer he dreamt the more real it became; the more real it became the stronger he felt. He made a fist and clenched it hard.

In his mind he had already started the journey.

The next morning Oby was able to stand up without wobbling or feeling faint. He waited patiently for the wife of Moussa Khaliffa to appear.

She finally came out of her hut, stretching and yawning. As if she had forgotten he existed, she stood with hands on hips, eyeing him up and down. Without a word she handed Oby a yellow bucket and pointed in the direction of the little oasis.

He had seen yellow buckets like this before, when the UN peacekeepers had come to his village to help build new huts and drilled new wells for water five years ago. One well had clogged up because everyone threw in their rubbish. One had never been used because it was where all the bad spirits lived. Only one had water in it and there was always a long queue of people.

Some people used the buckets to collect camel dung for burning. But, best of all, they were good for making kupti in. The men argued and stole the water buckets from the women and made kupti and the women had to go back to using clay pots. There had been hundreds of fights about the buckets. Real fights. Mostly women fighting their men to steal back their buckets.

Throughout the day Oby fetched water. He whistled. He tossed the bucket from hand to hand and then tried to spin it on one finger. He whistled louder and louder. Whistling drove away bad spirits.

As the sun began to fade and the Chagat Hills turned purple, the hiss, hiss, hiss of feet came from across the Salt Lake. Two dusty men and two languid camels emerged.

The wife of Moussa Khaliffa went out to meet them with bowls of camel's milk. They drank noisily.

The new man had two rows of gold glittering between his lips. He affected a wide smile.

Oby had never seen gold teeth before, but he knew about them. Gold teeth were a sign of wealth. The man had one gold cap for each year of droving, which meant that he now had a full mouth of gold teeth. He took his grubby white head-wrap off his head and gave his scalp a good scratch.

He hunched down next to Oby. "Moussa Khaliffa's been telling me what happened." He paused and grunted. "Sorry, boy. Sorry." He cleared his throat. "So, you want to go to El Malla to find your father?"

Oby nodded.

"Well, you can't."

Oby scowled.

"You're too young to cross the Zuda Desert alone. How old?"

"Sixteen."

Gold Teeth leant forward and pushed his nose into Oby's face, waiting.

"Thirteen."

"You wanna be dead? An inexperienced man could be dead in a day in that heat. You're safer here. You'd better stay here."

"My father ... he'll think I'm dead."

"Maybe. Maybe." He scratched his beard and gazed lengthily at Oby, as though judging his character. "On this trip I'm only going as far as Tembo Dolo. I have a relative there ... he often organises safe routes across the desert. From there, travellers continue north-west, to the dam. After that, it's easy because there are trains that travel straight north to the delta, even to El Malla. He'd do something for you, if I asked." He paused. Then his eyes became slits and he leaned forward and said quietly, "You got any money to pay for all this?"

"No." Oby didn't want Gold Teeth to know about the few coins tied in the corner of his sleeping rug.

"Travellers always need money because they have to pay fares. So, how can you travel?"

"Walk."

"Okay... and eating? If you have no money, how can you eat?"

Oby dropped his gaze and slumped back onto the sheepskins. He stared into the sky. Its expansiveness was as empty as his plans. He rolled over onto his side and turned his back on the two men.

He hated Gold Teeth.

Chapter 6

Plans

Oby could hear wind rustling through palms. When he opened his eyes he realised that his head had stopped trying to split itself open. He spotted Gold Teeth standing up high on the black rock, facing into the wind and winding his head-wrap very precisely around his head.

"Ever loaded salt?" Gold Teeth called down.

"No."

"Then you're no use to me."

Oby sat up. "I can learn."

"Good! What about handling a camel?"

"Grandfather had camels."

"Answer my question."

"Yes."

"Can you work your way to El Malla?"

Oby's chest began to thump.

"Answer my question," yelled Gold Teeth.

"Yes," yelled back Oby.

"Good!"

Yesterday Gold Teeth had said he couldn't go, so he must have had a rethink and changed his mind overnight.

Gold Teeth jumped down from the rock and went to his camel saddlebag and pulled out some leather sandals. He threw them at Oby. "Put them on," he ordered. He also pulled out a crumpled head-wrap and wrapped it around Oby's head. "If the wind gets up, wrap the end round your mouth and pull the top down, over your eyes."

The sandals were stiff. The leather thong between his toes was fat. Oby slid his foot out. Gold Teeth scowled, then spat on the leather and bashed the sandals together. "You'll get used to them," he barked. "Keep spitting and beating to soften them up."

* * *

The sky was alight with stars.

Moussa Khaliffa came and sat on the soft stinking sheep-skins with him. He pushed twenty likits into Oby's hand. "Be careful how you use this. It'll soon be spent. Work to pay your way – that's how I would do it. But be careful. There are rogues out there who will only want to fleece you, even of your old sleeping rug. Just be careful."

Oby clutched the money tightly, fearful that the wind would whisk it out of his fingers. He folded it over and over and pressed it into the corner of his sleeping rug and sealed it with a knot.

Moussa Khaliffa also gave Oby a small pouch in which he could carry a few lumps of salt. "You need salt when you work in this oven," he said. "A few licks every now and again with your water, or you'll get cramps. The heat in the Zuda is even worse than this, so don't forget the salt."

"Yes, Moussa Khaliffa."

"Come with me."

Oby followed onto the edge of the Salt Lake. His pup trotted at his side. This part of the Salt Lake had not been worked recently, so was not discoloured by the constant tramping of feet.

By light of the moon, Moussa Khaliffa drew shapes on the ground with a stick. "What's your memory like?"

"Good."

"Then memorise this map." Moussa Khaliffa waited whilst Oby studied the map of the Great White River, then said, "Now, repeat what I've just told you."

Oby stumbled over his words.

"Okay, I'll repeat it, but listen more carefully this time."

Four repeats later and Oby had it, word for word.

Moussa Khaliffa got out a small compass. "Do you know how it works?"

"No."

"See! That's north." He moved the compass round and showed Oby how to find the direction in which to travel. "Like this. See? El Malla is northwest from here. When you get to the river, stay with it. Always chase the river. And don't forget your prayers, boy. Prayers help you stay strong."

Oby didn't move. Neither did Moussa Khaliffa. The moon seemed to be shining a blessing. They stole time from sleep to talk, their voices warm in the cool night air.

Moussa Khaliffa said, "Why don't you stay here, boy?"

"No."

"This journey you want to make. Are you sure?"

Oby put his hand down to touch his pup.

"You can't take him with you."

"I know."

"I need workers here."

"I have to find my father."

"Be careful."

"Yes, Moussa Khaliffa."

"Are you really sure?"

"Yes."

"Don't lose the compass."

Later, as Oby was falling asleep, he thought he could hear the Great White River racing by.

Chapter 7

Wolves

Oby's final glimpse of the pup was of him licking the small fat feet of one of the babies. The wife of Moussa Khaliffa hung back in the doorway of her hut. She gave him an encouraging nod. Oby took a deep breath, stepped onto the Salt Lake and walked out to meet the camel caravan.

With Moussa Khaliffa's lack of workers, Gold Teeth did not have a full load of salt. He was forced to make a detour and journey to the south east of the Salt Lake to buy from another merchant.

This place was even more barren. Windy. Flat. Roasting, with mirages that turned into quivering ghosts.

Whilst the camel drovers spent time loading blocks of salt, Gold Teeth put Oby in charge of two old camels which needed to be rested.

Oby fussed over them. He rubbed their necks and the smells they gave off filled him with memories of his grandfather's camels. A wave of sadness swept over him at the familiar feeling of camel hair, but he managed to snap out of it again. Now and again a devil got into his fingers and he tugged at the camels' moulting skins which were hanging down like curtains from their stomachs – skins that were not quite ready to fall off. The creatures grunted and shifted sideways, throwing their weight at him, thumping him out of the way. But these old camels didn't present much of a challenge, only wanting to spend time rolling their jaws from side to side, chewing at a few prickly stalks with their worn-down teeth.

Looking for something to do, Oby pulled on a handle protruding from one of the panniers which had been removed from a camel and was now on the ground. Was it? Or not? He turned it over. Yes, a salt cutter's knife. He swished it over his head. It hissed. He stabbed the salt, then hacked at it until slivers and chunks flew in all directions.

Oby gouged squares and rectangles into the surface of the salt, to the exact size that he thought he could lift. The cutting wasn't that difficult. He dug down deeply, half sawing, half jack-hammering, but the salt didn't want to be prized off the lake floor.

Jerk and lever. He had seen it done before, but he hadn't quite enough strength to raise the block any further, so jammed his foot under it to prevent it falling back into place. Even then he couldn't lever the block any higher. His hands were neither wide enough nor strong enough. With no experience, his style was clumsy. The knife slipped. He snapped back his fingers in time, but the slab of salt wedged his foot. "Owwww!" An arrow of pain suddenly shot through his ankle. It was so awkwardly wedged that Oby could neither pull out his foot nor lift the salt slab.

He searched the horizon. It rippled in a heat haze. If it

hadn't been for the scarlets, crimsons, sapphires, emeralds and marigolds of the woven panniers on the camels, Oby would not have known that camels were moving about in the distance. Their buff hides blended completely into the Salt Lake. He yelled and screamed and hollered, but his cries were blown by the wind in the opposite direction.

A couple of pigeon-toed crows strutted back and forth, cackling like witches. Oby yelled at them. They flapped a few feet off the ground but were too curious to fly away. He wanted to sit down, but the surface of the Salt Lake was too hot.

Beyond the two crows, and trotting fast, two lean jackals were heading straight for him. Oby swallowed hard. His other leg was aching. The sun was hammering his head, because he had taken the head-wrap off and flung it around a camel's neck. The jackals were yipping and yapping, getting bigger and bigger as they loomed towards him through the haze.

But there was something else moving.

Oby shaded his eyes.

Gliding steadily nearer. Brown and grey ... trotting lightly ... heads fixed straight at him ...

"Wolves! Wolves!" Oby yelled so hard his head spun. He snapped his eyes shut to clear the dizziness. He searched the horizon again, in the hope that the camels and salt-cutters were returning. It was time they did.

The wolf pair trotted daintily, howling to attract attention. Three more wolves, young fearless things, emerged from the heatwave, sniffing the air, staring straight at Oby. They had eyes only for their target.

And it was him.

The two jackals, brazened by the presence of the wolves, sped up. Now eyes shone on him from almost every angle. Two of the wolves swung round to the right and the others to the left. Oby twisted left and right.

He yelled, "Clear off! I'll kill you if you come near me."

He picked up a couple of chunks of salt and threw them. The wolves stopped. Sweat poured off him. Suddenly, going dizzy again, he jammed his eyes shut.

A breathy growl came from his right.

Oby swiveled his head.

Face-to-face. A wolf. Its eyes held his.

"Yuk! You stink!" Oby spat at it. He whirled his arms.

The pale-grey eyes remained unblinking. Fixed.

Oby stiffened to rock.

The wolf remained motionless.

Oby blinked.

The wolf raised a paw. Its weight shifted forward. The paw was only five metres from Oby.

He shrieked.

Chaos! Yells! Yelps! Squeals!

Salt rocks rained down all around him.

Wolves and jackals scarpered and scattered, yelping and yipping, back into the haze.

Gold Teeth laughed. "What's this? You're shaking. Have you never met a curious young wolf before? I heard them howling. Believe me, there's worse in the Zuda." Gold Teeth flicked his cutter, twisted the slab and lifted it.

The injured foot had blood streaks and grazes. Oby rubbed his toes.

"It takes months to be a good salt worker," said Gold Teeth.

Oby stood up. He winced. He limped a few paces.

Gold Teeth scratched his chin. "It's swelling."

Oby didn't want Gold Teeth to change his mind about taking him to Tembo Dolo, so he stood up straight, not letting on about the sharp twinges in his foot.

Chapter 8

Sandstorm

This was not the best day to be on the Salt Lake, though. The wind was whipping up and massive tangle-weeds like huge ferris wheels were rolling by.

"Cover your head," ordered Gold Teeth.

Retrieving his head-wrap from the neck of the old camel, Oby fixed it around his head, but gusts of wind charging across the Salt Lake soon whipped out the ends. It uncoiled in seconds, flailing like a kite tail.

Gold Teeth chuckled, his gold teeth glistening even brighter. The other camel drovers laughed at Oby. One of them waved his arms in circles around his head, illustrating how the head-wrapping should be done. "Boy, look, like this," and the joker twisted his arms around his legs, tripping himself up.

The drovers roared and chortled, slapping their thighs. "No, like this!" laughed another. "This way, that way, pull it tighter, tuck it under."

Oby gritted his teeth. Why couldn't they shut up? He tugged impatiently at the cloth and coiled it a different way.

No ... he wasn't going to cry. He fixed it with a slant to the left, then readjusted with a slant to the right, then stood defiant.

"Not bad," laughed Gold Teeth.

Oby guessed he looked stupid, but he didn't care, as long as they could see he was fit to travel with them. Dust and sand scooted along the ground, stinging his legs.

The drovers had to shout at each other above the roar of the wind. On top of that, the camels started shifting restlessly and kicking up a din. Pebbles began rolling. A sandstorm was heading straight for them.

It was impossible for the camel caravan to move. The sky turned orange as sand whirled all around them from the desert ten miles away.

The drovers hastily curled the camels around, facing away from the direction of the storm. Oby pulled his head-wrap over his mouth and eyes and dropped down between the two old camels, clutching at their moulting skin. Then he closed his eyes.

The wind gathered pace. Sand hit even harder. The camels growled. Sand lashed. It cut into Oby's back. It flailed and stung. It piled up against his back and was driven inside his torb-shirt.

Hunkered down next to him, one of the old camels began making strange noises. Along with the hubbub of the wind, Oby began to confuse sounds.

Screaming! His mother's eyes. The flash of red. Crying! Running! Thumping! Falling! Falling ... falling.

* * *

As the evening approached, the storm relented, but Oby's ears continued ringing. Quicker than a snap of fingers came a cacophony of different sounds. Camels and men began clearing nostrils: blowing, snorting, spitting, burping, grunting, wheezing, snuffling, hacking, hawking, phlegm-throwing – they did it all.

Lodged between the camels, Oby had been a small, tight ball. As he unwound, he could feel thousands of grains of sand cascading down his back. He could feel them in his throat and up his nose and in his ears.

"Hah!" Gold Teeth laughed. "So, you're on your feet. How are those skinny legs of yours?"

"I'm better. See!" Oby presented himself, forcing his back straight and holding his head high.

Gold Teeth laughed, but as he walked past he gave Oby a shove which sent him sprawling onto the ground. "To travel the length of the Great White River you need to have a strong body and a strong mind," he called over his shoulder.

"Well, I have," Oby shouted angrily, gritting his teeth as he picked himself up. The camel drovers all started laughing again. Why were they all making fun of him? He studied the pebbles dotted on the ground and to show he didn't care how much they teased, picked a few up and tried juggling. When that failed, he arranged them in patterns on the ground. And still the drovers continued laughing for no reason.

At that point he knew he would have to fight his own battles; he would have to be strong and think strong. He would do it.

* * *

Gold Teeth carried two pots of camel milk over to Oby. He sat down, then sniffed and snorted and spat until he had cleared all the sandy, salty mucus from his nostrils.

"Camel caravans are not easy," he said. "Camel caravans are hard work. It's hard because the work is heavy. Camels need respect. You can't train a camel to obey commands, like training a dog to sit, and you can't make it obey by beating it. You have to love your camels and work together in harmony."

"I know."

"Then there's another thing. The heat. The heat sucks at you like a leech. And when you are tired your camel still needs to be taken care of. Do you know what I'm saying?"

"Yes, I know."

"I don't suppose you want to hear any more?"

"No."

"Good!" Gold Teeth slapped him on the back.

Oby said, "A camel will never forget and if you treat it badly, one day it will get its revenge and trample on your neck when you're sleeping."

"Your grandfather taught you well."

It took them six hours to cross the massive roasting oven, the Salt Lake.

Chapter 9

Fud Shifta

Beans. And more beans. Oby was already fed up with eating beans and this was just the start of his journey. It was sunset and conversations were beginning to run thin.

Gold Teeth strolled over to squat beside Oby. "We need to talk."

Oby didn't want to have anything to do with talking. Talking meant questions and he had had enough of questions. Questions were upsetting. And he didn't know all the answers. He moved to sit on the other side of his two camels. He could feel Gold Teeth's grin following him.

Casually, Gold Teeth moved to the other side of Oby and squatted, as if nothing had happened.

Oby shifted round, turning his back on Gold Teeth. He knew that from now on every day would be a hassle.

Gold Teeth shuffled to face Oby again, taking his time. "See over there," Gold Teeth said, pointing to a shabby hut strangely angled on a slope of rubble. "That's Fud Shifta's place. He and I sometimes do business. He'll have something very useful for you. Come on!"

Oby didn't move.

"Come with me."

Oby fidgeted uncomfortably, but remained on the ground beside the camels, re-knotting his sleeping rug.

"Come."

Oby fiddled with his sleeping rug to appear busy, but Gold Teeth had another angle.

"Bring your sleeping rug with you."

Oby slipped his hands in and out of the camels' bridles, then rubbed their hairy chins, as though these were essential tasks.

"Stop dithering! Come!" Gold Teeth's voice rose. A couple of drovers glanced over in curiosity. "What's wrong with you, boy? You want to get to El Malla, don't you?"

With a huge sigh, Oby wobbled his sleeping rug into a parcel, trapped it under his armpit and reluctantly tagged along behind Gold Teeth.

Once out of earshot of the other drovers, Gold Teeth said, "You can't tie up your money in your sleeping rug. It's too obvious. You need to keep it safe."

"Haven't got any money."

"Okay. So, you haven't got any money."

They picked over rough ground, heading in the direction of a small hut. The nearer they got to it the fouler the air became. From the hut emanated such a stench that Oby could feel his meal of beans trying to climb out again.

In front of the hut Gold Teeth yelled, "Get up, Fud Shifta, get up. You got a customer." He slammed his fist onto the wooden shutter that served as a door. "Get your skinny butt out of there. Come on! We haven't got all day."

A huge rattling and clunking of wood followed and the door of the small hut fell back.

Yuk! Oby's beans sprang up and down inside his belly as the sickly smells of rotting flesh shot out. He screwed up his eyes to try and focus on the shadowy figure inside. He stared only into blackness.

"How can you live with this filth?" Gold Teeth batted the foul air with his arms, trying to make the immediate spot where he was standing stink a little less.

Flies spewed everywhere.

Gold Teeth gave an almighty swing with his right leg and kicked the shutters off the window spaces. Light poured into the hut.

A scrawny shrimp of a man emerged.

"Filth makes money. Don't you know that?" Fud Shifta blinked and squinted at Gold Teeth, as the flame-red sunset streamed directly into his hut. "What do you want this time?" A strip of leather dangled from his lower lip, with dried camel flesh still clinging.

"We're in a hurry," said Gold Teeth. "I want a bag."

Fud Shifta was clearly not a man to make friends easily, living in such a stench. He continued chewing at the leather and muttered to himself as he walked around the side of his hut to inspect the condition of the window shutters. "So, where you put your camel? Now I kick your camel," he squeaked, as though wanting to punish Gold Teeth for this disturbance.

Oby had never seen such a den before, of skins, piles of freshly shorn wool and needles of numerous lengths and thicknesses. Amongst all this, Fud Shifta's stained sleeping cushion shared space with offcuts of leather and knives. Even the huts in Oby's village had been bigger than this.

"The boy needs a bag," said Gold Teeth.

Fud Shifta kept on chewing as he spoke. He was skilled

at doing both at the same time. "Bag? Bag? You need to say what sort of bag. Big, small, soft, hard. Not just 'bag'. How should I know what sort of bag? You got eyes. Look for yourself."

Gold Teeth leaned forward and tossed leather pieces around and pulled pouches and bags from under the offcuts. He removed some bags hanging from nails on the wall.

"*No!* Get your hands off those." Fud Shifta snatched them back. "They're special order for the market at Tembo Dolo."

"Come on, old grumbler, I'll give you a better price for these than the market."

"You heard. I said *not* touch. Customer orders."

So Gold Teeth continued to drag bags out of a corner that had not seen daylight for a very long time, revealing a plate with beans dried rock-hard onto it, mouse droppings, scurrying cockroaches and a pile of hairs from a goat's hide.

"Filth!" muttered Gold Teeth and flung all the bags that he had inspected back into the corner. From under a mountain of dust he pulled out a bag which was compact, with a secure fastening on it. He strode outside and beat the bag against the side of the hut to get rid of all the layers of muck. Then he held it up for Oby's inspection. "Yes? Good?"

Fud Shifta pressed forward between them. "That's a soft bag. That's expensive. Takes a day's chewing to get it that soft."

"There's always a catch with you, Fud Shifta. Always a reason to make it more expensive. This bag's been sitting under a pile of junk for about ten years so how can you remember it, let alone the price? Eh?"

"I don't need it," Oby protested. His money and the

printed document were tied safely in his sleeping rug and he wanted to keep it that way.

"Shut up, boy." Gold Teeth threw some coins at Fud Shifta and started out the door.

No sooner had they begun to walk away, than the shutters slammed back over the windows.

Gold Teeth handed the bag over to Oby. "I know what you're thinking. You don't want the bag. Take it."

The bag dropped onto the ground.

Gold Teeth turned around.

Oby stepped back two paces, thinking that he was about to be swiped about the head.

"See what I have here," said Gold Teeth.

"My father's photograph! How did you get it?"

"You dropped it ... and this ..."

"Mum's papers ..."

"You tied them with knots in that old sleeping rug, but it's wearing so thin in places..." He didn't need to finish. "Anyway, don't you think everyone will be asking, 'what's he got tied in that sleeping rug?' Have you seen anyone else clinging onto a sleeping rug like their lives depended on it? Y'know, there are thieves out there who will fleece you, even for a thin old rug like this. Listen! You must *think* like a man now, d'you hear? You must *live* like a man. Men have bags to protect their money."

Oby sighed and lowered his head as this *big* truth fixed itself in his mind.

"Pick it up."

Oby did.

"Keep the bag tied round your middle. Don't take it off. Ever. Understand?"

He nodded.

Gold Teeth suddenly raised his long torb-shirt, revealing his long underpants; and firmly attached to them was his money bag. "This is where I keep my personal belongings. Now, put your money and your documents in your bag."

"I don't have any money."

Gold Teeth roared with laughter. "You think I'm a fool? What's that you've got knotted in the corner of that old rug ... and the other corner?"

Oby's nose twitched nervously. "How do you know?"

"I've done a lot of travelling." He pointed and wagged his finger. "Learn to observe. Heed my advice."

As he was pointing and gesticulating to get his argument across, the sleeve of his torb-shirt worked its way down his arm towards his elbow, revealing an arm of dark tattoos. When he saw Oby's raised eyebrows, Gold Teeth chuckled. "Hah! One tattoo for each place I've traded. It's a reminder of my travels," he said proudly.

"Can't you take them off?"

"No."

"Never?"

"Never." Changing the subject, Gold Teeth asked, "How's your head doin' now?"

"Better," said Oby.

Gold Teeth pointed at Oby's head-wrap. "At least that stays on your head now." He patted Oby on the back. "You look better." He took Oby's arm. "And what are these? Muscles? My word, you even have a few muscles!"

As they swished back through the dry grasses towards camp, Gold Teeth said, "Why are you too impatient to wait for my return to the Salt Lake?"

"My father ..."

"If you could wait a month, I could take you all the way

up to Salima ... or ... I have a good friend in Mokolee, a few miles ahead. You could stay there until I come back, then continue ..."

"No, I want to find my father quickly, so he knows I'm alive."

"... and you want to travel with Abdul Sid when we meet him?"

"Yes," said Oby firmly.

"It's up to you. You're a man now." Gold Teeth stopped suddenly and shoved his face straight into Oby's. "Some big advice. Don't ... trust ... *anyone*. You hear me good? Not anyone." He thrust a large coin into Oby's hand then strode ahead towards camp and his camel.

Oby stared at the large gold piece shining back at him. He had never seen a coin like this before. He pushed it into his new bag before the other drovers saw it.

Chapter 10

Fida

Oby peered into the distance. Small whirls of dust were rising. He instantly recognized the gentle sway of a camel caravan creeping towards them. It was still some way off, but Gold Teeth gave instructions, and his drovers began preparing tea in their large pots so they could offer refreshment.

At the head of the approaching caravan rode Abdul Sid.

The two teams of camel drovers greeted each other with nods and raise of hands. As the new arrivals manoeuvred their camels into well-spaced resting positions, a bull piled high with boxes had other ideas and kicked and bellowed, swinging round, stamping, and spitting. One of the boxes loosened and crashed to the ground. The crash and splitting of wood and alarmed shouts of the drovers agitated the rest of the camels and the air was suddenly thick with growling and bellowing. It took half an hour of rope-hauling to get the animals settled down.

"Greetings, Brothers. God be with you."

"Blessings on your children."

"How is your family?"

"I'm sure your children are quite tall now."

"How is the road ahead?"

Gold Teeth invited them to sit down. Then he said to Abdul Sid, "See this boy. He needs to get to Salima ... safely. He needs your help."

A voice snorted, "Why should we?"

"Shut your mouth, Fida." Abdul Sid's rebuke was sharp.

Oby felt blood of embarrassment rushing to his face.

Abdul Sid's old head turned slowly to observe Oby.

Oby's toes began to wiggle. *Oh, please, no more questions. I don't want to answer any more.* He felt very alone and very out of place.

But no, Abdul Sid didn't ask any questions at all. He continued listening to Gold Teeth, at the same time picking at his teeth with a slender stem of dry grass.

Someone got up and moved away from the group. It was the bad-tempered one, Fida, but the rest of the men began chatting and drinking pale cardamom tea.

Just as Oby was beginning to forget himself and enjoy their strange tales, he felt a sharp sting on his ear. He flicked his ear with his hand. Dratted insect! Glancing around Oby noticed that the one called Fida was peering at him from behind a rock. He was wearing a twisted grin and fiddling with something in his hand.

Oby ducked.

The flying object missed. It clattered against the rock just behind Oby.

"Stupid! Brainless!" Abdul Sid yelled, then gestured, and one of the drovers jumped up and wrested something from Fida's hand and handed it over to Abdul Sid who studied the sling shot. "It could have taken his eye out." He turned to

Oby and held out the sling shot. "You can have it. You want it?"

Oby shrank back and shook his head.

Abdul Sid pocketed the weapon.

"Now, about this new gold rush in Mokolee," said Gold Teeth, "have you come across any of those get-rich-quick boys yet?"

"Some of them are up there already, stinking like hyenas, and the rest are hanging around in Tembo Dolo, because they haven't got mules or money to get to where they're panning for gold."

Fida moved.

Oby's eyes followed.

"And how much gold?" enquired Gold Teeth.

"Not much so far, but enough to feed a mule."

Gold Teeth laughed. "Now, when they find real gold – and I mean enough gold to decorate a tomb with – then I'll ditch all these camels into the Great White River and become a gold miner. I love gold!" And his smile widened further.

Abdul Sid gave a wry smile. "When you decide to do that, give me your camels. Don't forget."

The sun sank out of sight. The sounds in the darkness were camels snorting and men snoring.

Oby couldn't sleep. His ear was still stinging. Somewhere near him was Fida. He needed to keep an eye on him. All the time.

* * *

The sun rose. The sounds at dawn were of camels snorting and men snoring. Very shortly, the camel drovers stirred and coffee pots rattled. Then the caravans moved on in their separate directions, snaking past each other. Oby fiddled with tying his sleeping rug and pretended to be distracted so that he would not have to look anyone in the eye.

Gold Teeth said to Abdul Sid, "Don't forget to show the boy where the Great White River begins." Then, "But watch him, because he's got two left feet and glue fingers that can't tie knots. He'll have you all tumbling into a crocodile-infested swamp."

The drovers roared with laughter.

As the two caravans departed on their separate ways, Oby glanced across at Gold Teeth. He grinned, winked and nodded as if to say, *take care.*

Abdul Sid beckoned Oby to walk close to him. "That Gold Teeth! Just a noisy peacock."

The caravan moved into the hills; not in a perfectly straight line, but taking on the mood of the animals, swaying, edging to the left or the right. Mostly, the camels' heads remained fixed straight ahead, snooty, and occasionally sending out a dull bellow.

Abdul Sid was an old camel drover who refused to give up working. He had once said he would die with his camels. He never hurried. "I would miss everything around me if I hurried," he liked to say. He didn't think in a hurry either. Once he sat for three days at a wadi, where the water was sweet and there were date palms to provide some shade, and all because he couldn't decide which camel should take the lead after his best camel dropped dead. His old best camel had been black. His new best camel was white (although a bit grubby).

Oby matched the old man's pace. Right foot. Left foot. The rhythm was easy and comfortable. The old man moved loosely. His head was like a fat-budded rose atop a skinny stalk. He glided, and although the route was steadily climbing, he moved effortlessly.

Abdul Sid had two sons and two grandsons that made up his team of drovers. Oby had barely noticed three of them, but he had certainly noticed his youngest grandson, Fida.

Whenever Oby glanced up Fida was blasting thunderous glares in his direction. His face had a permanent sneer.

As the camels moved further into the mountains, the air became noticeably cooler. It helped to clear Oby's head from the heavy heat of the Salt Lake which had sat in his skull like an overfilled sack of corn, ready to burst. The camels snorted more frequently in the fresher air. The land became greener.

The sky was noticeably different too. Wisps and puffs of cloud shot across the sky. The mountain air currents, lifting and falling, clashing and disagreeing, tossed clouds back and forth.

Oby had a young female camel to look after, tan-coloured with a cute face but breath like dead fish. Her name was Mo.

The dirt road headed up a steep-sided valley. Dotted over hill slopes were moving shapes, brown, black and cream – sheep, shepherds and dogs.

"Watch out for boulders," warned Abdul Sid. "Slice your head off if one rolls down. Keep watch!"

Oby knew that stones sometimes rolled: first one, then another, dislodging smaller rocks, somersaulting faster, gathering speed and setting off landslides. He could always find shapes in boulders – a cat, a crow, a man's bald head – which absorbed his attention. So he failed to notice the trickle of stones.

Abdul Sid *had* noticed though, and he pushed two

fingers into his mouth and blew. The whistle echoed across the valley.

The caravan stopped.

The trickle of stones grew into a roll. The clatter of rock and dust, moving faster and faster, dropped like a waterfall, sent up a choking cloud of dust. The avalanche crashed and clattered into other rocks, ricocheting like an unpredictable firework. It roared directly across the path ahead of them, before finally settling on the other side of the drovers' trail, clouds of dust swirling lazily in the air.

Frantic yelps and howls came from the area below the rockslide. The shadowy figures of two wolves emerged from the dust cloud and began to scramble over the rubble. They moved back and forth, yelping.

The nearer one was different from the others, nearly totally cream and fatter than its thin-muzzled companion. Both wolves' ears were pricked. Then others appeared at a distance, pacing and nervous.

Abdul Sid grumbled to no-one in particular, "What did I tell you? That white male is half shepherd dog. Just look at him. Won't be any pure wolves left soon. They'll all be mongrels. Shepherds should keep out of wolves' territory."

The wolves began pawing the rubble, sniffing and whining.

Joe, the elder grandson, scrambled his way down to the rock mound. The animals backed away and paced agitatedly. Joe pulled away rock after rock, intermittently listening.

A scrappy young cub squeezed out of a crevice, wobbly, but strong enough to yelp. One of the adults had enough courage to dash forward and snatch up the cub in its jaws and carry it to a safe distance.

Joe bent down again and was hidden from view.

He called, "There's another one. It's alive, but its hind legs are broken." He held up the cub.

"Kill it," ordered Abdul Sid.

"No! Wait!" Fida dropped his camel rein and scrambled over the scree to join his brother. "*I* want to do it!" He grabbed a stone, then snatched the cub from his brother's hand. Then changed his mind and looked towards Oby ... grinning. "Boy ... you come down here. Come on! *You* do it. I want to see *you* do it."

Oby didn't move, nor did he reply.

Fida sneered. "Pathetic! Feeble!"

Oby kept silent.

Fida screamed, "Come on, you parasite."

"Shut your big mouth," yelled Abdul Sid. "Just get on with it."

Fida raised his arm.

He brought down the stone.

Dead with one blow.

He threw the corpse towards the waiting wolves.

They sniffed at it.

Oby turned his head away.

Scrambling back up to the track Fida passed close to Oby. He hissed, "Is that the way they killed? The killers that came to your village, did they do it good, like me?"

Oby jammed his teeth together hard. He was so tight inside he could barely breathe. He stared at the sky instead.

Fida whooped and shouted, "I love killing!"

Oby shook inside. He wished lightening would strike Fida dead.

As the caravan began moving again, two vultures circled above the dead wolf cub.

Oby stayed well behind Fida, where he could see him; he knew there would be more trouble to come.

Chapter 11

Mokolee And The Mob

Oby lurched back and forth, constantly adjusting his balance on Mo's back. There was little space for him amongst the lashed blocks of salt, but with so much walking earlier his leg muscles had become tight and painful. The ground was still rising and underfoot was rutted. The track became narrower. Mo picked her way daintily but surely.

They rounded a sheer rock face. Spread out ahead was a plain of semi-rough grass, occasionally pinpricked with small flowers. The plain was dotted with a dozen goats and a couple of shabby huts, and surrounded by even higher mountains.

There was little talking, only the soft footfalls of the camels. Oby thought about his father. What a reunion it would be! They would laugh and chat. He looked forward to hearing his father's stories about the old days ... about when his grandmother dressed up as a man and took the goats to market and got a good price. Everything would be all right. Yes, everything would be all right.

At the end of that afternoon the caravan meandered to the lowest point of a hammock-shaped pass. Below, in a patchwork of greys, lay Mokolee.

Mokolee's houses squatted low on the ground with their flat roofs blending in with the gun-metal colours of the rocky surroundings. Narrow paths between houses were just wide enough for a camel. Everything in Mokolee was economical in size – doorways just wide enough, walls just high enough.

Mokolee's central square was the hub of the town. It was a market for camel traders to sell their wares and haggle over prices. Mokolee's fame was its market, a crossing point of drovers' trails.

Abdul Sid led them to a series of wide troughs. Grubby boys ran bare-footed back and forth with rusty buckets, collecting water from rivulets tumbling down from the hills, then hauling back to fill the camel troughs.

Abdul Sid left the camels with the boys and headed for a spot on the edge of the market. He ordered his sons to dump two panniers of salt on the ground in front of him.

Customers suddenly appeared from everywhere. They bartered noisily about prices.

"What about this piece?" said a humped old man, hobbling up to stand directly in front of Abdul Sid.

"Twenty likits," said Abdul Sid.

"Twenty likits? You're a thief."

Abdul Sid cocked his head, pursed his lips and stroked his long fingers. "Nineteen then."

"Mean old fart!" the old man shouted. "He thinks cut-price is one likit! Hey, everyone! He's a robber. First he says twenty, now he says nineteen. He can do better than that. Look at his clothes, just look at the fine cloth they are made of. Look at my cheap clothes! Why should we poor men have to pay so much for simple salt, just so that he can wear fine cloth? It's robbery! I'm telling you, I'll pay no more than twelve. I bought last month for no more than twelve."

"It's my business. I charge what I want," replied Abdul Sid, calmly.

"I can buy cheaper from Gold Teeth," the old man shouted.

Oby's beans started pushing around in his stomach again. He stepped back.

A curious crowd slowly gathered and pushed forward. Most of them were newly arrived gold prospectors: some had torn shirts, some had dirty head-wraps, one was wearing odd sandals. They listened eagerly, their eyes not missing a thing on the two faces as they hurled insults and argued. The crowd started agreeing with the hunched old man and sneered at Abdul Sid.

Abdul Sid said, "Go and buy your salt from Gold Teeth then. Is he here? I haven't seen him."

The crowd peered around, looking for anyone who might be Gold Teeth.

Oby looked across towards Abdul Sid's two sons, but they stayed well back and Oby couldn't understand why they were not attempting to defend their father. The only one to take a keen interest in what was going on was Fida, standing near his grandfather with his arms folded, with an expression that indicated he would love to see a fight.

"You're a crazy old fool and a cheat!" shouted the humped one.

"I'll cut your fingers off one by one!" Abdul Sid whipped out a shiny, thick-bladed knife, from a sheath dangling down from his waist, and waved it menacingly.

The crowd gasped and stumbled over one another in order to get away. Oby got knocked over. He scrambled to his feet to see Abdul Sid looking ferocious and lunging towards the humped one. Oby gripped his hands together to stop them shaking.

The hunched one limped aside and sneered, "Lousy thief, trying to rob the poor!" He swung around and addressed the crowd. "He's trying to fleece you. Kick his salt into the Great White River. Teach him a lesson." He swung around to face Abdul Sid again and spat. Not once, but twice, aiming straight at Abdul Sid. Spittle dribbled down Abdul Sid's beard.

In a flash, Abdul Sid raised his knife and lunged forward, but it only sliced air for the humped one had already vanished into the crowd.

Oby's legs were shaking, but he noticed excitement on Fida's face.

As Abdul Sid put his knife away, the crowd suddenly changed their loyalties and milled round and offered Abdul Sid sympathy. "Spitting!" and "The worst king of insult!" and "He's bad, that humped one!" and "Only last week I saw him arguing with a policeman," and "His mother should have taught him manners," and "They say he's always in trouble," and "I say we don't need him in this town," and "Yes, let's run him out of town," and "You should have hit him. Why didn't you hit him?" and "No, the knife is better," and "Kill the humped one next time," and "Why don't we find him and kill him now?"

The crowd slowly turned into a mob.

Oby hid behind Abdul Sid's two sons as the mob yelled and jumped about. Abdul Sid looked dejected and fed up. As if he had had enough of the whole business of selling salt, he offered the remainder for a bargain price of fifteen likits.

Miraculously, the mob became a smiling crowd again and money began changing hands. Every slab of salt was sold faster than you could count to fifty.

Chapter 12

Icy Water

The sons of Abdul Sid collected the well-watered camels and led the way along even more narrow passageways. Glumly, Oby followed as they zigzagged along routes that looked the same but gave off different smells: cooking, animals and sweat. They halted in front of a building, larger than the others. The guard at the metal gate had to use two hands to lift the heavy bar that secured it. He grunted a greeting as they entered. Across a wide courtyard, white-painted buildings rose on all sides.

Leaving the camels with several boy-guards, the drovers followed Abdul Sid to a room which had huge cushions encircling the whole of the floor space. They sat down. A man brought drinking yoghurt, water, and rice with chicken.

Abdul Sid turned to Oby. He pointed across the courtyard, "You can sleep over there with Fida and Joe."

Oby's heart thumped a warning at the thought of spending a whole night in the same room with Fida. He tried hard to reason with himself that since Joe would also be there, maybe the night would pass comfortably ... or maybe

Joe was like Fida? But what could he do? He knew there was only one thing he could do. If things became unbearable, he would run away.

Just as everyone got up to leave the room, Oby said, "Where does the Great White River start?"

Abdul Sid grunted. "Wait until tomorrow, it'll soon be dark."

"Is it near?"

"Near enough."

"Tell me and I'll find it," said Oby.

"Pest! Wait until tomorrow. Don't bother me, boy. Go and make a final check on your camel. Remember, you're working for me," and he flicked at Oby's ear with a finger. "You two as well," he ordered his grandsons.

The camels were tethered under a canvas shelter and were steadily chewing. Mo was well-settled. Oby rubbed her neck.

"Where's the Great White River? Which way?" said Oby to Joe.

"Not far." Joe glanced around, then whispered, "I'll show you, if you like."

"Now?"

"Yeah."

"Okay."

They had only walked about five hundred metres when the sounds began to change. Tinkling and splashing replaced the noise of people-movement of the town. Water bustled along, slipping around stones and jumping over pebbles, dancing in a glittery dress.

"Put your hand down there," suggested Joe. Oby flopped onto his belly and lowered his hand into the racing stream. It was icy cold. "That's your river."

"The Great White River! It's fast ... but it doesn't look so great."

"This is only the start. There are hundreds of streams like this. They come from up there, just above Mokolee, hundreds of them and they just go on and on, all joining up into a giant. You wait 'til you see it. And plenty dangerous in places ... hippos and crocodiles and things like that. Down in Tembo Dolo the kids throw palms in the river from one bridge, then race like mad to try and get to the next bridge before the palms get there, but they never can. It's that fast. Sometimes they throw in kittens."

"Why?"

"Dunno."

"The kittens die?"

"Yeah."

Oby thought about all that for a moment. In his village there had been kittens; sometimes the kittens died when they were born, sometimes the jackals took them, sometimes the kittens went somewhere else but he didn't know where. He couldn't remember killing any.

The cold water splashing over his hand brought Oby back to the present and he scooped some over his head. Nothing in his life had been this cold before. His fingers began to turn numb.

Then he was tumbling.

Headfirst into the river.

A wave of ice clawed at him.

The water was travelling fast, sweeping around his body, twirling him round and round, bashing him onto its stony bed. His knees and elbows rammed into boulders. He tried to lift his head, but his neck muscles had gone stiff and he gasped and spluttered in the torrent.

Swirling around.

Bumping.

Floating away.

Fading away ... drifting into faint dreams ... drifting into the sky ... floating ... like a feather ...

A juddering halt!

His foot was caught, wedged between stones, but the water was still pulling him downstream. His neck strained to hold onto his head, as though every bone in his spine was going to spring apart. His arms flailed. He grabbed at rock, but his head was like a lead weight. It wouldn't lift. He couldn't lift it.

Watery dreams began to float by ... soft dreams ...

Suddenly, a strong, firm hand grabbed him and hauled him upright onto his feet. Oby spluttered and gasped to take air. He brayed like a donkey, coughing and rasping. He threw up water, from nostrils and throat. He had never heard his body kick up such a racket before.

"Stupid bloody idiot!" yelled Joe.

Oby locked his arms over his head, waiting for the beating. Nothing came except a coughing fit. He retched again. Even more water from the Great White River spurted out.

When at last his running heart began to slow down, he opened his eyes.

Joe was pushing Fida, slapping him around the head. "Idiot! Stupid idiot! You gone crazy or something?" Joe kicked Fida's backside. But Fida only ran off a few steps before turning. With arms folded he smirked with a look of triumph on his face. "Why'd you do a stupid thing like that?"

Although unsure of it before, Oby was in no doubt that he had an enormous enemy. Fida was much bigger than him. He had tried to kill him. Oby knew.

Joe grabbed Oby's arm and led him back towards the house.

With dry clothes he felt better, although still nauseous. Even though he was exhausted and only wanted to drop onto his sleeping rug, Oby needed to say a prayer. He had found the Great White River – his guide to his father. He needed to say a prayer of thanks.

He walked out into the silent, empty courtyard and stared up at the stars, straining to hear if the sounds of the river carried this far. Then he knelt. The ground was still warm and the sky was glittering and silent.

He saw a figure step out of the shadows, so jumped to his feet. In the moonlight the face looked familiar. As the figure drew nearer, Oby stood rooted to the spot in disbelief.

HIM!

It was the one who had spat at Abdul Sid in the market, and he no longer looked hunched nor old.

And his right hand was clutching something metal.

Chapter 13

The Humped One

The man took long strides. His feet made no sound on the blue-tiled courtyard. His hump had gone. He was erect and tall. A gun dangled from his right hand and the sight of it gripped Oby with such fear that his fingers began to tremble uncontrollably. He wanted to shut his eyes, but couldn't. *Shoot me quickly. Do it quickly and don't make a mess, and don't break my legs first.*

Oby burned. Sweat lay between his toes. He felt as though flames were licking up his legs and over his chest. There was no one to protect him here. He had to face this danger alone.

Unpredictably, his fear began to turn to something else. Anger. He stretched tall, pushed out his chest, lifted his chin high and faced the man square. With each of these movements his anger grew. So did his courage. Oby clenched his small fists, getting ready. These were his weapons. *Come on ... two more steps ... can't you see my fists... they're ready for you... don't think I can't defend myself.*

The seconds seemed like minutes as the man neared.

Droplets of sweat on Oby's forehead collected to form a trickle over his eyes.

The man swung his gun casually. Now clean-shaven, his chin folded into three fleshy rolls. He seemed to have sensed Oby's fear and a grin parted his lips. It grew wider and wider.

Oby gritted his teeth and took a deep breath, then another.

The man was now no more than six steps away when there was a distraction from the house.

Abdul Sid emerged and strode fearlessly across the courtyard.

Oby rushed forward. "No! No!" He threw himself at Abdul Sid and tried to push him back into the building. "Get back in! Get back in! He's got a gun." Oby pushed, but Abdul Sid did not move back. He stuck to the spot where he had come to a standstill. "He's got a gun, he's got a gun! You've got to listen to me, you've got to listen," cried Oby.

"Pesky boy! Pesky boy!" Abdul Sid attempted to dislodge himself from Oby's grip.

All of a sudden, Oby was lifted from behind, but he was still clinging to Abdul Sid's torb-shirt. A drawn-out tearing sound, a ripping of cloth, drowned out everything else. Shocked, Oby stared at his hands. He was holding a large piece of fabric from Abdul Sid's torb-shirt and Abdul Sid's very hairy legs were now on full view.

"Pesky boy! Look what you've done!" Abdul Sid gave him a kick.

Oby overbalanced and his forehead hit the ground. The pain was worse than last year's bad toothache and his eyes watered. Eventually, he lifted his bloodied forehead and looked from one man to the other, completely baffled and afraid of another kick.

"Ben!" Abdul Sid opened his arms widely. The two men slapped each other's shoulders and kissed each other on both cheeks. "A fine show today." They laughed loudly. Abdul Sid poked Oby with his foot. "Look what you have done to my torb-shirt, boy!" Oby stared from one man to the other in disbelief. "You'd better treat my brother and me with a little more respect."

"Brother!"

Ben Sid and Abdul Sid looked down on Oby, one grinning, one scowling.

Oby could see they were waiting for him to say something. "You were going to attack me."

"Me?"

"Yes"

"Why should I attack you?"

"You were waving that gun at me." Oby pointed. "You had an argument with Abdul Sid in the market and you spat into his face. I saw you. You tried to get the crowd to attack Abdul Sid. Then he threatened to slice off your ears with his knife ..."

"... and that means I want to attack *you*? Why should I want to do that?"

Oby wiped the dribble from his nose with his arm. "You were coming straight at me ... just now ... with that gun."

"With this old gun! Ha! I usually carry this." He swung it around his head. "It's my, shall we say, good luck charm. Try shooting with it." He held out the gun towards Oby. "I carry it for effect. It's useful. I use it to scare away troublemakers, that's what. Go on! Take it!"

Oby scowled and put his hands behind his back, but saw that the gun had a chipped, rusty-edged barrel. He began to believe the man might be telling the truth.

"Now, this one ..." From under a fold in his long, gold-embroidered coat Ben Sid pulled out a new pistol. It shone in the moonlight. "This is for real trouble."

It looked alive in Ben Sid's hand, ready to spring. Oby scowled. "Why do you keep the old gun when you have a new one?"

"This new gun is very expensive." Ben Sid turned the gun over in his hand lovingly. "Top of the range. Brand new. Very powerful." He huffed on it and gave it a little polish with the sleeve of his torb-shirt, then held the gun up to admire in the moonlight. "A lot of men would love to get their hands on such a fine gun. There are a lot of thieves about – you know what I mean?" He played with the trigger and rubbed the barrel again. "I keep it hidden."

The handle glittered with shiny stones in the moonlight, as brightly as the stars above.

Oby wrapped his hands around his knees and rested his chin on them. He had been deceived. Brothers ... how could they be brothers? In the marketplace earlier, Ben Sid had looked old and mean and had fired off a mouthful of insulting language at Abdul Sid. Oby stared blankly from one man to the other.

"Look at this boy! See how you've confused him, Abdul." Ben Sid pulled Oby to his feet. "If you'd forewarned him about our little game, he wouldn't be standing there now pissing his pants."

Oby gulped as he felt a warm trickle of fear beneath him.

Ben Sid laughed, tossed the pistol into the air, caught it and slipped it under his torb-shirt again. He said, "Old age is making you forgetful, Abdul. Why didn't you tell the boy about the game?" Abdul Sid grunted. "You forgot, didn't you,

Abdul? You forgot to tell him. That's the truth. You're absent-minded."

"You talk too much," said Abdul Sid.

"You tell me that every time I see you." Abdul Sid ignored his brother and pulled at an irritatingly long hair that was growing out of his nose. "Have you eaten?"

"Yes, yes we ate well," replied Abdul Sid. "Your house is always the master of hospitality."

"*Your* house?" said Oby.

"Aaah, so Abdul also forgot to tell you that you'd be staying at my house." Then Ben Sid asked, "What about our performance in the market today? What did you think of that?" Oby didn't answer. "Come on! Come on! A truthful answer."

"You were tricking people."

Ben Sid looked thoughtful and rubbed his chin. "Tricks? You think it was tricks, do you?"

"Yes," said Oby.

"Business is business," said Ben Sid. "Abdul sells salt and people buy. How he sells it is an art. Don't you think it's art?"

Oby scowled. He had never been asked such a weird question before. Selling, buying, he knew nothing about these things. Nor art.

Ben Sid made a suggestion, "At the market tomorrow, why don't you try selling? Yes? Let's see if you have any clever ideas for selling salt. Do you accept the challenge?"

Oby's hands ran nervously over his head. Fortunately, his brain seemed to click into another gear. His father! He had to get to his father. So, he had to accept every challenge, beat away his own sadness, let everyone see who Oby Malassa really was. *I am the son of Boudi Malassa ... and I'm not afraid of anyone.*

"Well?"

An idea was already beginning to form in Oby's mind. He managed a brief smile, the first for a long time. "I'm ready." He hoped he was.

Ben Sid slapped Oby's shoulder, sealing the challenge, but Oby noticed that he winked at Abdul Sid. So! They didn't really believe he could do it. He would have to prove to them. Just have to.

"Selling salt can be terribly boring," said Ben Sid. "Just look at my brother. Have you ever seen a man more bored? Have you ever been to a more boring place than the Salt Lake?"

Nod. Yes. Nod. No. Oby's head went this way and that.

"So, we like to liven things up a little to make things a little more interesting. When Abdul's caravan passes through this way we put on a performance or two, to relieve the boredom."

"Everyone must know your tricks by now?" said Oby.

"Not everyone. Those gold panners didn't. Just so you know, boy, we aren't stupid. We don't use the same trick every time. And sometimes we sell without tricks at all. We just smile nicely. Ladies like to buy from us when we smile. Now, boy, you stink really badly." Ben Sid called out to a hovering servant, "This boy has peed himself. Get him cleaned up."

Oby hung his head in shame. He suddenly felt extremely hot. Everyone would now know about his embarrassment.

The hovering servant rapidly steered Oby at arm's length along a corridor and through a door to a small room covered in marble. Then he turned a large handle that protruded from the brim of a vast white bath, the likes of which Oby had never seen before. From a long spout beneath the handle poured a stream of warm water, which slowly rose up the sides of the bath. The man left the room momentarily, returning with a clean torb-shirt. He threw a great slab of olive oil soap into the water and told Oby to get into it.

It was strange to sit in warm water. Oby usually squatted under one of the village pumps to get rid of dirt, as long as water was running fast enough. He always had to be quick, though, because older boys would push in, push him out of the way. Now he sat in quiet water, naked. The warm water wrapped around him so soothingly that he couldn't help but lean back and close his eyes.

* * *

The following morning everyone gathered in the room with the ochre and sandstone-coloured cushions, because there was business to do. The conversations were about salt: selling, buying, pricing, quality. They talked about who were the most difficult people to trade with. They also spent time suggesting new selling techniques for Joe and Fida to try out at local markets. Mostly, they discussed selling to large companies.

Oby paid attention to most of it, but found the whole business of selling salt strange. They talked about twenty likits, eighteen likits, twelve, ten, eight and six. He couldn't stop himself from asking, "What's the real price?"

There was a pause as Ben Sid poured cardamom tea, raising the pot high above his cup and jetting the pale liquid down with a perfect aim. "Ah now, you're really getting down to fundamentals," he said. "There isn't a real price. It changes all the time; it depends on supply and demand." Ben

Sid was as talkative as his brother was silent. "What d'you think it should be right now?"

Oby gazed at the patterns on the cushion for a few moments and made a wild guess. "Seven likits," he said, ponderously.

"The boy's a genius. Take good care of him, Abdul."

"Am I right, then?"

"Nearly. It's six."

"Six likits! Then you're robbers."

"Why're we robbers?"

"You tried to sell in the market for twenty."

"Why not? They were gold panners. They might have had pockets lined with gold."

"Then you finally sold for twelve. You tricked them into thinking twelve was cheap, but even eight wasn't cheap, was it?"

"If they think it's cheap, that's fine. Let them think it. It's business," said Ben Sid, clearly amused.

"Another thing, Gold Teeth only paid Moussa Khaliffa four likits for salt. I heard. He said trade was so bad that the worry of it all made his bones ache. So bad, he couldn't get more than six likits himself. He lied." Oby's voice rose higher. "Moussa Khaliffa's a hard worker ... Gold Teeth cheated him."

Ben Sid laughed. "Where did you find a boy like this? Did his mother *beg* you to take him away? Or did she *pay* you to take him away?" He guffawed loudly.

Fire rushed through Oby, making his ears burn.

Fida smirked and raised himself rather grandly on his cushion. Wicked words spewed from his mouth. Oby tried not to listen, but Fida's tongue was running away with itself; words like *'ransacked and ravaged by raiders'* and *'they deserved it'* and *'they were stupid village people, so it doesn't matter'*. Fida flicked his fingers towards Oby and tossed his nose in the air. He went on and on.

Oby leapt. He sprang upon Fida, lashing him with fists, digging his knees into Fida's belly and pulling at his hair. Oby sliced at Fida, aiming anywhere and everywhere, with karate chops – one, two, three, faster, faster, four, five, six ... Fida squealed and yelled, but Oby didn't stop. He wanted to hear Fida howl.

Ben Sid pulled Oby off.

Fida had a bloody scratch on his cheek. Oby had a chunk of Fida's hair in his hand. Fida was spluttering and crying.

Oby breathed steadily, ready for more. He stood ready.

"Where did this boy come from, Abdul?" Ben Sid's arms waved about in front of his brother's face. "Come on, Abdul." He banged his hand onto his cushion. "Abdul, speak!"

Abdul Sid readjusted himself on his cushion and raised his eyes to the ceiling. He blew steadily into the air. "He's from the village ... from the village near the Salt Lake. He was there ..." He poked at Oby's leg with his finger. "You tell him."

Oby wriggled and shrank low into the cushion, as though trying to disappear.

Ben Sid adjusted, getting himself more comfortable. His eyes were shining with an abnormal curiosity, and Oby didn't know how to escape from telling what had happened. *No, I mustn't cry... I don't want to speak ... I wish I was dead ...*

Ben Sid waited. They were all waiting. Oby clenched his teeth, his breath surged in and out in huge waves. He could hear it rattling around like a cyclone. His chest ached.

Still, they waited. And waited.

Oby started ... he stopped ... he started again ... Eventually, he spoke slowly about that night.

... his mother's voice pleading his younger brother and sister to hurry, hurry, run, run ... telling them to be silent, not to cry out... run, run ... his little sister's small, bare feet trotting as fast as they possibly could ... the flash of his mother's red dress ...

That night he lay like a rag on the soft mattress with his head safe in the smells of his own old sleeping rug. He was not used to such softness beneath his bones, that wrapped around his feelings, soaked up his tears and helped to dull all his pains ... and allowed him to slither into sleep.

Chapter 14

Injury On A Dusty Mountain Trail

Crackle. Bzz. Crackle.

An old radio buzzed in the news. Crackle, bzz crackle. "New government of ..." crackle, crackle ...

Abdul Sid stopped chewing his breakfast and cocked his head to one side to catch every word.

Oby continued scooping up brown beans with a piece of flatbread.

Abdul Sid smacked his lips together. "Ah! The rebels have been pushed back. The airport has been re-taken by Government troops. Maybe it's safe for you to go back home now."

Oby stopped eating. "There's nothing left. They smashed all the houses down. I don't know what happened to my mum ... so I have to find my father. How will he know I'm not dead? I have to go to Madame Betcha's farm in El Malla. I know that's where he is."

"Take my advice, boy, go back."

Ben Sid interrupted. "Take him with you, Abdul. Take him. The boy has lost his mother and needs to find his father." After a pause, he said, "Listen here, boy, I have a very good friend in Tembo Dolo. I know he could help you. Abdul could take you to the house of Yaki Zakariah." He turned to his brother, "Okay, Abdul?"

Abdul Sid shrugged.

Ben Sid continued, "Believe me, he's the best. He's a reliable friend and I know he would help you get all the way to El Malla. I could write a letter for you to take. What do you say?"

Oby could feel his feet twitching. He suddenly had enough energy in his legs to dance all the way to El Malla. "Yes! Yes!" He felt his journey was almost over.

After resting the camels for two days they headed out of Mokolee and West, towards the Zuda. Oby was happy to be with Mo again. She moved gently, with a small swagger and whenever she turned her head Oby rubbed the side of her neck.

"Is Ben Sid a salt trader?" asked Oby when he finally caught up with Abdul Sid.

"No."

"What then?"

"Spices, gold, and a few other things."

Oby thought about dealing in gold. He looked down at his hands and tried to imagine a large gold ring sitting there, having a big house with a courtyard and sleeping on a soft cushion ... and a big bath of warm water.

"And guns? Does he sell guns?" asked Oby.

"No."

The image of the gun handle, sparkling in the moonlight rested in Oby's mind. He said, "Was it a real diamond in the handle of Ben Sid's new gun?"

"Might have been."

"He likes sparkly stones, hey?"
Abdul Sid only grunted.

The trail down to the Zuda played switch-back with the Great White River. When the stream tumbled in waterfalls over cliff faces and jutting rocks, the road left it and meandered in snaking loops behind rocks until the two met again. When Oby could not see or hear the stream he felt anxious, as though he had lost hold of the string that was leading him to his destination. However, the stream always appeared again and sometimes they even crossed it, so he found it on his right one moment and then on his left. Stream and trail plaited like ribbons.

The trail met a junction crossed by a wide dirt road that followed the contours of the mountain. They took the road which zigzagged towards the Zuda. Oby caught glimpses of desert peeping between peaks in the distance.

Parts of the road were still in the making and enormous digging machines were grinding and gobbling into the hillside, sending up whirls of choking dust and filling Oby's ears with an almighty racket.

The road was a circus of activity. The camel caravan had to share the road with rainbow-painted lorries loaded with stone and moving constantly in low gear, crunching and squealing. The roadside itself was littered with used oil cans. Discarded drink cans shone in the hot sun. A couple of overturned and burnt-out vehicles lay abandoned.

Suddenly, Abdul Sid was not so placid. "A curse on your noises! A curse on your bloody machines!"

As lorries rumbled, the ground vibrated; hot air slapped

Oby in the face as each vehicle thundered by. The camels grumbled down their snooty noses.

Behind him a horn blasted with impatience. He twisted around to get a better view, but before he knew it, he overbalanced and fell headfirst past Mo's flank. With a yell he crash-landed. The road had teeth of stone and a hot spur stabbed Oby's right shoulder, followed by an oozing blood stain that quickly spread down the front of his white torb-shirt.

Mo started to chew at roadside thorn scrub. A dumper truck roared past. The driver hooted, purposely braked, then skidded, which sent up a cloud of dust, before accelerating away. Dust stuck to the damp blood and turned it a dirty pink.

The elder son of Abdul Sid stood with his hands on his hips and laughed. "Come on! Get up!" He had a grin stretching from ear to ear.

Oby couldn't even lift his left arm. As he struggled to his feet, pain shot through his shoulder. He pretended. He pretended there was no flame burning in his bones. He pretended he didn't care. He pretended there were no tears ready to spring from his eyes. He decided to walk. With every step his shoulder burnt with pain and the blood dried stiff. His head began to throb as they walked towards heat.

As they left the higher slopes, grasses became patchy. Breezes were getting hotter. From a point where the road widened Abdul Sid stopped the caravan to rest. Spread below was a narrow valley. It had been carved out slowly over thousands of years by the Great White River. Oby could not actually see the river from where he was standing, but a line of twisting trees and bushes marked its course. In the near distance the greys of the hill slopes abruptly ended and beyond them a wide sheet of flat biscuit took its place.

"The Zuda," announced Abdul Sid.

Oby didn't reply.

"You're not too good, hey?"

Oby still said nothing.

"But I can see you're brave. Not a moaner."

Oby met Abdul Sid's eyes. There was some kindness there. It was a sign that everything would be okay.

* * *

They finally arrived at the last village before the Zuda. It hung to the cliff like a limpet. The vertical drop of the hillside formed the walls of small houses. Narrow holes had been cut into the rock so people could see across the valley.

The camels' feet made a soft echo as they all filed through a dark, cold tunnel which had been hand-carved through the rock and led to the centre of the village. Men were squatting outside a building, smoking and sharing a hubbly-bubbly pipe. They passed the pipe along, each one sucking on the mouthpiece before passing it to the next. Brown mouths with teeth stained from tobacco and coffee sucked seriously at the pipe; the water bubbled in its clear glass container. The hubbly-bubbly owner came along the row refilling the pipe with tobacco and topping up with water and collecting payment. Gold Teeth had said that travellers needed money. He was right, because even smoking a dirty old water pipe needed likits.

Abdul Sid dropped down next to an old man with a face like wrinkled newspaper. Oby watched. No one spoke. Nor smiled. Just a nod of recognition towards Abdul Sid as the pipe was passed to him. He sucked at it and closed his eyes, as if it was the sweetest thing in the world, as though he had been waiting all day for this moment. As he let out a stream of smoke, a fit of coughing started and the contents of his mouth suddenly spewed out. Abdul Sid's eyes expanded and rolled and he flung aside the mouthpiece which smacked into the dust. "Filthy muck! What cheap muck have you put in there? Are you trying to kill me?"

The coughing fit continued as Abdul Sid walked his camel caravan through the village and past a field where men were mowing grass with hand scythes. At the end of the field was a house. Two servant boys ran out and grabbed Mo's lead to relieve Oby.

Abdul Sid gave a final splutter and spat onto the ground. "Filthy pipe!" he wheezed. "Come on, boy. Come on, follow me."

A woman appeared wrapped in brown from head to toe. She flung her arms in the air when she saw Oby. "Look at the state of you!" She called out, "Isda, come here!" A young woman appeared. "Get him cleaned up."

Within twenty minutes Oby had been shown how to work a shower handle, been given a clean torb-shirt (although a little too large) and had a glass of yogurt drink thrust into his hand.

The all-in-brown woman steered Oby into a room where the sons and grandsons of Abdul Sid were already sitting on floor cushions. "Sit there!" She pushed Oby to where she wanted him to go. "Move over, Joe, that's Abdul's place." She bossed Abdul Sid to make space. She bossed the girl to bring rice.

Oby was left to guess that this was Abdul Sid's house and the woman was his wife.

After eating, one of Abdul Sid's sons asked, "How many days do you want to rest the camels?"

"Three ..." Abdul Sid pursed his lips. "... no, four days, because I need to replace Joe's camel. It's been a good animal, but it's done enough. I need to get down to the market early and find a replacement."

When he heard the word market, Oby asked, "Will you sell any salt there?"

"Yes, tomorrow."

"Is that where I can sell?" Abdul Sid ignored the question. "Remember we had an agreement."

Abdul Sid pursed his lips and muttered, "Just a stupid idea hatched up by my brother."

"Abdul Sid, have you forgotten we had a deal?"

"But boy ..." Abdul Sid gave a weary sigh.

"Please ..."

Abdul Sid sighed again. "Pesky boy. Okay, tomorrow take Joe with you ... he'll show you where to sell."

Chapter 15

Ghost

Oby stood in front of Abdul Sid, grinning, holding out fifty likits.

The old man raised his eyebrows. He looked over Oby's head at Joe who was also grinning. All of a sudden, Abdul Sid was asking questions and it was the most Oby had ever heard him speak.

"Why are you wearing those grubby old shorts and T-shirt? Where did you get them from? Why have you got all these bloody scratches on your legs? Have you been fighting with Fida again? Joe, you were there to ..." Abdul Sid didn't finish because both Oby and Joe had such smug expressions on their faces and were obviously so satisfied that clearly there had not been a fight. There was something else going on. "Well?" he said, his eyes flashing with curiosity.

"Scrub thorns make good scratches. People feel sorry when you're scratched and there's blood."

"You did all this ... all this mess to yourself? Didn't you have enough blood on that shoulder from yesterday?"

Oby proudly explained, "Joe stood over the other side of

the marketplace pretending to be a salt trader ... and he had an enormous stick and walked up and down like he was my master ... and so I begged them to buy the salt otherwise he would beat me and not feed me." Oby ran out of breath.

"Did you grin like this all the time?"

"Oh, no, I was like this," and Oby dropped his head onto his chest, lowered his eyes, pushed out his stomach, so that it looked swollen from lack of nourishment and allowed his arm to drop, with the hand twisted back, so that it appeared injured. He sucked in his cheeks and looked dejected, hungry and ill-treated. He grinned. "See! So, they bought all my salt. And I sold for one likit more than you sell."

"One likit more! It's too much to pay."

"I know, but they didn't want to see me beaten. Anyway, I begged really hard. So, they paid."

"What trickery!"

"No, it's art," grinned Oby. "Remember?"

In an unusual outburst, Abdul Sid threw his head back and chortled loudly. "Let me see your profit."

Oby opened his hand.

Abdul Sid stared into the small palm, then picked up half the coins. "Now put your profit away ... and get yourself cleaned up."

* * *

As Oby slid into sleep that night, he realised that Fida had kept his distance from him all day.

* * *

Three days later the camel caravan met the Zuda. Oby had often heard the men in his village telling tales about its power: about dryness sticking your tongue to your mouth, about sandstorms that could scrape away your skin and leave your flesh raw, about wadis that disappeared overnight, about sand that changed form so rapidly that overnight you could lose your direction and walk in circles and never return.

The Zuda scorched.

Oby secured his head-wrap and pulled the top down over his forehead and the bottom up, over his nose, as Abdul Sid and his sons had done.

The sand was pushing to the foot of the hills. It nestled in every rock crevice. Where the road met the Zuda lay a village. Empty and in ruins, it had been taken over by sand. The sand piled itself wherever it could, using abandoned houses as scaffolding, slipping into every nook and cranny and suffocating everything in its path.

The caravan halted and Oby climbed a dune to a roof top where he found a sun-bleached animal skeleton. He jumped to another roof and another and another. Something glittered in the sun.

It was a knife. A very beautiful knife with a wide, curved blade lay cleanly on the sand, as if in a presentation box. Oby picked it up, jumped off the roof and showed it to Abdul Sid.

"Belongs to a gold panner, I expect. They carry knives. It can't have been there long, otherwise it would've been covered by sand."

Oby tied the knife into his sleeping blanket, then ran to another ruin, whose entrance had yet to be concealed by sand. He extended one foot inside, then ducked low in order to squeeze through the entrance. He was going to explore.

Then he heard an angry yell. "Boy, get back here. Stop

wasting time! You've got a camel to look after. She needs water. There's no time for playing. Pesky boy!"

Disappointed, Oby walked away from the ruin, but he felt sure he had heard a sound in there. In fact, he knew he had heard a sound.

At the well, which camel caravan traders kept protected by covering with corrugated tin and huge planks of wood, Oby sidled up to Joe. "Go and see," Oby urged him. "Honest! There was a sound in there."

"Ghosts. I bet it was ghosts. Or wind."

"Go," urged Oby again. "It was like someone groaned ... there was a groan. I know there was a sound."

Abdul Sid prodded Oby with his stick. "Enough chattering. Water."

Oby hauled up the bucket of water, hand over hand. It pulled on his sore shoulder and made him wince. Whilst Mo drank, Oby checked the strapping on the saddle, to ensure the salt was secure, and that the strapping was not twisted or rubbing against her belly. She slurped up every drop from the bucket in seconds. Then more. And every time Mo removed her head from the bucket water jewels fell from her long beard, showering Oby with cool relief from the heat.

In the meantime, Joe had drifted over to the ruined building.

Impatient to move on, Abdul Sid motioned for everyone to mount the camels. He snapped his fingers. "Where's Joe? Where's he gone? We aren't explorers, we're traders."

Oby thought, what if it was an injured wild animal in there? Or a man with a knife? And what if Abdul Sid made him go and look for Joe? What if he got attacked, too?

Then from out of the ruin Joe appeared, tightlipped,

carrying a boy; a lifeless form with maggots crawling over sores on his feet and ankles.

As they approached Oby noticed the large blotch of a pale pink mark on the boy's left leg. He knew that leg. That leg had played football with him. His heart thundered in his chest and his stomach heaved at the sight of so many maggots. Suddenly, without any warning, he vomited onto the baking sand.

Chapter 16

Death In The Zuda

The road from the ghost village poked into the Zuda like a bony finger and vanished into shimmering heat. Oby remembered his grandfather's tale of men's livers cooking from Zuda fire.

Flaf! Flaf! Flaf! Everyone was silent, slouched on their camels without wanting to talk. The only sound was a rhythmical flaf, flaf, flaf of the camels' tread. The sky was a sheet of washed-out blue, with not a single cloud wisp. Vertical blue and red striped poles on either side marked the route. Spaced at regular intervals, they broke the flatness. In the event of a sandstorm when the route might become covered in sand, the protruding poles marked the way.

Oby couldn't take his eyes off the boy. Kibo. Where had he been for the last year or so? Kibo slumped in Joe's arms, his bones sticking through his chest, his eyes sunk deeply into their sockets seeing nothing. Oby wanted to look away but couldn't. He wanted to stare new life into the boy. He wanted to say, *Hey, Kibo, we need you for our football team.*

He steered Mo close to Joe's camel in order to be as close as possible. Being close was better. *Kibo, wake up! Hear me! You have to live!*

But it was already too late. The boy's fingers twitched. Both arms dropped. Two glass stones sat either side of his nose.

The same panic swept over Oby as the night when the raiders came. Inside he was screaming. *No! No! No!* The screams inside his head had to stay there, though. Oby was getting used to hiding his heartaches.

* * *

"Dig!" Abdul Sid ordered his sons.

Camel drovers never move across deserts without a few tools and so they set about to dig a grave a short distance from the trail. Joe held the body; Fida and Oby stood back and watched. Oby continued to grit his teeth, his thoughts drifting back and forth. The Zuda was a lonely place under its clear and beautiful sky.

There was nothing to wrap Kibo in. There was no cloth to enfold him except a spare head-wrap that Abdul Sid always kept in his saddle bag. Joe wrapped Kibo gently and lowered the boy and they covered him with sand.

"We shouldn't have to bury a boy like this," muttered Abdul Sid.

They all crouched around the grave in silence for a few moments. Then stood, as Abdul Sid murmured, "Rest your wings, young butterfly."

"Rest your wings," they murmured in reply.

Abdul Sid said to Oby. "From your village, you say?"

"Yeah."

"Sure?"

"Yes, Abdul Sid. His name's Kibo. You saw the pink flesh. He was born with the pink flesh around his leg. Everyone knew him because of that. His father had the same."

"God go with him," said Abdul Sid. "How did he get here, so far away?"

"Don't know ... but he went with a lot of other boys from the village. Some men came looking for workers. They wanted servants for important people's houses and farmers for the fields up in the Delta. They paid for the boys. Some of the families had no corn ... they said it was a good thing. Kibo left during last year's heat."

Their procession across the Zuda had been silent before the burial and continued so. Oby was so tired that he felt little interest in the journey.

* * *

By mid-afternoon the distant view began to change, not only because the sun was lowering in the sky and changing from white light into warm orange, but because shapes were growing out of the horizon. As the caravan moved forward, the hazy shapes transformed into squares and rectangles, became solid, transformed into low buildings that hugged the desert floor and reached widely to east and west.

Tembo Dolo sat on the Zuda like a massive cake decoration.

The camel caravan of Abdul Sid neither quickened nor slackened, the camels needed no guidance. They passed through a shanty-town on the outskirts, where makeshift homes were made from heavy-duty, corrugated cardboard boxes with words that Oby was unable to read, like Omo, Ariel and Tide. Washing hung over the ropes that were binding the shelters together and tethering them to the ground. Women pummeled laundry in an old oil barrel, joking as they beat the dirt out of clothes with long sticks. Gold circles of sequins were stitched onto their black head scarves and glittered as brightly as their laughter in the fading sunlight.

Oby tried to pull his thoughts away from Kibo, but couldn't. Kibo had had huge goalkeeper hands and skipped so lightly on his feet when defending the goal. So absorbed with his thoughts, he didn't pay attention to Mo who was now placing her huge feet a bit too close to a cardboard home. Her skinny legs got caught in rope and, as she kicked and stomped to free herself, some wooden pegs in the ground dislodged and the box home slithered sideways and collapsed.

Immediately, two screaming women leapt towards him like panthers. They lashed him with sudsy washing, slapping with such ferocity that he was swung from one side of Mo to the other. Mo snorted and pitched into a run, tipping him to the ground. He wrapped his hands around his head as wet laundry slapped him all over.

Fortunately, Joe had seen. He snatched the camel's rope and yanked with all his might to stop Mo charging off, pulling so hard that his head was thrust into the panniers of salt on his own camel. But Mo was stubborn and kept stamping her feet and bellowing.

Two more women rushed forward with sticks. Thrashings landed on Oby's back. A fifth woman leapt up to steal salt protruding from the top of Joe's pannier. She clung to the pannier and pulled herself up high, straining to free the block.

Joe's camel stepped sideways and lurched forward, pulling Mo with it and the woman fell to the ground, landing beneath Mo's legs. Children began screaming and more women ran forward and clustered around, assessing the situation, before picking up stones.

Oby's arms were still wrapped around his head for protection when the first stone split the skin on the back of his hand. As seconds passed, the beating got worse. His right ear was bleeding. His thigh had gone numb. The pain in his ribs was excruciating as someone kicked him over and over.

All of a sudden, Oby was being dragged away. Pedalling his legs furiously, someone hauled him onto his feet. He grabbed the arm of his rescuer and ran and ran. Someone was keeping him steady so he could get away. Someone was hanging onto him. At a safe distance, Oby turned to his rescuer.

Fida!

Oby stumbled. The ground came rushing up. His nose met hard-packed earth. The pain made his eyes water so much he couldn't see.

Then Joe yanked Oby back onto his feet. Between them, Fida and Joe grabbed hold of him and threw him like a sack onto Mo, before leaping onto their own camels. Behind them the women were screaming. Curses and threats and a volley of stones followed, causing the camels to buck and snort and bellow.

Far ahead was Abdul Sid, who seemed to know nothing of the commotion behind him, or was ignoring it.

Fida had saved him. He looked across, but Fida didn't look at him, just flicked the reins and continued on his way.

He saved me because he's trying to say sorry. Or was there another reason?

They twisted through the outskirts of the town for half an hour, finally arriving at a large open square where camel drovers collected. Huge troughs of water and piles of mown grass, brought by boat from farmland on the lower course of the Great White River, were waiting for the camels.

"Say goodbye to your camel," said Abdul Sid. "This is where you leave us."

"Here?"

"Right here."

Oby slid off Mo but his hand remained on her soft neck and he could feel movement in her throat as she chewed. "Shall I give her some water?"

"No, we can look after her now." Abdul Sid's oldest son took the rope from Oby. "You'd make a good drover."

Oby's eyes creased into a small smile. He put his face to Mo's muzzle, to feel her warmth and to get some of her familiar stinking breath for the last time, but she was too interested in chewing grass and edged away.

"May God give you strength," said the oldest son. "Lead you safely."

Fida stood in the background, not moving, not speaking.

* * *

Oby walked a stride behind Abdul Sid on their way to find the house of Yaki Zakariah. In passing each house, Oby adjusted his sleeping rug to tie it more firmly round his middle. That's when he noticed that the corner of his sleeping rug had been neatly cut off.

So that was it! Fida's knife had done it! He had wanted to

steal Oby's money. That's why he had rescued him. So Gold Teeth had been right about the importance of having a concealed money bag and not telling anyone.

He smiled to himself.

Fida would now be holding a handful of stones.

Oby walked tall.

Chapter 17

Yaki Zakariah

The streets were strewn with pockets of desert dust. As they walked, there were changes: houses increasing in size and the spaces between them greater. There were giant walls separating each house. And there were guards.

They came to a bridge that crossed the Great White River. Here, the water was much wider, flowing smoothly, but far too dirty to see into its depths. It wasn't playful as before, but wide and flat and dotted with small boats.

Abdul Sid hesitated as he glanced right and left. "Come! This way."

Hanging over the bridge, Oby could see the contents of boats: bulging sacks, a couple of goats tied together and sprays of dates still on their stems.

On the other side of the bridge there were fewer houses. They walked swiftly on, Abdul Sid counting as they went. Each property had a fringe of palms rustling high above its walls. Some walls stretched for two hundred metres and more.

They stopped outside a massive wrought-iron gate. Two

beggars squatting beside it sprang into life, planting themselves at Abdul Sid's feet.

A guard put his nose through the gate's bars. "What do you want?"

Abdul Sid had to speak over the heads of the two beggars, who were touching and tapping to find a money bag. He shoved at them.

"You! Who are you?" demanded the guard.

"The brother of Ben Sid. My brother is a friend of Yaki Zakariah."

By now the two beggars were slithering their fingers into Abdul Sid's pockets and up his sleeves. He bellowed and pushed them both away.

The guard gave a performance, rattling his heavy keys, taking his time. No sooner had the gate opened than one beggar dashed forward, holding out thin hands. The guard immediately flew into a stamping rage and knocked the beggar sideways.

The hood fell off. An old man lay at Oby's feet, looking as though he hadn't eaten a solid meal in years. As the other beggar dashed forward to help him the hood fell back to reveal a girl, younger than Oby, with a grubby face. Abdul Sid threw some likits in her direction and she scooped them up.

The guard slammed the heavy gates behind them. Then gushed, "Oh yes, your brother, Mr. Ben Sid, I know him, he's a very good man. Very generous man to me. Very generous." He suddenly turned, grabbed the branch of a shrub at the side of the path, shook it vigorously and yelled, "Ratface!"

From under the bush's leafy canopy crawled a bleary-eyed man.

"Get a move on, lazy good-for-nothing," screamed the

guard. "Go and tell Yaki Zakariah that the brother of Ben Sid is at the gate."

The man shuffled towards the house, muttering. Fifteen minutes later, he shuffled back and gave a lazy wave to follow.

In the great hallway of the house Oby and Abdul Sid stood in silence, whilst the man rubbed his eyes feverishly. At the hall's centre a brass urn dripped with plants that smelled sweetly of jasmine. It was cool away from the oppressive heat outside.

At the end of the long hallway double carved-oak doors suddenly flew open and through them glided power. The man was tall, his neck was long, he strode with huge confidence. His polished, black-patent shoes clicked against the marble floor that shone in random swirls of grey and white. He was wearing a startlingly white silk torb-shirt which had been pressed so perfectly that not a crease could be seen. His face was freshly shaved and shone, as though it had just been pampered with fine cream. His fingers were pale and nails finely manicured. On his left hand a large yellow diamond flashed, and around his neck hung a heavy gold chain embedded with pale blue stones. At first Oby thought they were goats' eyes. As Yaki Zakariah drew near, Oby could smell a musky perfume.

"Greetings, my brother." He looked only at Abdul Sid. Then he turned to the guard. "Get out of here!" Yaki Zakariah turned to Oby. "You can have his job. He keeps falling asleep and he stinks. He's been warned." Then he scowled. "What happened to you? Looks as though you've been rolling in dust. If you want to work here, you'll have to smarten up."

"I'm not here to ..."

Yaki Zakariah turned away. "Abdul Sid, how is your dear brother? A fine man. We do a lot of business together."

"Blessings on your family, Yaki Zakariah, and on your house." Abdul Sid gave a small, polite bow.

Oby was getting anxious already, since Yaki Zakariah had yet to hear why he was there. He certainly wasn't looking for a job.

They were led to a simple side room. Yaki Zakariah wiggled his fingers towards a mat with pictures of camels and palms. Abdul Sid and Oby sat down on it, cross-legged. Yaki Zakariah sat on a large ornate chair forcing them to look up at him.

Oby and Abdul Sid were brought lemon juice, freshly squeezed and sweetened with honey.

"From my farm," said Yaki Zakariah, and he tipped back his glass and drank it in one long gurgling gulp. "You can work there if you like." Oby must have looked surprised, or even frightened, because Yaki Zakariah said, "You'll like the farm."

Oby appealed to Abdul Sid with his eyes.

"If you please, Yaki Zakariah, we are here to ask for your help for Oby."

"He isn't here to work?"

"No ..." Abdul Sid hesitated and coughed and looked as though he didn't know where to start his story.

Yaki Zakariah scowled, then stood up and looked very pointedly and impatiently at the enormous gold watch on his wrist. He leaned forward expecting a rapid explanation.

For once Abdul Sid could not escape from speaking. He gave a lot of detail about the raid on Oby's village.

"Yes, yes, yes, the news has been full of it," said Yaki Zakariah. He said to Oby, "You're lucky to be alive."

Abdul Sid said, "My brother said that you have many business connections and would be able to help get this boy to El Malla."

"Yes, yes, of course I can help." Yaki Zakariah stroked the arms of his velvet chair with long nails.

Oby replied excitedly, "Thank you, Yaki Zakariah, thank you." Then he fumbled under his torb-shirt, to his money bag, and brought out the crumpled letter.

"Oh, yes!" Abdul Sid said, "You nearly forgot the letter, the letter."

Yaki Zakariah used a fine, thin dagger to open the envelope. His eyes screwed into slits as he read it, and a slight smile appeared at the corners of his mouth. He placed it on his desk. "Yes, of course I can help you."

Abdul Sid stood up. "I am grateful to you." He then turned to Oby who had already scrambled to his feet. Abdul Sid's mouth opened, then closed again. He placed his hands on Oby's shoulders and let them rest for a moment before finding his words. "God give you strength on your way. God give you strength, boy." Abdul Sid gave a small bow to Yaki Zakariah and quietly departed.

Yaki Zakariah took Oby to a long, low building hidden amongst date palms and orange trees. "You need some decent clothes."

"Thank you, yes, thank you." Oby felt safe. His hopes surged high.

Blue, plastic pipes snaked to the base of every palm where pools of water collected. Jets from other pipes spurted up into the branches of palms keeping them fresh looking.

The building Oby arrived at consisted of six rooms in a long line, all with two narrow beds, a small table and a cupboard. He had never seen beds on legs before. In the very last room was a young man with his nose pushed into a book, wearing wire glasses supported only by cotton threads twisted round his ears. He looked up, blankly.

"Look after this boy," said Yaki Zakariah. "He'll share with you."

Chapter 18

Ramu

Oby fidgeted in the doorway.

"Come in, if you like."

Oby stepped inside.

"My name's Ramu."

"Oby."

Oby didn't know what he was supposed to do and there was an awkward silence. Ramu ran his fingers through his hair, then gestured for Oby to sit on a bed. Ramu scratched his ear repeatedly, red from where the cotton threads holding his glasses had irritated the skin. He flicked through the pages he had been reading, weighing up the situation. Then stood up. "I'll get some bedding for you." He returned and proceeded to show Oby how to organise the bed, covering the mattress with a white sheet, then wrapping a white cloth round the pillow. The second white cloth he left folded on the bed. "Cover for when you sleep."

Oby untied his sleeping rug. "I've got this."

"Use that if you want." Then Ramu said, "Where're you from?"

"Triathia."

"I'm from North Triathia," said Ramu, smiling broadly.

Oby stiffened. He stood up, edged towards the doorway and felt for the doorpost, not turning his back or moving his eyes off Ramu.

Ramu frowned. "What's wrong? Why don't you rest?"

"Are you a raider?"

"A what?"

"Raiders came from the north."

"What are you talking about? What raiders?" Ramu's dark brown eyes swelled rapidly.

"They came from the north, ransacked our village, set fire to our huts and killed."

Ramu leaned forward. "Raiders killed? When? I don't know any raiders."

"North and South Triathia are fighting."

Ramu's glasses drifted onto the end of his nose as he rolled his head from side to side, as though loosening his neck would help him to digest the information a little better.

"You don't know anything about it?" said Oby.

"No."

"Why don't you know?"

"Because I'm here."

"How long have you been here?" Oby asked the question as though it was an order. He stared hard at Ramu.

Ramu's raised eyebrows were pushing his forehead into tight pleats. He glanced down at his hands, then replied, "I think, eight years."

"You've been here for eight years?"

Ramu nodded.

"When you go back home, they'll make you fight?"

"I can't go back."

"If you're a guest worker ... soon you will go back."

"No, I can't."

He was hiding something. Oby became more bothersome with his questioning, determined to find out why the youth believed he couldn't leave. "Why can't you leave?"

"Because I like it here," Ramu snapped with impatience. "It suits me here. I'm preparing, you see ..." He didn't complete what he had started to say.

Oby noticed his eyes drift through the doorway to the palm fronds swaying gently in the breeze. "Preparing for what?"

Ramu sighed and cracked his fingers. "Well, you see, Yaki Zakariah has an English nanny to look after his children. She teaches me English. I need English. So, it's good here ... and when I have enough money, I'm going to London."

"London?"

"Yes, it's a beautiful green place and it isn't hot. When I have enough money, I'll go to school in London and then I'll go to university."

"University?"

"I want to be a teacher. *Then* I'll go back to my village and teach—" A horn sounded. Ramu immediately stood up. "Food is ready. Wait here. I'll bring you some."

Oby tried the bed. He lay on his back watching the lazy ceiling fan loop around with its soft, low whirr. His eyes were beginning to droop when Ramu returned with a plate of rice and lamb. He beckoned for Oby to sit next to him and they shared the plate, using their fingers to mix the rice with the meat, making it into balls before dropping it into their upturned mouths.

A little later, Ramu took Oby outside, round the back of

the whitewashed building, to a washroom. He grabbed the long handle of the shower and yanked it down. Water hurtled out. "The soap is in the corner, on the ledge above your head," he called out. "Throw your clothes outside. I'll collect some clean ones for you."

Oby spread soapy lather all over himself. It was sweet-smelling. He remained under the falling water for ages. But he was naked and Ramu had not returned.

He might have known. Ramu was from the north. They were all thieves from the north and not to be trusted.

Oby wasn't sure what to do. He stayed under the shower for a few more minutes. Then, with one hand clutching the entrance post for support, he leaned out as far as possible in the hope of attracting someone's attention, but there was no one in sight.

He stood naked, rapidly drying, for five minutes or so, then slid out of the washroom and, facing the wall, moved along the length of the building. He was cautiously peering round the corner when a finger prodded him in the shoulder.

The man was tall and very, very bony. "If you're a new boy," he said, "tomorrow you help me."

Oby covered his nakedness with his hands.

At that moment, Ramu ran round the corner, his glasses half off his face.

The thin man reprimanded him. "Why are you letting this boy run around naked?"

"I left him in the washroom, Hassan. I went to get clean clothes for him but couldn't find the right size. When I got back, he wasn't there."

Hassan's arm flew out sideways and clipped Ramu on the back of his head. "Make sure he gets to me early tomorrow." He glided off.

Oby put on the clean clothes and followed Ramu back to the room. Maybe he wasn't so bad, after all. "Why do I have to go to that man tomorrow?"

"He's the cook. He's Hassan."

"Cook?"

"Yes, he says you have to help him."

"I have to cook? I can't cook. I'm not here to cook." Ramu only shrugged. "I can't cook. I'm not here to ..." But Oby could see that Ramu didn't want to talk any more. As he made himself comfortable on the bed, a lot of questions passed through his mind. Things were not right. Ramu was hiding something. "Why did you come here to work?"

In barely a whisper Ramu said, "Because Yaki Zakariah wanted workers. I came to work."

"Yes, I know you came here to work, but why? Why didn't you go to school ... like you wanted?"

"There was no money. So, when Yaki Zakariah's men came looking for workers, they said if I worked for him for a while then I would have enough money to go to school."

Oby nodded. "When will you have enough money?"

"He said he'll pay me soon. He said he will pay everything he owes me soon. He said he's keeping it safe for me ... for my education."

"So, he's never paid you?"

"Not yet."

"Nothing at all?"

"No."

"Nothing in eight years?"

"No... not yet."

Oby saw tears welling in Ramu's eyes. Even though his torb-shirt was warm and comfortable against his body, Oby felt icy stakes pinning him to the bed.

Chapter 19

Yaki Zakariah's House

"Boy! Where's that boy?"

Oby heard bellowing. It was his name. He opened his eyes. Just a dream! But ... no ... the booming was close. He saw the sandaled feet of Hassan in the doorway while spittle exploded from his mouth. All the veins in his temples were forming ridges. "Follow!" he barked and strode towards his kitchen.

Oby leapt from his bed and trailed behind. Shivering. The sun was hardly up.

Hassan began stirring his cooking pot. He grinned, showing a couple of black teeth. He stared out of one eye at Oby whilst the other eye concentrated on the swirling contents of the pot.

Oby waited for orders.

Hassan's stirring-spoon fell into the cooking pot. "See! See! See what your scrawny self has made me do! Get out of my sight, you skin-bag! Shove off!" He snatched up a filthy cloth: the same one he used to wipe the pots with, the same one he used to wipe his sweaty face with, the same one he used to wipe away grease and burnt meat with, the same one he used to polish his teeth with. He advanced on Oby, thrashing the cloth in the air in all directions.

Oby stepped aside, raising both arms over his head for protection. "Please, no, no, Hassan." He wasn't sure if Hassan was thrashing at him or simply beating a path through the swarms of flies.

"Get out of my sight! I'm sick of the sight of you already." Hassan screeched, "I'm telling you, clear off." He raised his arm again.

Skidding out of the kitchen backwards, Oby ran.

Ramu showed no surprise at seeing him again so soon. "That's normal for Hassan. He gets mad at everyone and changes his mind a hundred times a day. Stay out of his way."

"So what am I supposed to do?"

Ramu shrugged.

Oby decided to hang around the main entrance of Yaki Zakariah's house in the hope of meeting him ... to discuss his journey to El Malla.

Ramu stopped him. "That's not a good idea. We're not allowed there. You'll be punished." He put a bucket and shovel into Oby's hands.

"What's this for?"

"You'll soon see."

At the far end of the gardens, there was a large, semi-shaded enclosure. The metal fencing was high and inside were four gazelles. They bucked and leapt into a corner as Ramu opened the enclosure gate.

Ramu began shoveling gazelle muck into his bucket. "Come on, use that spade."

"Why do I have to do this?"

"It's better you do."

So Oby shoveled muck, filling and emptying several buckets. Each shovel-full sent up a wave of stench. And every time he held his breath for as long as possible. The only sounds were the scraping of the shovels on the ground and the clicking open and the clicking shut of the enclosure gate as they moved in and out, dumping waste onto a donkey cart.

"How can you work in this place?"

"There's worse."

After hosing the ground, they threw down fresh bedding of straw. Oby sucked in the sweet perfume of dried grass feed that arrived once a week on a felucca. Ramu told him that it was brought along the Great White River, from the delta to Tembo Dolo.

Oby wondered if perhaps his father had had anything to do with growing or cutting this grass. The thought of his father made his heart thump erratically. He needed to be moving towards the delta, not stuck here in Tembo Dolo.

Ramu gave him a nudge. "Stop daydreaming. Get on." He nodded in the direction of the water trough. "You only have to clean it out, because it fills with water automatically." In the next breath he said, "Try and catch their tails."

Oby grabbed at one of the gazelles. He tore around the enclosure, his hand snatching up and down, but the stubby tails rotated like propellers and his fingers got stung.

Ramu locked the enclosure gate and headed off. "Come on."

"Where're you going now?"

"Clean out the drain."

At the back of the house Ramu lifted a metal grate and then thrust a long rod with a metal hook down the drain which plunged underground. There were surprises down there: thin, fat and ugly. Oby watched with curiosity as

Ramu pulled back the rod slowly, heaving a slimy stench-ball of hair, bone and grease. He used bare hands to transfer the stench-ball into his bucket.

Oby stepped back.

Ramu worked in silence, his back hunched over.

Oby felt badly for him. The longer he watched the more uncomfortable he became as sweat trickled down Ramu's face.

The smells that arose from the drain were the worst that Oby had ever experienced. He turned away. Date palms were swaying in the desert wind, throwing themselves into a rhythmical salsa. His eyes moved back to the bent form of Ramu whose glasses were now hanging by one thread from one ear.

"Let me do it." Oby pushed Ramu aside. "Fix your glasses."

Congealed sludge clung to cracks and crevices like glue. Oby lay on his stomach and brushed vigorously with a wire brush.

Fattening by the day, stench-balls sometimes grew until the drain became totally blocked. When that happened, oily black waters had nowhere else to go except to shoot above ground and form vile swimming pools.

Oby found a half-drowned kitten, trapped by its paw in a wire netting guard. He needed to work quickly at untwisting the wire before the next shoot of dirty water came along. But it was already too late. Dark grey foam rushed towards him and this time it was steaming hot. He snatched his fingers away in shock and the kitten was dashed away and swallowed by the black-hole drain. He closed his eyes.

"What's wrong?"

"The water came too quickly. The kitten. I couldn't save it. I couldn't help it."

"You tried." Ramu showed little feeling. "It will join all the other dead kittens in the river."

Rats and rubbish. The two belonged together like desert and sand, date and palm. To keep the rats away rubbish had to be removed twice a day. Oby helped Ramu load the metal bins from behind the kitchens onto a donkey cart. As each bin was lifted, scrawny rats scattered, racing towards the drains. No sooner had the cart squeaked away than the rats returned, chasing every morsel remaining on the ground. Ramu flushed the area with a high-powered hose which sent one rat high into the air.

Throughout the day, Oby listened out for footsteps, kept his eye open in case Yaki Zakariah came into view and gave him the opportunity to ask about going to El Malla.

At the end of the day, smelling sweeter and wearing a clean torb-shirt, Oby watched Ramu tie fresh string around his glasses. Under the cool relief of the ceiling fan Oby slowly drank a tumbler of water. "Where's Yaki Zakariah?"

"At his office."

"When will he be home?"

"I don't know. Sometimes he's away for days."

Oby turned over on his bed to face the wall and closed his eyes.

* * *

The following day, using rope supports, Oby and Ramu scaled date palms with bare feet to reach stalks of ripened dates. The fruit hung thick and pale, but when some fell loose, Oby hurriedly retrieved them for his own mouth.

* * *

It was now five days since he had arrived at Tembo Dolo. Every morning he woke up wondering. At these moments the journey to find his father seemed far away. He wondered how he would travel there. Perhaps in one of the big limousines, polished every day until you could see your face in it; or would it be by felucca, sailing north on the Great White River?

Oby was still trying to understand why Ramu had been working for Yaki Zakariah for eight years, yet never been paid. He thought a lot about the boy, who struggled to answer his questions. Ramu seemed muddled. His replies didn't make much sense. Oby also considered something else: Ramu was from the north, so it wouldn't be good to trust him. Maybe everything that he told Oby was a lie. Yaki Zakariah had promised he would help Ramu ... he was saving the money for him. It was obvious to Oby that Yaki Zakariah could see that Ramu wasn't responsible enough yet ... he was saving it for when he was more mature.

Oby decided not to ask Ramu any more questions.

Chapter 20

Fire

It was the start of Oby's second week at the house of Yaki Zakariah. Hassan appeared at the door of the boys' room.

"Come on," he ordered. "Lazy waster! You didn't come here to waste time. You're here to work."

"No! That's not true. I'm waiting for Yaki Zakariah to help me. He's going to help me."

"Help? What help?"

"He's helping me to go..."

"Go? No-one goes from here. Except to Hell."

Oby did not move from the bed. He scowled. Ramu gave him a push and suddenly Oby knew why, as Hassan's hands, clenching and unclenching flew forward and struck him over the head.

He did not touch his head after he received the blow, or make a sound, even though pain shot from left ear through to his right ear and left them buzzing. Momentarily, he became dizzy and hung his head between his knees, only to be faced with Hassan's filthy feet.

Ramu helped him to his feet and whispered, "Do what he says."

Oby quietly followed Hassan to the kitchens.

The dry heat of the kitchens burnt his breath. The sweat on Hassan's brow sizzled in the heat. Half of the windows in the kitchen were shut, because when opened it created such a strong draught that the gas cookers blew out. The mosquito screens were covered in a thick, black blanket of flies, but hundreds still got into the kitchens and hovered lazily over meat which was sitting in large chunks on chopping blocks. Two fans whirred above, only disturbing more hot air, and slashing through flies.

Flies divebombed Hassan's hands as he threw oil onto the dough he was stretching across a wooden table. He swatted flies as he pulled and eased the dough, until it was finer than a sheet of paper. He ordered Oby to pick the flies out of the dough and after that he ordered him to cut it into equal squares. He stood breathing over his shoulder, so Oby made every movement with extreme care, lest he should make a mistake. But Hassan was the kind of man that could always find a mistake.

"Do it faster! Do it faster!" He jabbed Oby in the ribs with his finger. "Faster! Faster!" Jab. Jab.

Hassan filled some of the squares with a soft white cheese. He folded the dough over the cheese, lapping it over and over into a triangle. "Now, you." Hassan grabbed Oby's collar and yanked him nearer.

Oby's fingers were not dexterous, so some of the triangles were big and some were small. Hassan snatched the ones that were not the right size and threw them at Oby's head.

"Fry them in that," yelled Hassan, indicating a large pan of bubbling oil.

Oby dropped a dough triangle into the oil. Immediately, it exploded into the air. Hot oil leap like a geyser, out of the pan, over the gas burners, and in an instant, flames were leap-frogging over the cooker and up the walls. He stumbled back as flames leapt greedily in all directions.

Hassan snatched at a pile of blankets, already patterned with scorch marks, and threw one after the other over the flames. He raced out of the kitchen, and round to the outside wall of the building, to the exact spot behind the gas cookers where gas cylinders were lined up. He quickly turned them all off. Oby followed Hassan and found him leaning with his back against the wall and his eyes closed, sweat pouring down his face.

A gaggle of servants suddenly appeared, laughing and pointing. Oby stayed well back. Hassan slowly opened his eyes and fixed them on Oby. He moved forward with his hands making fists.

A woman appeared from nowhere, like a billowing fluff-puffed cloud. She smelt of flowers and was adorned with a long, floating scarf made of hundreds of dyed feathers.

Hassan's attack halted before it began. There was sudden and complete silence all around. The group parted to let her through.

Brightly painted red lips opened. "Hassan," she shrilled, pointing her red painted fingernails at Oby. "I don't think I've seen this boy before. Is this a new boy or an old boy?"

"New boy," Hassan muttered.

"New boys start in the house. You know that."

"Yes, Madame," Hassan muttered again.

"Where's the other boy?"

"He ran away, Madame."

"Did you go and look for him?"

"Yes, Madame," said Hassan, dropping his gaze.

"He's lying," whispered Ramu, coming up behind Oby.

The bright red lips continued. "Well, he won't get far in the Zuda, will he? If he isn't dead already!"

Oby stood staring at the red fingernails; cold shudders went through him as he somehow knew exactly which boy she was referring to.

She turned towards Oby and rose to her full (but still very short) height. "I am Madame Zakariah. You call me Madame." He gazed at the teal-blue gems sparkling around her throat.

She then paraded up and down like a queen, inspecting her troops. The gems scattered light in all directions, creating patterns over the plain white torb-shirts of the servants.

Turning to Oby again she said, "The Zuda does a better job than prison walls. You'd better remember that." Gazing round, Madame Zakariah then pointed. "Jama! You will go into the kitchen with Hassan."

Hassan and Jama glowered at each other.

"Clean up that disgusting mess in the kitchen, and do it quickly," she added, before tottering on her thin high heels back to the house.

"Jama and Hassan hate each other," Ramu said to Oby, as the group dispersed, "and Madame knows it."

"Why did she do it, then?" asked Oby.

"She's like that."

Chapter 21

Awad Sha-Had

Oby waited in the back hallway. A few seconds later the housemaster Awad Sha-Had rolled down the stone stairway, wide and sturdy as a bulldog.

"Can this skinny boy make a bed?" His buffalo boom filled every space.

Oby began to feel sick with fear. What was this loud man going to do? Was he like Hassan? He winced when an arm stretched towards him, but it landed around his shoulders. A sweaty, fat-fingered hand ruffled his curls and picked out bits of pillow fluff.

"You'll be alright with me, boy," Awad Sha-Had rasped between coughs. He steered Oby up two flights of stairs. "Are you okay? You don't seem so good to me. Your eyes are bloodshot. Getting enough sleep?" A tear collected in the corner of Oby's eye. "Come on now, boy, you'll be all right with me. Didn't I tell you so? What's your name?"

"Oby."

* * *

The house made Oby shiver. Air conditioning machines slotted into the walls of every room spewed out cold air. Awad Sha-Had handed him a large blue cloth and showed him how to clean a bath. As it was wide and deep, Oby climbed inside to work. It had a large flowery curtain on a high track that could be pulled completely round it.

Oby had his own ideas about cleaning. He twisted the cleaning cloth around his right foot and swept it back and forth. In the background he heard click-click-clicking, but paid no attention.

The large form of Awad Sha-Had suddenly loomed. "Shhhhhhh!" and with one deft swing the curtain was swung round to conceal Oby.

His heart skipped.

The click-clicking sound came nearer and nearer. He heard the shrill voice of Madame Zakariah the other side of the curtain. "Why are you hanging onto my bath curtain?" she shrilled.

"Just cleaning it, Madame," said Awad Sha-Had.

"Cleaning! Don't you normally take it down to clean it?" and she pushed in front of Awad Sha-Had and swung the curtain back.

Oby stood nose-to-nose with Madame Zakariah.

"What are you doing in my bath?" she shrieked.

Awad Sha-Had quickly spoke up. "Please, Madame, you can see he's just a kid. Madame, he'll soon learn. This is his first day in the house. He's new ... I'll teach him better."

But Madame was already click, click, clicking away.

"Madame, Ma—" Oby's voice suddenly rose to a cry he'd never heard before.

She swung round, causing the pale blue icicles dangling from the ends of her ears to dance in circles. "Well?"

"Yaki Zakariah. When will he help me?"

"He's helping you now. You've got a job, haven't you?" She clicked away out of earshot.

Awad Sha-Had mopped his brow. He said, "You're lucky! She's a real mountain cat. One pounce and you're dead." He waggled a finger at Oby. "She flies into terrible rages over silly little things and then we suffer with dreadful food for a month. So, learn to listen, Oby. Use your ears. Ears are for listening. You have two. Use one, at least. Don't forget. Right?"

"Right." repeated Oby, swallowing hard.

* * *

Oby swept up and down long hallways with a wide broom, collecting Zuda sand that crept into the house every day. He threw buckets of water over the same hallways and then swept again, forcing the water to run like a river, down the marble stairs and out through the doorways, washing away every grain of sand.

The days rolled by.

Oby liked cleaning the children's rooms because of televisions which stayed on most of the time. Occasionally, when the children were at school and he knew that he was completely alone, he sat quietly on the edge of one of the children's soft beds and watched cartoons. He loved *Kung Fu Panda.* It made him laugh.

Sometimes he saw families, with a mother and father laughing and joking and children playing together. Sometimes tears came. Sometimes the tears would not go away. At these moments Oby wished he was a bird and could spread his wings and fly away to wherever his mother might be. It always took ages to clean the children's rooms.

Sometimes, he was sent up to the roof where there was a laundry. Two sisters, Gulum and Giddy, lived and worked on the roof. There were two rooms up there, the laundry and the ironing room. Gulum's and Giddy's beds were tucked away into a corner of the laundry.

They showed Oby how to hang out washing on lines that stretched across the flat rooftop. All the hanging made his arms ache. They taught him how to iron. The iron was heavy and that also made his arm ache. The ironing room was as hot as the kitchens.

Oby didn't mind working in the house, though. Even when he made mistakes, Awad Sha-Had only laughed.

* * *

"Come on," Ramu called to Oby, fixing his glasses with fresh thread and tying them round the back of his head. "Yaki Zakariah and Madame have gone away."

"Where?"

"Don't know, but they've gone for three days." Ramu ran off, excited.

Three days for Oby was three days more of waiting for the opportunity to speak to Yaki Zakariah. Dragging his feet, he went to see why there was so much noise in the courtyard.

Gathered were the house servants, gardeners, drivers, cooks, the five children of Yaki Zakariah and the English nanny, Ruth. The men had tucked their torb-shirts into their underpants. Gulum and Giddy wore trousers under their dresses. Everyone was bare-footed. Nanny Ruth wore jeans; so did the Zakariah children, all but the smallest girl, who wore her prettiest dress, stitched with pink flowers and a big ribbon tied at the back. They were all shouting and laughing and Awad Sha-Had picked up the little girl and swung her around as she cried for, "More, more, more."

The fourteen-year-old son of Yaki Zakariah produced a brand-new football. He and Awad Sha-Had organised the teams and a football game began. They all rushed back and forth, screaming unreservedly every time someone scored a goal. The shouting got louder and louder, scaring the feral cats over the walls, and a pack of dogs lingering at the gates began howling.

Oby raced back and forth, all the tightness in his head loosening away. First left foot, then kick back with a heel, now right, right, right, over to Jama, then the oldest son swept the ball away, up the pitch and into the arms of goalie, Awad Sha-Had.

The noises attracted street children. They peered through the gate. Two came in and played football with them.

Oby began to tire and his mouth felt sticky and stale. The symphony of cries and yells and shrieks began to muddle into sounds from the past. He suddenly felt sick, so he walked away towards the date palms. The smell of jasmine coming off the wall of the house brought back memories of the wife of Moussa Khaliffa and the scented water she had washed his brow with. The laughing footballers, tearing back and forth, were the sounds of donkey races round his village. Oby sank into a corner of the garden.

Awad Sha-Had thrust a yoghourt drink under Oby's nose. "You need this, you skinny boy. You've got no energy. Now, come on, come and have some fun."

They played football into the night, until Nanny Ruth

swept the little girl into her arms and carried her off to bed, crying and protesting. Awad Sha-Had whistled through his teeth and the football game continued.

They played on and on until, one by one, the teams shrank in size, until the last few players were exhausted.

Throughout the following morning the house and gardens were silent. No one got up. No one worked. The house and gardens were still. Work returned to normal in the afternoon and that night there was another football match.

At noon on the third day, several people were still sleeping soundly at the house of Yaki Zakariah when suddenly the guard at the gate whistled through his fingers and everyone ran. They ran to wherever the servants were expected to be.

Yaki Zakariah and Madame went straight to their private rooms, and did not appear for the rest of the day.

Oby could barely walk; sleepiness kept dragging his eyelids down. The other servants worked in silence throughout the day. By six o'clock there was not a sound at the house of Yaki Zakariah.

* * *

He was helping Awad Sha-Had to change beds when Oby said, "When do you think Yaki Zakariah is going to help me?"

"What sort of help?" Awad Sha-Had lifted his eyebrows in surprise.

"To get to El Malla."

"El Malla?"

Awad Sha-Had turned to Oby, his eyes immediately serious. "You're not here to replace the boy that ran away then?"

"No. Didn't Ramu tell you?"

"No, Ramu doesn't tell much to anyone. He keeps his thoughts to himself."

"So, you don't know why I'm here?"

Awad Sha-Had propped himself on the edge of the bath. "I'm listening."

Chapter 22

Secret Meeeting

"That's what the letter is for."

"What letter?"

"The one I gave Yaki Zakariah."

"What does it say?"

"It asks Yaki Zakariah to help me."

Awad Sha-Had scratched his stubbly face. He wriggled his toes feverishly in his sandaled feet. "Who brought you here, Oby?"

"Abdul Sid. His brother Ben said it would be best because his friend Yaki Zakariah could help me get to El Malla."

Awad Sha-Had repeated Oby's words. "His brother Ben, his brother Ben," just letting this information settle in his mind. "Then that would be Ben Sid, wouldn't it?"

"Yes, yes," said Oby eagerly.

"Ben Sid sent you ... mmm. And he wrote a letter?"

"Yes. I gave the letter to Yaki Zakariah myself."

"Have you read this letter? Silly question! No, of course you haven't." He gave his nose another little scratch. "Oby, we *must* see this letter." Awad Sha-Had stood up and immediately started to hurry off.

"No!" Oby ran after him, pulling at his torb-shirt. "It's for Yaki Zakariah. And he's got it."

"I know, but I have a very good reason." Awad Sha-Had kept walking.

"No, it's not your letter." Oby shouted. "You can't steal it."

"Sssh! Not so loud." He turned and patted Oby's head. "You're jumping around like a cockroach! I don't want to steal it, just borrow."

"No! Listen to me—"

"No! If you want to get to your father, then *you* listen to *me*." Awad Sha-Had scratched his fat nose for a third time. "I need to speak to Gulum and Giddy about this ... and we'll need Ramu's help"

"No! No! Ramu doesn't believe me."

"He believes you, but he probably doesn't know how to answer. Ramu locks everything into his head. It all goes in. This place is the end of the road. Once here, you stay here. Until one day ... *Zap!* God takes you. *Zap!* Just like that."

"When Yaki Zakariah pays Ramu, he's going to go ..."

"Yes? Go to where?"

"To school ... train to be a teacher ..."

"Ramu still hangs on to his dreams, but only just. Now then, we can't stand here wasting time." Awad Sha-Had pushed Oby aside. "No more discussion. Make sure you are at the gazelle enclosure in one hour. That will give me enough time."

"*No, what are you going to do?*" yelled Oby, but his words only landed on Awad Sha-Had's broad back.

* * *

On the way to the gazelle enclosure Oby skirted the back corridors of the house and exited through the infrequently used beggars' door. He ducked along a path between high walls and a band of shrubs that grew in front of them. Ahead, he caught a glimpse of Gulum and Giddy making their way beyond the male servants' quarters. He caught up with them. Gulum pressed her fingers to her lips for him to be silent, but placed a reassuring hand on his arm. All three ran, dodged under fig trees and over fallen palm leaves. They met up with Awad Sha-Had, running from the direction of the kitchen area. Ramu was snipping away at jasmine tendrils that climbed in haphazard haste over the gardening sheds and store rooms. Startled, his forehead puckered into a frown when they all appeared.

Awad Sha-Had beckoned Ramu. "We need to talk," he hissed, breathlessly.

They ran to where there was a narrow gap between the gazelle house and the garden wall. Behind it was dense foliage which they tunneled through. Oby feared that Awad Sha-Had would never get through, but he was as supple as plasticine and his large stomach contorted and squeezed as though he was a snake.

They arrived at a very small shed which used to be part of the gazelle house and was now closed off. Awad Sha-Had hastened them inside.

Oby noticed that everyone's eyes were darting like rabbits.

"Sit! Sit!" Awad Sha-Had pointed to the piles of dried palm leaves.

Palms crackled as Oby landed on them and rough stalks pricked into his backside.

Awad Sha-Had went straight to the point. "Let's face it, we are here to work. We get paid only sometimes. Yaki Zakariah pays us a few likits, but usually it's when he feels like it, when it pleases him. We have nowhere else to go, no families to return to. Well, except possibly Ramu, but he can't remember anything much about his family, except his sick old aunt and she's probably dead now. Since we have no family then there's no-one to be concerned about us. That's why it's easy to keep us. Anyway, why would we want to leave? Food! Bed! What more do we need? This is home." Oby jammed his knees together and bit his lip. "And Ramu told you he was going to save his money and go to England, didn't he, Oby? Ramu has been paid *nothing*, have you, Ramu?"

Oby stared first into Awad Sha-Had's face and then at Ramu's, but Ramu kept his eyes lowered.

"I'm *not* here for work." Oby's voice lifted higher and higher. "I'm on my way to El Malla to find my father. Yaki Zakariah is going to help me. That's what the letter is for, asking him to help. If he doesn't help me ... I'll ... I'll ... just run out of the gate and find my way. I know how to chase the river ... I have my compass."

"You're in the Zuda. This town sits slap in the middle of the Zuda. How can you leave? You'll just replace the boy that ran away," said Awad Sha-Had.

"But they promised."

"Who promised?"

"Moussa Khaliffa, he promised. When Gold Teeth brought me from the Salt Lake he promised, too. Then Abdul Sid promised. Then we stayed at his brother's house for one night and his brother, Ben Sid, wrote the letter. He said that Yaki Zakariah was a very reliable friend and the best man in the Zuda to help me."

"I don't know this Moussa Khaliffa," said Awad Sha-Had, "but I have heard of Abdul Sid. They say he is a good man ... an honest trader. Unlike his brother, Ben Sid."

"Ben Sid ... he's ... well ... he's funny."

"Funny! And you think he's to be trusted just because he's funny?"

"Yes! He said he would help me. He was nice to me."

"And you believed him!"

"When Abdul Sid brought me here, the guard at the gate told him that Ben Sid was a good man; he said that to Abdul Sid. I heard him."

"Hah! That's because Ben Sid throws likits at that guard every time he comes here. That's why the guard likes him. Ben Sid is not what you believe he is. He is greedy and you can't trust him, believe me," said Awad Sha-Had.

Oby ran the back of his hand across his nose. He suddenly remembered Gold Teeth's words. *Not to trust anyone.* So, he wasn't going to trust these four. He would stand up for himself.

Awad Sha-Had continued, "Ben Sid would sell his own mother for a single diamond."

"No! No! No! He's not like that." Oby wiped away the tears of frustration that were beginning to dampen his cheeks. "Ben Sid deals in spices and gold ..." he said with a hint of triumph in his voice, "... because I saw them ... bags of spices wrapped in brown cloth. He's an honest trader."

"He and Yaki Zakariah steal gemstones from our government's own mining company."

"You don't know that," shouted Oby.

"Yaki Zakariah has a fire burning in his belly for the biggest gemstones that he can get his hands on. And he'll get his hands on them by any means." Awad Sha-Had turned his head towards Ramu for confirmation and Ramu nodded.

Oby didn't want to hear any more of this. He folded his arms firmly across his stomach. Why should he listen? His head was swimming. Gold Teeth said not to trust anyone.

Awad Sha-Had prodded Ramu. "Are you going to tell him?" Ramu didn't move or speak. "What Ramu doesn't want to tell you is that Ben Sid was the person who brought him here to work down an illegal mine. Ramu was just the right size at the time, like Kibo who ran away: thin with long legs and long fingers." Oby stared down at his dry hands. "Yaki Zakariah gives Ramu titbits: a bed on legs, best jobs working with the gazelles, new sandals, and once ... some glasses. But money! Yaki Zakariah tells Ramu that this month's income is poor so next month he will pay treble. There is never any treble of anything." Awad Sha-Had paused, watching Oby carefully. "Yaki Zakariah says he'll do many things for Ramu. He lifts Ramu's hopes, then changes his mind. Ramu is like a football, kicked wherever the player wants it to go. He is still waiting. He is always waiting and can do nothing. There are many broken promises."

"It can't be true ..." Oby's voice was getting thinner. The fight was leaving his tongue.

"Ramu was first brought here to work underground in tunnels that he could only just squeeze through. He chiseled at the rock day after day for a couple of years. Then he became too tall. Ramu knows what's underground. He knows too much. So, Yaki Zakariah will keep him here waiting, for years and years, tossing him a few likits now and then, buying him titbits to keep him sweet, but never paying him any regular wages."

"He can't do that! It's slavery." Oby expected a look of shock on their faces.

But none of them flinched, not a flicker in anyone's eye.

"I said, it's slavery."

"Yes, that's right."

"He can't ..."

"He can. He does ..."

Gulum and Giddy both started gabbling at once, shaking their heads, cursing Ben Sid, telling Oby he should never trust anyone. "Only trust your God," they chorused. "Only God."

Oby flopped back onto the palms like a lean, stray dog. Gold Teeth had warned him. He felt the freedom he had always known being squeezed out of him. His freedom was being stolen.

Awad Sha-Had beat his chest with a fist. "Let me tell you something, Oby. In Yaki Zakariah's eyes I am nothing. Nothing. But see this?" He jabbed at his chin, at the dark blue mark there. "He can't ever make me forget where I come from, because I have this." He jutted out his jaw proudly. "This tells me who I am. The mark of my tribe."

Gulum and Giddy sat either side of Awad Sha-Had like supporting pillars. He asked Gulum, "Did you get it?" She nodded. "Let's see then."

She drew out of her pocket a letter.

"That's my letter." Oby leapt up. "It's the one I gave to Yaki Zakariah. You've stolen it." He tried to snatch it. Giddy held him back.

Gulum quickly handed the letter to Ramu.

"Ramu is the only one of us who can read," said Awad Sha-Had.

Oby sank back down onto the palm leaf pile, trembling. Giddy kept her arm around him.

Ramu's eyes narrowed and his lips began to move. "... *at last, I think we have a boy perfect for crawling down to that narrow seam where we know the pink diamonds are. He's very thin and agile and has a bit of intelligence, too. He'll figure things out. He's desperate to find his father, so he'll be keen to do what you ask and get those stones out as quickly as possible.*"

"No, no, no, no, nonono ..."

Giddy clasped Oby even tighter.

"*I am even dreaming of pink diamonds. Delicious! I have already informed our man in Europe that the stones will soon be in our grasp and he's very excited. If those crystals are as massive as we believe, then riches await us. Delicious pink diamonds! This could be the most remarkable discovery ever and the biggest gem will have the name we decided: Princess Seraphina Starlight. I shiver with excitement knowing that we shall have wealth to make the whole world envious.*"

"No!" Oby screamed and tried to jump up, but Giddy's arms were now wrapped around him. All the muscles in his face looked ready to burst apart. "No, I'm not. Not for anyone. I'm not going down any mine! Do you hear me?"

Gulum spoke rapidly, "Stay calm! We shall help you. Awad Sha-Had will think of a way."

Oby's breaths were now coming so fast that his stomach pumped up and down. He slapped his fist into his palm. "I'm going to find my father *now* and no-one is going to stop me."

Giddy was quicker than him and blocked the entrance to the shed as he tried to leave. Gulum took hold of his arm and gently pulled him back. "Shh! You must be quiet. Quiet. If Yaki Zakariah suspects anything, even knows your smallest thoughts about leaving, he'll lock you in the rice room at the bottom of the house where no one can hear and send one of his bodyguards to beat you."

Awad Sha-Had was gentle. "Listen, my boy. See us here? We work, we smile. We don't grumble. We pretend that we are grateful to Yaki Zakariah. He trusts us. Ramu is clever, but Yaki Zakariah thinks he is stupid, because that's what Ramu wants him to think. He suspects that Ramu can read a few words, but he doesn't realise that Ramu reads fluently. And the other thing he doesn't know is that Nanny Ruth secretly teaches Ramu English. She is on his side."

Gulum bent closer to Oby and stroked his hair. "Be patient," she said, "we all have our pains too."

Oby turned to her. With her serene smile she looked contented, so what kind of pain could she possibly have?

She must have read his thoughts. "When I was twelve and Giddy ten our father died and our mother was too poor to look after us, so we went to live with an uncle. He didn't want the expense of looking after me so he married me off to his friend. The man beat me when I didn't have a baby and demanded to marry Giddy instead. She didn't have a baby either. So, he gave us ..."

"No, he didn't give us away. He sold us. We heard them arguing about a price," said Giddy.

"He sold us to Yaki Zakariah. We've lived here for seven years, but it's nice for us, better than before. We are together. We are okay."

Oby's hopes were siphoning away, fast.

Awad Sha-Had wrapped his fat arms securely around Gulum. "Now I look after her." He had his ample lips very close to her ear. She giggled and wriggled and they rolled back onto the palm leaves. Ramu and Giddy beckoned Oby to follow them out of the shed and as they left Oby could hear Gulum laughing and Awad Sha-Had growling like a tiger.

Giddy whispered to Oby as they squeezed out of the gap between the gazelle compound and the wall, "Go back to the house quickly. Go by the back wall. We must go one at a time. Be very quick and quiet. Don't worry. Awad will think of something."

Oby ran through the tunnels made by the fig trees and skirted the house along the back wall, dodging from shrub to shrub. Just round the next corner was the beggars' door. Parked in front of it was a cart. As he ran around the tail end of it, he couldn't fail to see its contents and gulped in discomfort, making him dash even faster.

Slap!

Oby fell sideways. His head hit the ground.

Directly in front of his eyes were a pair of highly polished shoes.

Two hands yanked him to his feet.

A hand smacked across his face a second time.

"Where've you been, boy?" Yaki Zakariah shouted, grabbing Oby roughly by the collar and swinging his feet off the ground. "Are you a time-waster? Where've you been? Who's teaching you the art of laziness, you time-waster? Eh? Speak! Speak!" He flung Oby onto the ground, but Oby gritted his teeth and said nothing.

Two bodyguards, never far behind their master, came around the corner. One of them grabbed Oby's leg and pulled him at speed over the concrete path towards the beggars' entrance. Then, with one holding each of his arms, hauled him up the stone stairway until they reached a window. Yaki Zakariah followed close behind. They grabbed Oby's legs and dangled him, upside down, out of the window.

He could feel sickness welling up as his teeth accidentally sank into his tongue.

"Now, tell us what you were doing," yelled Yaki Zakariah. "Come on! Come on! Speak up. I haven't got all day."

Oby remained tight-lipped. His tongue was swelling fast.

He was yanked back through the window and then Yaki Zakariah's face miraculously changed ... into broad smiles and from his lips poured charming words. "Oby, boy, Oby. It is Oby, isn't it? Well, I'm going to help you."

"Thank you, Yaki Zakariah." Oby managed to splutter. The punishment was over.

"Before I help you to find your father, before we send you on this expensive journey, I'd like you to do a little work for me ... as payment for my hospitality ... just for a few weeks."

"But my father will think ..." His words were blurred mumbles under his swollen tongue.

"Boy, stop making noises like a baby. You are not listening to me at all. You must surely agree with me that my generosity is good. You have a comfortable bed and plenty of food. So, in a few days I have some very special work that I want you to do for me. Very special."

Yaki Zakariah led Oby down into the bowels of the massive house where it was only very dimly lit. "First, you must be taught a lesson."

He was pushed into a bare, airless room and then had his legs kicked from under him so that he landed heavily onto the concrete floor, falling on to the shoulder that he had injured when he fell off Mo.

At that very moment Oby knew that everything Awad Sha-Had and Ramu had told him was completely true.

The two bodyguards then dragged in a large sack of rice.

"Open it," ordered Yaki Zakariah.

One of the thugs pulled a thread at the top of the sack. It opened its wide jaws and the rice spewed out across the cellar floor.

Yaki Zakariah smiled at Oby. "Now clean it," he ordered. "Remove every piece of grit and bug and put the rice in these buckets."

The second bodyguard threw four large buckets at Oby.

"No water and no food 'til it's done, boy. Do we understand each other?" Yaki Zakariah patted Oby's cheek and gave him a sickly-sweet smile, before walking away.

One of the thugs gave Oby a triumphant grin, raised his leg and booted his right thigh with such force that the excruciating pain forced him to curl up and a horrible nausea swept over him.

... thumps of bodies hitting the ground, grunts as men threw their weight into kicking people who were already on the ground and helpless ... the flash of his mother's red dress.

Oby heard the door slam.

He didn't clean the rice. He didn't fill the buckets.

The pain got bigger until darkness swept over him.

Chapter 23

Patched Palace

Oby could feel the gentle waves of a breeze on his face. His hand was resting on something soft and he knew it was a sheepskin. He opened his eyes, but everything was a little blurry. He thought he could make out blue sky through a doorway. He thought he could hear Ramu sneezing. Next, he heard Ramu's voice, "I'll get away from this place ... one day ... one day I will."

"Are you talking to me or yourself?"

"So! You're awake! You okay?" Ramu stepped into the tiny shelter-hut where Oby was recovering and dropped onto his knees.

"Get off! Don't touch me," Oby cried as Ramu's hand came towards his bruised and swollen thigh. He rolled his head from side to side on a soft cloth that was cradling his dull head. He tried to raise himself, tried to lean on his elbow, but flopped back again like a rag doll. His eyelids drooped and he dozed through muddled images.

Day after day he dozed, between eating mouse-size bites of fruit. At night he shivered. Daytime baked him. He got sprinkled with wind-blown sand from the Zuda that spiralled through the entrance of the shelter-hut.

Oby could feel a tenderness in the care that Ramu was giving, in the way he slopped water over Oby's brow in the noonday heat and covered him with a fusty-smelling drover's blanket at night. Little did Oby know that, as a child, Ramu had watched his aunt make all these moves as she hovered over his parents' fragile forms in the months before they died.

* * *

Oby could hear Ramu giving little grunts of satisfaction. "Well, that's more than you ate yesterday, and you're breathing more easily and managed to stay awake for four hours today. That's progress."

* * *

It was the second week. Oby positioned himself in front of the doorway. He was not quite perpendicular, but at least he was standing unaided. He wanted to surprise Ramu when he returned from his usual morning trip to collect breakfast from the farmer's wife.

As Ramu strode towards him, he said, "How's it feeling?"

"It still hurts." Oby winced.

"It's good that you are on your feet, but the leg needs more time. You have to be patient."

Oby smiled. Just.

"Didn't think you'd smile again. Awad Sha-Had thought you were dead when he found you."

"Me? Dead?" Oby felt himself all over, partly mocking and partly to reassure himself. His eyes fell onto the dish in

Ramu's hands. Ramu held it out. After only a couple of bites the bread and beans did not sit comfortably in his mouth. The chewing got slower. His jaw hurt with every movement. He pushed the dish away. "I can't eat any more."

"You've been unwell for nearly two weeks."

"Two weeks?" Oby's face changed, as memories of the beating came flooding in. He half expected Ramu to laugh at him, or get angry with him for having got caught after their meeting in the disused gazelle house.

But Ramu did neither.

Oby stepped back into the shelter-hut and began fumbling with his bedding. "My money bag! My sleeping rug!"

"It's here. Safe." Ramu rummaged under his own sheepskin. As though reading Oby's thoughts, he said, "It's okay, I didn't touch anything. I didn't put my nose into your bag."

Oby clutched his belongings to his chest and gave a brief smile. "Thanks, boy from the north. Thanks." His father's photograph, the document, the money, the gold coin, the salt chunks, the compass, a fine leather bag. He had a lot of possessions.

He looked up to find Ramu fiddling with the string around his glasses. He knew that Ramu had no possessions. He had nothing to tie in a sleeping rug. He didn't even have a sleeping rug.

Ramu held out the half-empty bowl of beans. "Why don't you try to finish them?"

"You eat them," said Oby.

Whilst Ramu ate, Oby unknotted his sleeping rug and untwisted the knife hidden so carefully away – the one he had found at the ghost village in the Zuda.

"I didn't know you had a knife," said Ramu.

Oby held it out. "It's yours."

Ramu shrank back. "No, no! I don't want your knife."

Oby pushed the knife into Ramu's hands. "It's yours."

"Why?"

"You deserve it."

Ramu's head rolled from side to side. He turned the knife in his hands, over and over, studying the shining blade and trying to understand the design on the handle. "But how can I carry it?"

"In your head-wrap ... conceal it in your head-wrap." Oby took the knife from Ramu and rolled and knotted the knife in place. "You'll have to be careful when you wear it, though. Roll it around three times, then keep the blade at the back of your head and pointing upwards."

They tried and tested until Ramu felt the position was comfortable.

Neat rows of squat orange trees just a short distance from the shelter-hut gave off sweet smells. Enough to encourage Oby to explore. All around the periphery of the orange grove tall palms rose like frothy umbrellas. Loitering at the foot of the nearest palms were six dozing donkeys.

Oby studied the shelter-hut. He hobbled round it and poked a finger into a small hole which, at one time, had been stuffed tightly with mud. There were many holes like this, and clearly an attempt had been made to repair the roof with palm leaves.

"Did you do this fixing?"

"Yes! Welcome to my patched palace."

"Not bad, but why have we been sent here?"

"Yaki Zakariah always sends me here when I start wheezing."

"Wheezing? What's that?"

"Trouble with breathing. Sometimes, when we have a dust storm or I catch a cold, my chest rattles. Sometimes it's hard to breathe."

"Why?"

"Don't know. Yaki Zakariah is scared stiff of sickness ... any sickness. When anyone's sick he sends them here," said Ramu. "Nobody else wants to come here, they make a fuss. But I like it here. There's no one here to shout orders."

"Why did Yaki Zakariah send me here?" Oby shuffled towards a tree. He leaned against its trunk and slithered to the ground.

"Awad Sha-Had fixed it. He told Yaki Zakariah it would be a good idea to send you here with me until you were better. He also said you were a clumsy house boy, always knocking things over. He thought you would be better doing something simpler, like picking and packing oranges."

"Me? Clumsy? That's not true!" Oby scowled and snorted. "Was I really clumsy?"

Ramu shook his head. "No, no, no, you were okay. It was just Awad Sha-Had's way to get you out of there. To give you a chance."

"Chance?"

"Well, those thugs of Yaki Zakariah would have beaten you again, because you hadn't cleaned the rice. Any excuse. Next time you might be dead."

"Dead?"

"Maybe."

"I can fight."

"Don't talk stupid. Anyway, there's a better chance you can escape more easily from this place than from the house. Awad Sha-Had is trying to think of something. We're ten miles from Tembo Dolo. Yaki Zakariah never comes here and the farmer sees to everything. Some people think that Yaki Zakariah got rich from farming, but I know differently. There aren't enough oranges here. You can't get rich selling this number of oranges, can you?"

"I don't know. There are lots of trees. Just look."

"You need thousands of trees to get rich on oranges. No, this farm is just a cover."

"Cover? What do you mean?"

"For his illegal diamond mining. Yaki Zakariah steals diamonds from right under the government's nose." Ramu was the most talkative Oby had known him to be. "When they sent me down a secret shaft into the mine, I had to work in a space nearly thinner than myself ... I could barely move ... only slide like a snake ... hardly breathe. I used to have nightmares about getting stuck in those tunnels ... dying there, struggling to breathe."

"Well, I'm not working in any diamond mine!" snapped Oby.

"When I got too big for those small spaces, Yaki Zakariah put me in his office in the middle of Tembo Dolo, cleaning and tidying. That's when I saw lots of things. Some letters were in English and I sometimes got the opportunity to read them. He had lists of clients in a book. I think they were people who wanted to buy diamonds."

"Why did you stop working in his office?"

"I don't really know why, but ..." Oby stared impatiently at Ramu as he paused for a mouthful of water. "There was once an English visitor who came to his office and I had to make him tea. He thanked me in English, and I answered in English. Yaki Zakariah looked up at me in surprise, and after that, I wasn't allowed to go to his office again. I wish I hadn't spoken. Yaki Zakariah ordered me out of the room and told me never to speak to his visitors again. Afterwards, he tried to find out how much English I knew, but I just kept repeating the same words to everything he asked me – the same words that he heard me say to the English man. 'It's a pleasure. It's a pleasure'. Yaki Zakariah moved me back to the main house to look after the gazelles."

Oby sat in silence for ages. He gave a sigh. "It's nice here. I never want to go back to the house. Never."

Ramu said, "When Yaki Zakariah sends his thugs out here to see if you are better, you must limp badly. We'll find you a walking stick. You could fall over on purpose. Pretend you cannot get up without help."

"I'm not going to work in any gold mine!"

* * *

The farm clung to the banks of the Great White River and this great waterway was Oby's hope. Every day, as he squatted on its banks and gazed into the depths of its lazy flow, his plans grew. His hope grew. As days passed, he felt less restless, but never far from his mind was all of Moussa Khaliffa's advice.

It wasn't long before Oby was able to help Ramu pick oranges. In late afternoons they sat side by side on the banks of the Great White River, staring into its biscuit whirls. Often, a few paces away, sat the farmer's son, with his legs dangling over the riverbank, hauling in his fishing net. It had been mended over and over, but still caught fish efficiently. The farmer's son never spoke. Swift-fingered, the boy ripped fish from the net mesh and flung them behind him onto the bank. With three or four fish tied together he ran home with his haul to his mother.

"We could do that," said Ramu.

They created a mesh net of sinewy palm threads, all stripped individually and twisted together to form a trap. It had taken three days to complete, with changes in design as they went along. They made a fire from dried palm branches and threw their fish catch onto the charred stalks. They picked at the smoky fish with bare fingers, then flung the bones and scraps back into the river.

For two months Oby picked oranges with Ramu. The farmer seemed pleased with their help. The donkeys were not so easy, though. They were stubborn and protested at everything. They were best at doing nothing. When the orange baskets were saddled onto their backs, they kicked out, braying in that ridiculous voice that ends like a squeaky door. The farmer never bothered to yell orders to the donkeys. When he wanted them to move, he used his small stick: whack, whack. It seemed he was the only person the donkeys didn't try to kick.

Every evening the farmer's wife prepared for them beautiful fish, rice and custard fruit which they feasted on in the quiet of the little patched palace. Every night, as Oby closed his eyes he wondered if he would find the chance to run away the following day.

But all around the orange grove sat the Zuda.

He was trapped.

Chapter 24

Escape

Then one morning, a bellow broke through the dawn.

"Hey!"

A roaring voice catapulted through the doorway of the patched palace, exploding over the ears of Oby and Ramu.

"Hey! Hey! Get up! Get up!"

The bellowing got louder.

Oby pressed his hands hard against his ears, curled into a protective ball and snapped his eyes shut and waited. It was the end. Yaki Zakariah's bodyguards were on the loose.

There was roaring in the air. There was clunking of metal, buzzing and rattling ... buzzing and rattling that seemed to fall out of the sky ... of machinery ... of something enormous ... coming straight at them.

Was he awake or was he asleep?

Black sky. Black weapons discharging bullets. Screams and howls. Black shapes running towards him ...

. . .

"Get up! Get up!" The bellowing voice was almost on them.

"Get up, you two!"

A large body filled the doorway.

"Get up! Get up now!"

Oby nudged Ramu who sat up as though in a trance, then slumped back down. Ramu shouted, "Awad Sha-Had, you noisy farter, I can smell it's you."

"Get up! Get up! Come on, hurry!" Awad Sha-Had pointed towards the noisy object which was standing nearby. "It's your journey to freedom." He gave Oby and Ramu nudges with his foot to stir them up.

"Hey!" squealed Ramu.

Oby followed Ramu in crawling to the doorway. His eyes were stinging, resisting the early morning light, but through the blur he saw a lorry. From the cab of the ancient vehicle a driver stared down at them through filthy glass, unshaven and chewing a mouthful of brown leaves, leaving a tell-tale thick stalk sticking out of the side of his mouth.

The driver yelled, "Move it. I haven't got all day."

"Get a move on! Git! Git!" Awad Sha-Had's voice was loud and firm. "There's no time to waste. Just *go!*"

He hustled Oby and Ramu along, pushing into their backs and yelling, *"Get a move on! Faster!"*

Oby had a sudden surge of energy; the lorry was like a magnet as he realised that his moment for escape had arrived. Ignoring his stiff leg and its reluctance to move, he grabbed his belongings and scrambled up the back of the lorry and dropped inside. There were already two companions there – young, grumbling camels.

But Ramu stood blinking.

Awad Sha-Had pushed him forward. *"And you as well. It's your chance,"* he hissed. *"Just git!"* He grabbed Ramu, picked him up like a sack of rice and flung him into the back of the lorry.

Ramu swung his leg back over the lorry, protesting, fighting to get out.

Awad Sha-Had thrust him in again.

Ramu had terror in his eyes.

The thread veins in Awad Sha-Had's cheeks began to brighten, the way they did when he drank too much kupti. *"Don't you dare try to climb out of that lorry. Don't you dare!"*

The lorry began to roar.

The camels started to bellow and tried to shift about.

"You've been drinking kupti," screeched Ramu. "What are you doing to us?"

"Git out of here," shouted back Awad Sha-Had. "Just go while you have the chance. Chances don't come often. This driver is taking a risk helping you."

"He might be one of Yaki Zakariah's men," protested Ramu.

Awad Sha-Had raised his arms over the back of the truck and grabbed Ramu's collar. "Listen! This man hates Yaki Zakariah. Yaki Zakariah owes him more than five thousand likits. What are five thousand likits to a rich man? Without that money this man wasn't able to buy new tyres for his lorry. I ran with him in the middle of night all the way to Yaki Zakariah's lorry depot and we stole two tyres and fixed the truck, so now he can work again. He's doing this for me, because I asked him."

The driver began crashing the lorry into gear.

Ramu tried to wriggle free from Awad Sha-Had's grasp, but he was being held very firmly. "Listen to me! Culum overheard Yaki Zakariah say he wants Oby down in that diamond mine as soon as he's recovered. D'you understand me? Once the boy is down there there's no chance to escape. This is your chance, too. Take it ... *just git!*"

The lorry shuddered.

Ramu became tearful. "I can't go ..."

"Listen to me, you coward-who-wants-to-be-a-teacher, do you want to die in the Zuda? Never teach? Never have your dream?"

The lorry began to roll forward.

Ramu looped a leg over the back of the truck.

"Get back in there!"

Ramu heaved himself forward again.

Oby pounced. He held Ramu fast.

Ramu was shaking feverishly. "*But you!*" he called pathetically. He tried to reach out.

The lorry rumbled faster.

Awad Sha-Had was no longer within reach. He cupped his hands around his mouth. "I can't come with you. Gulum and Giddy, I have them to look after ..."

... but his last words never reached them.

The heavy lorry rolled over the bubbled ground, spraying out small stones. Oby sat on Ramu until Awad Sha-Had's face was no longer visible and he was a blur in the distance.

Dreaming of freedom for so many years, of cool breezes and a class of talcum-powdered school children under a great acacia tree, Ramu was unprepared for this moment and he sank into a corner and wept uncontrollably.

Oby lifted his face to the wind.

Chapter 25

Freedom Lorry

The camels shifted in the lorry, their rope tethers stretching and creaking under the strain. They blew foul stinks into the air, rolling their jaws so that thick spittle made beards beneath their chins.

The lorry picked up speed and Oby and Ramu were tossed and flung around, until they learnt to grip the sides more tightly. They swept north, curling round wind-sculpted sand humps, before slowing to rock like a cradle over stones.

"*He's mad!*" screamed Ramu.

"We're getting away! I don't care how he drives."

For some reason, the driver didn't shift into higher gears, so the engine roared and droned in protest. Every time the driver picked up speed another pothole seemed to appear. Every time the front wheels vaulted, the springs squealed and clanged, the camels roared and Oby gritted his teeth and clung on for dear life. Ramu had his eyes closed and seemed to be mumbling prayers.

The road followed the course of the Great White River,

then suddenly veered west. Animals and men appeared in increasing numbers from all directions.

The lorry crunched onto firmer ground. It was now gritty and flattened. The journeys of animals, people and vehicles were now combining. In some places the route was wide enough for four lorries and sometimes so narrow it was little more than a single track.

Two boys in grubby T-shirts and torn shorts suddenly appeared from amidst the traffic. With darting eyes, they slipped between animals and under carts, seeming hungry for an opportunity to steal. Oby saw them leap and disappear, so he knew they must be clinging onto the side of the lorry. He kept watch and eventually two hands appeared over the side, then two more. One boy lunged at Ramu's head-wrap and he was knocked forward. The boy's lightning fingers gripped the head-wrap with one hand and the other hand gripped the side of the lorry as he fought to regain his balance. The head-wrap began to unwind. Oby lunged. He bashed the thief's fingers with his fist and wrenched the head-wrap out of his hand, then punched him in the chest with his free hand. The lorry lurched. The thief flew into the air. The second thief leapt away.

"Your knife! Is your knife still there?"

Ramu nodded and replaced his head-wrap more firmly.

The lorry wove through dusty alleys to a large, open square. A battered metal sign hung on a nearby building with the words JUNKA LIVESTOCK MARKET. The lorry parked at the side of the market amidst neglected cars which had been dumped because of no spare parts to fix them. Camel traders stood on the dumped cars, using them as sale platforms. Shouting got louder and louder as traders attempted to be heard over the perpetual noise of camels.

The lorry driver completely ignored Oby and Ramu. He dropped the back of the lorry with an enormous clang, jumped on board and untied the camels' legs. Two traders jumped up behind him and heaved at the bridles of the two animals. The camels baulked and fought against the ropes. Oby and Ramu pushed back against the cab. A stream of camel pee suddenly pumped straight across the lorry towards them. Oby wriggled out of the way, causing pain to shoot up his leg. Biting his lip to control the agony, he couldn't move for several moments.

With the camels gone, Oby finally rolled off the back of the lorry. With sitting hunched for so long, his legs were stiff and he could only hobble, but he still managed to move with amazing speed. "Let's go this way, Ramu, we have to move fast."

But Ramu wasn't with him.

"Ramu! Ramu!" He scanned the immediate area, then looked back at the lorry. Ramu hadn't shifted. He was huddling in a corner and shaking in fear. Oby limped back towards the lorry. "Come on! What's wrong with you?"

But Ramu didn't move a muscle.

"Please yourself, but I'm not hanging around here waiting to get caught." He turned on his heel. He hadn't gone far before he heard the sound of running footsteps behind him.

"Wait for me!" shouted Ramu. "I don't have a place to go ..."

Oby grabbed Ramu's arm. "We have to keep moving. Come on! We have to keep following the Great White River."

"I don't have ..."

"I'll help you. We'll find a way," Oby encouraged. He

started to trot away, but Ramu suddenly slumped, cringing, against the side of a burnt-out lorry. Oby's right leg wanted to move on but his left leg pulled him back to Ramu.

"So, you're a coward!" Oby knew he had to shift Ramu in some way, so he spat on Ramu's foot. But it didn't make a scrap of difference. "A dead dog has more courage than you have. Do you hear me? Do you?"

Ramu tucked his head into his knees and ran his long, thin fingers over his head, as though this would save his life.

Oby raised his voice again, "You want to be trapped in this dump all your life, is that it?" He started to move away, then turned back and lobbed a stone at Ramu. "You're a loser! Listen to me, you'll *never* be a teacher."

Ramu's head sank even lower onto his chest. "Stop yelling."

"Loser!"

"Go away."

"If you go back, Yaki Zakariah will kill you. First the rice room, then he'll kill you. Your guts will get mashed all over the floor ... and he'll scrape out your eyes, fix them on a gold chain and hang them around his wife's neck. You hear me?"

"Shut up! How can a kid like you make up so many ugly things?"

"Because I've seen them," yelled Oby.

Ramu began shouting back. "You can't scare me. You're full to your skinny neck of rubbish. Keep it to yourself." He rolled his head from side to side. "What's there to go on for?" His voice cracked. "Well, I can answer that. *Absolutely nothing!*"

Oby poked Ramu in the chest. "So, you want to go back, hey? Is that it? And what about Awad Sha-Had? He's taken the biggest risk in his life for you. If you go back, Yaki Zakariah's thugs will make you talk and after that they'll drag Awad Sha-Had out to the middle of the Zuda and dump him there. You want to do that to him?"

"I won't tell them ..."

"No, you *won't* tell them. I *won't let you* tell them. Come on! Let's go!"

Ramu raised his head slowly. Immediately, the browns of his eyes grew huge like a gazelle facing a lion. He hissed, "*No!*"

Oby swung round to see where Ramu was looking. "*Nooooo!*"

Two men the size of heavy-weight wrestlers were talking to the lorry driver who had transported them. They gazed all around, scanning the area, casting a lengthy study on every person there. Even from this distance Oby and Ramu knew exactly who they were – the thug bodyguards of Yaki Zakariah.

The thugs began to move among the traders, with a word here, a word there. Oby knew they were asking questions. He hissed, "Come on; if we stay here, we're dead."

Oby limped and dodged through the market towards an old mud wall that had been built by boys, then repaired by boys, many years before. Bending low he followed the length of the wall until he reached a point where the wall began to crumble and its mud slabs had become cracked and eroded almost to the ground. He scrambled over at this point and dropped into a sandy pit on the other side, made by a succession of boys' feet dropping over the wall over the years. He waited. It was only seconds, but it seemed like minutes. A body catapulted over the wall and landed on him.

"Come on, Ramu, we have to keep running."

They sprinted. Between buildings, Oby caught glimpses of sail tips of feluccas gliding on the Great White River, so he knew they were running in the right direction. They kept moving until heat stole their energy.

Water. They desperately needed water. Their thirst had now become more important than running away. They ducked into an alley. Here in the shade was a small market-place of custard-fruit sellers. Snaking amongst the stalls Oby stuck out his arm, and suddenly in his grasp was a custard fruit. He kept running, then ducked behind a water carrier's cart.

"You're a thief," said Ramu.

"You think of a better way."

Oby pushed half of the fruit into Ramu's hands.

The water seller was so busy gossiping with his neighbour that Oby was able to snatch two cans of water from under his cart. After speeding around the corner into the next alley, they stopped long enough to gulp down the spoils.

Then on they went, hot and tired in a ragged route, only stopping in the narrowest alley – barely one boy's width – to pee. The gradual fishiness of the air, the sound of wood banging on wood and the high-pitched shouts of boatmen and construction workers told them that they were near the river.

Oby gave a backward glance, "There's no one following, but we have to keep going." For a while he had almost forgotten the pain in his leg, although he was limping.

They moved almost in silence, only nodding to agree a route.

Their path took them through a small clearing with a

massive acacia tree at its centre. Under the tree was a group of children with their teacher, reciting poems and rocking in rhythm as they chanted. The teacher gazed after Ramu and Oby as they skirted the clearing.

Suddenly the teacher yelled. "Bring that boy here! He should be in school."

Even though Ramu put a hand on Oby's shoulder and steered him swiftly away, the teacher's voice kept right behind them. The voice had long arms which seemed as though they might pluck him off his feet and catapult him backwards to the poetry lesson.

Oby grabbed Ramu's hand and they ran faster and faster, jumping over someone's sparse vegetable patch, then scrambling over a steaming heap of rotting vegetation and goat dung.

They dared not stop.

The ground was pitted with hollows and littered with stone. Gradually, the grasses changed, got thicker and spikier and the ground became damp. They could now see why. In front of them, the Great White River widened out and separated into hundreds of channels, moving around islands of rushes. Which way to go now?

They agreed on a route and followed what they thought was the most promising river channel, but it split into more arms and fingers and spilled over the land, creating a marshy puzzle. It threaded around clumps of shrubs and skirted boggy pools. It narrowed and headed further and further into the unknown. The ground became springy and occasionally their feet squelched under foot.

Very soon they were ankle-deep in water. Oby balanced on top of a dense thicket of marsh grass and gazed around.

He searched for a route, but all he could think was they had made a bad decision. They could not go back and they didn't know how to go forward.

To complicate the situation, daylight was fading fast.

Ramu squinted behind his grubby glasses. "Come on, eyes. Find the path. Come on!"

From the top of the grass clump, Oby grimaced at Ramu. "This path keeps vanishing." There was now a weariness to his voice. He tried to force his eyes to penetrate the gloom.

"You're not trying enough," grumbled Ramu. "You have to concentrate harder. Go on. Keep your eyes fixed on one place and *make* them work, go on, *make* them find the path. My eyes are no good, so you just have to do it ... otherwise ..."

"Shut up!"

"You got us into this."

"Shut up! You agreed." Oby pressed his lips together and concentrated hard. *"Path,"* he suddenly yelled, *"where are you? Any path, just any path ..."* He was dizzy. He could hear himself breathing hard and knew it was because he was scared. He jumped down from the clump and his feet sent sprays of water into his face. He grabbed Ramu's sleeve to stop himself toppling over.

As every second passed there was less light and retracing their steps was impossible. In the gloom were only the grey shapes of marsh plants, stiff and prickly.

"We'll just have to stay here 'til light."

"Standing in water?"

"We can balance across the top of these stumpy reeds."

The stiff reed clumps took their weight easily, but it was like lying on a bed of nails, with every slight movement delivering a shot of needles.

Worse, the marsh plants played host to greedy insects

that came out at night and quickly found human flesh, digging in their teeth and suckers, and feeding hungrily on every centimetre they could pierce.

Oby could feel creatures crawling up his legs. Insects began feasting.

Chapter 26

The Junka Marsh

Dawn awoke the marsh dragon. Its first bellow travelled miles in the still air.

Oby rolled off the prickly reeds and flattened himself onto the soggy ground.

The bellows were followed by rumbles that got louder and louder, before changing to a full bellied roar, increasing in anger until the air was so full of thunderous noises that the sounds were then forced downwards, into the ground, making the ground vibrate like jelly.

Ramu dived down next to him and they clutched their arms around their heads, too scared to move. Too scared to look up for fear of what they might see.

It flashed into Oby's mind, the warning of Moussa Khaliffa about the dangers of the marsh. Crocodiles! That was the warning. They were quick on land and even quicker in the water. And they could pull you under and drown you in seconds. Oby could hear no sound from Ramu; he wanted to hear something, anything at all, but he dared not lift his head.

The roaring continued but seemed to get no nearer nor further away. The noise went on and on.

Oby felt movement. He tentatively raised his head, to see Ramu scrambling to his feet and staring across the marsh. Oby got up and followed his gaze.

In the distance, a massive head of brilliant yellow rose above the marsh. With many mouths dangling beneath it, each one in turn swooped down tearing and gobbling into the ground, before swinging high and dumping its catch to the side.

Oby could feel his chest banging, as though his heart was struggling to burst through. He grabbed Ramu and dragged him back down. "Where there are machines, there are people. We have to be careful."

"I know," said Ramu.

"So, what kind of machine eats up the ground and spits it out again?" said Oby. "What thing does that?" Ramu shaded his eyes with both hands. "Those glasses are useless."

"They just need washing." But Ramu couldn't take them off to clean them; if he did, he wouldn't be able to fix them back on again because he had no thread. Picking a few stems of marsh grass, he buffed the glasses as well as he could. Then he looked across at the roaring monster again, "Just look at that! That's the biggest machine I've ever seen. See! There's writing on it. We need to get closer."

In the increasing light they both turned in circles, looking for a route out of there.

And there it was, right under their noses. Just two metres away the ground was firm. Two steps and two leaps and they were on firmer ground. Oby stretched his aching limbs.

Then the scratching began.

Oby noticed bulbous lumps on Ramu's face. Putting his

hands up to his own face he immediately could feel lumps there, too: tingling and itching. His fingers began clawing at his legs.

"Don't do it! Don't scratch them," Ramu pulled Oby's fingers away, "you'll only make it worse."

"Scratching makes them feel better."

"No! It *will* make them worse and they can get infected. Then you'll have a fever. Leave them."

But Oby was being driven crazy and as he walked ahead out of Ramu's reach, he scraped his fingernails along both arms. The bites were becoming bulbous. Blood droplets began rising to the surface of his skin. He could hear Ramu using the flat of his hand to try and slap away the annoyance.

As they moved around to see the machine more clearly, at its side rather than from behind, Ramu concentrated on the writing.

"What's it say?"

"Caterpillar Plant. Junka Canal Project."

"What's it mean?"

"Don't know. It's English."

"Nanny Ruth was teaching you English, so why don't you know?" said Oby. "She was teaching you the wrong things."

Ramu shrugged and grunted and Oby knew that he had irritated him with the comment.

The vegetation was changing, becoming thicker and more shrubby, taller than before. As they rounded the next reed bed, yet another kind of monster sat facing them. Metal again, but with four seats perched on the top of a tall platform; the platform was held up by fat metal stilts which were fixed onto a flat deck. It was floating on the marsh, like a boat. Further away from the water stood two large cabins.

Men were moving amongst the cabins and they all wore bright yellow hats. One yellow-head waded through the shallow water, over to the strange metal boat and climbed into one of the high chairs. Within seconds the machine began to shake and create a din. Its flattened base filled out into swollen lips that blew down into the marsh and the whole machine rose like a duck, skimming over the marsh towards the Marsh Dragon, spurting out water and flattening all the plants under its force. Even the water close to Oby's and Ramu's path began rippling.

The path was bone dry, a marker, dividing the dry land from the edge of the marsh and it led straight towards the two large cabins.

"We mustn't let them see us," said Ramu, "and they will if we stay on this path. Let's detour around, behind those huts."

"They aren't huts, they're cabins," said Oby.

"How do you know?"

"When some Americans came to our village with special machines to help us dig wells, they called them cabins. They made them in one day." Ramu started to walk towards the cabins. "We could go the other way," Oby called after him. "Now it's daylight we might find a way over the marsh, then no one would see us."

"Are you crazy? Look, we can't cross it. Just see over there. See all that water? Go ahead if you want to be a slap-up feast for a crocodile."

"Ramu, listen, I have got to chase the river."

"*Stop scratching!*"

"What if we lose it? We can only get to El Malla if we chase the river. *Remember?* What if we lose it?"

"Look at all those channels," Ramu spread out both arms. "It's impossible to know which one to follow."

"The biggest one," suggested Oby.

"Which is the biggest? You can't tell. *And stop scratching!*"

Oby yelled back, *"Shut it!"* Then he sulked a bit and fiddled with the marsh reeds, tying knots into the top of them. Every now and again his hand slapped against his leg, his arm, his cheek, to get some relief from all the bites.

The silence went on. They didn't look at each other. Just stared in opposite directions.

Finally, "Okay, have it your way!" Oby kicked into a tuft of grass. "You can lead, and if something goes wrong it's your fault."

The insect bites were now stinging and although it was a cool morning Oby's body was on fire. His eyelids were heavy through lack of sleep and the ferocious burning on his back felt like he'd been beaten with a plank of wood.

In front of each of the cabins was an area set out with faded-orange plastic tables and faded-blue plastic chairs, all slightly misshapen. Above them hung a tarpaulin for shade.

They slipped behind one of the cabins and found themselves at the entrance of a small store with a flapping cloth covering the entrance. Ramu ventured towards it and put his head inside. He beckoned Oby to follow. The store was piled high with crates of bottled water, the same kind that Yaki Zakariah had stored at his house (but only he was allowed to use).

Apart from marsh water, they had had nothing to drink since the previous day. They glanced at each other, then back to the bottles of water, longingly. Oby slowly fingered one of the labels on the front of a bottle. Simultaneously, they each snatched a bottle, ripping off the plastic tops and pouring the contents down their throats. Oby reached for another bottle.

"Hello there!"

Oby dropped the bottle behind him. He stared, scared stiff, at the man's heavy boots. He knew the man was speaking in English, but could detect there was no anger in his voice.

Ramu clutched the empty water bottle to his chest. "Well, we were thirsty, that's all," he said in a small voice.

The man tore two more bottles from the plastic wrapping and held them out. "Here you go, then!"

"He says it's okay. We can have them," said Ramu.

Oby glanced up. The man was tall, grinning, and chewing gum. His teeth were very white and he wore a yellow hat that had straps dangling either side of his face.

"Now, get away from here. Work sites are dangerous," said the man. He pointed back the way they had come.

Ramu shook his head and explained their forward route.

"Are you crazy! You'll drown, or bake out there. Look at you! Where are your supplies?"

"We have to find a way," said Ramu. "We can't go back."

"Why not, for God's sake?"

Ramu spoke, pointing at Oby. The man removed his yellow hat and scratched around his ears as he listened; the lines on his face changed from stretched to squashed, as he concentrated on what Ramu had to say.

"Jee ... sus!" he exclaimed. "Whaaaat!" He kept knocking his yellow hat against the side of his leg. He tutted and shook his head as he noticed their bitten faces. "Look at you both!" He paused. "Come with me. I don't need problems. I can't let you walk out there. Follow me."

The man walked with long, fast strides. Oby and Ramu

found the speed difficult to match and trailed behind. The man turned his head, as he walked. "I'm Bill Smith ... from Idaho. What are you two called?"

Ramu gave him their names.

Bill Smith flung open a side door of one of the cabins. Two men were sitting at a desk with papers spread in front of them. They looked bemused as Bill Smith came in with Oby and Ramu.

Ramu whispered to Oby as much of the conversation as he could understand. "They say they're going to try and help us."

"What if it's a trick?" Oby stepped back, ready to run, but tiredness and hunger were defeating him. His stomach was twisting in pain from hunger and he started to curl forward. He held onto the doorpost and spread his feet apart to retain his balance, but had barely the energy to stand. Voices shouted in his head.

Run! Run! Run! Run! His knees kept folding, his ankles wobbled and he crashed into the trunk of an acacia tree.

Oby felt himself lifted. His head swam. There was no control as foul-tasting bile rose to fill his mouth.

"It's okay. Spit it out."

Someone was holding him, wiping his mouth and gently rubbing something cool over his face. Someone was trying to spoon warm liquid into his mouth. Someone was dabbing at his painful, bleeding arm.

Bill Smith said, "Try and eat a little."

Oby opened his eyes.

He was on a narrow camp bed. Bill Smith was sitting on a chair beside him. Another man was giving instructions. "Just pass the medical bag." The man studied other bites on Oby. "We have to treat all these, to prevent the risk of infection." He turned to Ramu, sitting on the floor. "You, too. You both need to get cleaned up before we treat you. You need to take a shower."

The shower was in a special unit on the outside of the building. Bill Smith handed them a large plastic container of blue liquid soap. Some clean (although slightly large) shirts and shorts were found and then the sores and bites on their bodies were spread with a pink antiseptic cream.

One of the men gave Oby two pills, but they clung to the back of his throat like leeches. He kept trying to swallow, but finally spat them onto the ground.

"He says you've got to take them." Ramu picked them up and handed them back. "They'll stop you getting sick."

"Take them with water." said Bill Smith. "Now then, I'm going over to the canteen to get you something to eat."

He returned quickly with big plates of rice and ground meat. Whilst they were eating Bill Smith pumped air into two blow-up mattresses and put them in a small room at the rear of the cabin. "It's quiet here. Now, get some sleep." This was an order, not a suggestion. "Later, we'll talk."

Even with the ground vibrating, and the marsh dragon clanging its noisy rhythm, and the generator pop-popping not far away, Oby and Ramu sank into sleep.

* * *

When he woke up it was dark. There were boots clunking up

and down on the other side of the door; there were cooking smells. Oby could hear Ramu fumbling around.

"My glasses have gone!"

A shaft of light strayed under the door which helped Oby to search, but he couldn't find the glasses either.

Then the door suddenly opened and light flooded the room.

"Thought I heard you." He threw two cans of cola towards them. "There you go!" Bill Smith laughed at Ramu. "Can't find your glasses, hey? Wait up." He returned with Ramu's glasses now fitted with fine wires to go over his ears. "You can change the shape of the wires. Just try them."

Ramu slid them over his ears. He slipped them on and off a few times. Then he grinned. At long last he had wires on his glasses instead of scrappy pieces of thread.

"Come on, come and join us." Bill Smith was cheerful. Clutching their cans of cold cola, Oby and Ramu were faced with eight men. "Come! Sit here. Here's a place for you ... Jack and I are just leaving." Bill Smith introduced the other men. "This here's Bill and this is Bill. There are three Bills here ... makes it easy to remember," he said grinning. "I have to go now, got a few things to complete ... leave you in the hands of Bill B."

The food placed in front of them smelt good and tasted good.

Bill B said, "How are your glasses?"

"Good, good."

"Had those glasses a long time, have you?"

Ramu nodded.

"Look here, we've got several pairs of glasses that have been left behind over the months." From a shelf behind his chair he took down a box. There were more than dozen pairs of glasses in it. "Any good?"

Ramu tried them on. There was an oversized pair, which simply dropped off his nose, ones with enormous frames that simply turned him into a cartoon character, a pair with lens so thick that he couldn't see a thing through them and two that gave Ramu good vision. "Yeah! This is ... oh yeah ... mmmm ... this is good ... and this ..." He held them up, undecided.

"Keep both of them ... and hold onto your old ones for an emergency," said Bill B.

Oby had never seen Ramu smiling so much, but a little worry made his nose twitch. Was Ramu beginning to forget that they were on a journey?

Bill B continued talking to Ramu whilst the other men at the table listened attentively, frequently nodding and making the occasional murmur or grunt of agreement. As he spoke Ramu demonstrated with hand and arm gestures, as though explaining something in quite exact detail.

Oby was bored with not understanding. Was Ramu saying too much?

Bill B's next words made Ramu's mouth open wide. He turned to Oby. "He came to your village to help dig wells five years ago."

Oby didn't know what to say, or where to look, at the mention of his village. For the last few weeks he had been trying hard to push thoughts about it away. His last view of it was burnt out remains of ... everything.

Bill B gave Oby a warm smile and spoke. Ramu translated once again. "He's very sorry, about what happened. He says you're courageous."

"Bloody mess, that's what it is," said one of the other men. "Who is there to take responsibility for this kid?"

Ramu immediately replied, "It's me. I'm the one responsible for getting him to his father. So, we need you to tell us which is the best way to go."

"Tell me something, where did you learn to speak English?"

"English nanny, Ruth. She works for Yaki Zakariah."

"Do you have a special reason for wanting to learn it?"

Ramu gave a slightly embarrassed sway of his head and bit his lower lip before saying quite emphatically, "I like learning. I always dreamed of being a teacher."

"You speak okay English."

Ramu bit his lower lip again. His face glowed.

"Excuse me for asking," said Bill B, "but how old are you?"

"Nineteen."

"You look younger ... but I guess that's because you're so skinny. Stay here a few days and we'll feed you up ... get you a bit stronger ... find you a safe way up to Kaffassassee."

"Which is the best way to go?" said Ramu.

"One thing for sure, that marsh will kill you. It stretches for two hundred miles and it takes a boat two days and more to get through."

"Two days!" Ramu exclaimed.

"That marsh is a regular killer. You know, when killers get caught, they end up with a long jail sentence. That marsh is a regular killer and never gets sent to jail. Just free to kill whenever it wants to. It's a devil! You know, there are more human remains in that marsh than there are crocodiles."

And throughout this Ramu was interpreting for Oby.

"Crocodiles! How many?" asked Oby.

"I don't know, but one is enough, isn't it? And another thing, you already know that insects eat you alive out there. Some of them can strip the flesh from your bones. You want that?"

Only then did Oby really believe that the marsh was impossible to cross on foot. He sank back into his chair with a defeated look on his face.

"But there's no problem," said Bill B, patting Oby on the head. "In the morning I'll show you why."

* * *

The next morning Bill B was true to his word. Oby and Ramu climbed aboard the swamp hovercraft and strapped themselves in. The machine rose high on its rubber lips, then blasted across the swamp towards the channel which was being cut by the marsh dragon. Even though it was early, the air was already warm.

Bill B brought the swamp hovercraft to a standstill. "There it is! Your new river. The Junka Canal."

Oby stared at it longingly.

"It shortcuts across this side of the marsh, so boats will be able to sail the length of it, without getting lost in channels, or running aground.

"Where does it go to?" asked Ramu.

"It starts at Junka and goes all the way up to Lake Kaffassassee."

"All the way?" said Oby.

"Yep! Straight through the marsh."

There it was. Wider than ever he imagined a river could

be. Oby began to feel different. He could feel energy and excitement creeping in. This was his river flowing north. He could hear its lapping energy, and see its fast-flowing pulse.

Chapter 27

Maktoub

Feluccas gathered like hyenas at the northernmost section of the Junka Canal, from where the marsh dragon was working forward. They circled, sails flapping, booms swinging, nosing into each other's way, getting as near as possible to the marsh dragon. Impatient boatmen howled at the dragon to work faster. They were eager for the canal to be completed so they could sail straight south and avoid the meandering river channels through the marsh, thus saving two days of travelling time.

Bill Smith yelled out, "Hey, hey, over here!"

A felucca with worn and scratched grey paintwork turned. The sail, mostly good, had tattered edges that occasionally flapped and pasted themselves across the face of the boatman. Cursing, he hastily peeled the shreds away and every time he did that the rudder was left to snake its own path and the boat lurched. The surrounding boatmen yelled and called him a maggot.

This particular boatman paid no attention, because his

eyes were fixed on the American. The American wanted to do business.

"You want to go up to Kaffassassee?" called out Bill Smith, chewing hard on gum.

The boatman tilted his head slightly, considering. He didn't reply.

"Which direction you going?" called Bill Smith.

"Junka."

"That's no good. I want a boat that's going up to Kaffassassee."

"Just come from there."

"Pity," said Bill Smith, "Because I'm willing to pay good money."

The boatman's eyes screwed into horizontal lines. "How much?"

"Well!" Bill Smith watched the boatman's face stiffen, in anticipation of a good price. "Well ... I want to know how much *you* say."

Not a muscle moved in the boatman's face for several moments. Then, "A hundred likits."

"Last week it was fifty likits. Someone did a job for me last week for fifty."

The boatman threw up his arms, muttering into his armpit as he wiped his nose across his sleeve.

Bill Smith was now lassoing gum over his tongue. After a few seconds he shouted again, "You want to go there, or not?"

The boatman snorted and spat an arc of phlegm into the river. "I'll go! I'll go!"

"For fifty?"

"Seventy five."

"I said fifty."

"Make it seventy."

"Sixty."

"Okay! Okay! As much as you say," the boatman growled and pulled on the rudder and steered his craft into the bank.

"What's your name?" said Bill Smith.

"Maktoub."

"Okay, Maktoub, take these two up to Kaffassassee." He drew out of his pocket a wad of bills. Maktoub leaned forward, looking eagerly at the money. His hand came out.

Bill Smith waved the wad of money into the air. "I'm giving these bills to Ramu, here. When you get them safely to Kaffassassee, he'll pay you." He turned to Ramu. "Don't pay him until you leave the boat. Right?"

Ramu nodded that he understood only too well.

Bill Smith shook hands with them both. It felt very strange to Oby. He had never shaken hands before.

* * *

The felucca tacked north, its grubby sail filled with a warm south east wind. Maktoub sometimes hummed, sometimes grunted and sometimes swore. He swung from one mood to the next depending on how his boat was sailing. Wisps of white hair escaped from his dusty head-wrap and he recited poems about his felucca and the fanciful journeys it had made.

"... and my beautiful swan gliding,
gliding over and over clouds,
damp and grey, to the edge of night;
white and cool like the jasmine dawn
and crimson like a queen in the sunset ..."

It was as if the felucca had feelings and could be coaxed into sailing more smoothly. "Huh, huh, huh," chuckled Maktoub. He patted his rudder fondly.

"Why are you fussing over your felucca?" asked Oby.

"It's to steady her nerves. She's uneasy with strangers."

"I think he means us," said Ramu quietly.

Oby asked, "Why do you recite poetry about her?"

"Why not? She's my Queen. Queens must be given royal treatment."

"She doesn't look like a queen."

"What do two skinny boys know about queens? Have you ever met a queen?" said Maktoub.

"No," said Ramu.

"I'll tell you about *my* Queen," said Maktoub. "She doesn't answer back. She doesn't ask stupid questions and she's always graceful. Have you seen anything more graceful?"

The journey continued in silence for an hour, maybe more. Maktoub said, "Water is under the sack."

"Bill Smith gave us some water," Oby said. "D'you want any?"

Maktoub looked at the bottles of water with a suspicious eye. "That's *your* water." He kicked away a rough sack. "This is *my* water," and he banged his fist onto a plastic container, yellowed with age and dented with use. It had a filthy piece of cloth rammed into the top of it, acting as a stopper.

Yet another hour passed and the boat glided as easily as a soaring bird. Maktoub said, "You know anything about feluccas?"

"No." Oby shook his head and raised his eyebrows in apology. Ramu didn't turn his head nor attempt an answer, as if he didn't want to hear. He stared straight ahead.

"Been in a felucca before?"

Oby shook his head again.

"What *do* you know about?"

"Camels."

"I hate camels," proclaimed Maktoub. "They fart …"

Oby laughed.

"… and they bite …"

"You have to know what to do with them."

"Same with feluccas," said Maktoub, "and they never fart nor bite."

The felucca skimmed over the water as though it knew exactly where it was going. They greeted more and more water traffic, passing villages and small towns. They stopped for cardamom tea on the riverbank at a place where groups of tea sellers had congregated with copper urns.

A group of cyclists wearing shorts and skin-tight shirts had just arrived there as well. They said they were friends on their annual holiday and were cycling for two hundred miles along the banks of the Great White River for charity and picking up rubbish at the same time. They also said they were trying to persuade people to keep the river clean because it was important for the environment.

Maktoub watched the tourists without any expression on his face. He behaved as if he had heard nothing. As they climbed back onto the felucca and Maktoub pushed away from the shore he started to roar with laughter. "Crazy tourists!" he shouted. "Collecting stinking presents from the Great White River!" He roared and roared with laughter, slapping his rudder with enthusiasm. "Crazy tourists, taking all the rubbish as a souvenir." He drew out from under his seat an old piece of cloth which had dried stiff and was coated in fish scales. He flung it into the water and shouted,

"Here's a present for you. It's free." He then lobbed overboard an old oil drum.

The cyclists watched Maktoub's theatricals with sad eyes. His drama unfolded accompanied by howls of laughter. Overboard went black, dried banana skins, an old flip-flop shoe, a dead fish, an old razor, a torb-shirt with more holes than shirt, mouldy nuts, the bony remains of a sheep's nose, bits of wood, a comb with no teeth, a broken clock, rotten rope and stuff which was so mangled together it was impossible to tell exactly what it was. The trail of flotsam was like Maktoub throwing his life away. "Ha!" He chortled, "I haven't cleaned out my Queen for years. What a perfect time to do it!" Maktoub patted the rudder of his felucca, lovingly. "What do stupid tourists know? They weren't born on my river."

Oby simply observed, but Ramu said, "Those tourists are right, Maktoub. This river is a mess. Everyone should take care of it."

"*Silence, empty head. Shut up!*" He had plenty more to shout about. "You sit on my beautiful Queen with your nose in the air. All day I've been working hard sailing this felucca. You don't raise a finger. You don't even speak. Then you meet tourists and suddenly you're Mr. Smile. Chit, chat, blah, blah, chit, chat, blah, blah! Now you are trying to tell me what to do on my river. Am I not Maktoub? Is this not my river? Generations of my family have lived on this river and we know how to use it. It's our life. This river takes our rubbish away. That's what it's there for. That's what it does. So, *don't* tell me how to use my river. Or do you want to walk?" Such was his anger that spittle flew in all directions.

Oby wondered what Ramu was now thinking as he sat

there quietly. He then said very casually, "I am the one with the money. Kick us off and you won't get paid."

Oby felt his chest give a pump of pride. It was the first time he had heard Ramu speak with courage in his voice.

Maktoub's voice thundered. "Hold your tongue." He began to rise from his seat. "I'll give you ..."

"How far to Kaffassassee from here, Maktoub?" Oby quickly asked.

Maktoub didn't answer. He was leaning forward and breathing heavily. A massive scowl grew the width of his forehead. Oby wasn't sure whether he was sulking or plotting something evil for Ramu.

"Two days," he finally said, sitting down again.

* * *

Oby moved frequently in the boat; his leg throbbed constantly, unused to sitting for so long in one position. Occasionally, for a change, he squatted, resting his chin on his knees. Ramu remained silent, his back erect and always facing the direction in which they were sailing. He rarely looked left or right and didn't seem to take an interest in the passing landscape.

Maktoub said, "You come here, boy." Oby ignored him, unsure of what he meant. "Come here! Come and take this rudder."

"Me?"

"You can learn. I can teach you." He shifted a canvas bag so Oby could sit the other side of the rudder. "Hand on here," said Maktoub and indicated the rudder arm.

Oby sat down, a little unsure. The rudder was long and uneven, but polished smoothly by Maktoub's hands over the years. As Oby tightened his grip on the rudder he could feel its strength. It was weighty and tried to drag his arm away, but Maktoub reached out and eased the rudder back.

"*You* control the rudder. The rudder *must not* control *you.*"

So Oby tightened his grip and for some seconds he felt comfortable. Then the rudder started moving away again as the wind in the sail grew in strength. The felucca didn't respond immediately; it took time for his efforts to take effect and by the time he had got the rudder and the felucca in the right place again, his arm was aching and his fingers tingling. They tingled so much that he felt he was losing control yet again.

Maktoub grinned and reached out. He gripped and heaved on the rudder and the veins on his hand rose in purple ridges. "See how my Queen loves me," he chuckled. "She obeys me every time. She's perfect!"

Oby took the rudder again.

A tourist cruiser with three decks of passengers came gliding down river. She was adorned in small flags and waves of music floated across the water. She sent out ripples of wake that rolled bigger and bigger across the water and Maktoub's felucca started to roll.

"Look at that!" spat Maktoub. "Tourist boats getting bigger and bigger. Think they own this river. And it's going too fast. Slow down!" he yelled.

Maktoub's Queen began to roll.

"*Control it! Control it!*" Maktoub yelled at Oby.

But the rudder pulled away from Oby. He tried to pull back, but the rudder's strength was too much for him.

Maktoub laughed and leapt forward. He grabbed the rudder with both hands, jammed his feet into a wooden strut on the floor to get extra leverage, and pushed until the veins in his neck stood up. But Maktoub's Queen did not respond in the way he expected and began to roll even more heavily. He struggled to turn the bow of his boat directly into the wake of the tourist cruiser.

Oby was now trapped in a tiny space between the rudder and the stern of the felucca. Suddenly, Maktoub's efforts paid off. The rudder responded, but it slammed into Oby's chest, pinning him to the stern. Oby shrieked. Maktoub didn't seem to hear.

Water slapped hard against the sides of the boat and sent a shower of spray over both of them. The felucca rolled. Oby's legs lost touch with the floor of the boat. He shrieked again.

This caused Ramu to turn round. He saw the form of Maktoub hanging over Oby and pushing hard with the rudder, trapping Oby beneath. The only part that Ramu could see were Oby's legs peddling air.

"Get away from him!" yelled Ramu.

But Maktoub was looking at nothing but the direction of his boat.

"*Let him go,*" Ramu yelled. "*Get away from him.*" He scrambled over sacks and threw himself at Maktoub.

Maktoub overbalanced and fell over. The sail started flapping and the heavy boom swung wildly out of control and whipped across the boat. Maktoub was getting to his feet when the boom crashed into him and sent him flying.

The felucca shaved through reed beds at speed and rammed into the bank of the Great White River. Its timbers creaked and groaned as the prow became firmly embedded in deep, thick mud.

Oby slithered out from beneath the jammed arm of the rudder.

"What was he doing? Trying to kill you?" Ramu helped Oby to his feet. "You okay?"

Oby couldn't speak at first. He held his chest and panted heavily. Massaging his arm, he said. "I'll be okay." He stretched out his arm. "I'll be okay." He looked round. "What's happened to Maktoub?"

Chapter 28

Death In The Reed Beds

One of Maktoub's legs was caught in rope. The rest of him was dangling overboard.

"He isn't moving," said Oby.

"Hurry! He's injured. We have to get him inside the boat."

With the felucca at a steep and awkward tilt, Oby and Ramu crawled towards Maktoub. They peered over the side of the boat.

Maktoub's head was bobbing on top of the water. Beneath his head a widening pool of water was being dyed a very deep red.

Maktoub was dead.

Oby crumpled silently into the bottom of the boat.

Ramu's hands completely covered his face.

* * *

The felucca was concealed by reed beds and embedded deeply in mud. They lay on sacks in the bottom of the boat and did nothing. The sun's fierce rays were beginning to pull in their claws. Breezes rustled the reed beds. Occasionally, voices rose from the direction of the river. The only other sound came from Ramu. He quietly sobbed. Oby's legs could not stop shaking. He shifted position and his hand touched Ramu.

Ramu's fingers clutched Oby. Oby gripped Ramu.

As dusk descended, they untangled Maktoub's leg from the rope. His leg slipped over the side of the boat and his body drifted into the reed beds.

The night hid their tear-streaked faces; as many tears as stars in the sky.

* * *

Oby must have slept. An insect on his nose stirred him. His eyes opened as the sun's rays began to turn the sky pale pink. Breezes began to play with reeds on the riverbank.

"Hey, Ramu!"

"I didn't do anything."

"I know. It was an accident."

"I didn't do it."

"It was an accident, Ramu. It wasn't your fault."

"How could he be dead?" Ramu's voice was shaky.

Oby slowly uncapped a bottle of water, but took several more moments before lifting the bottle to his lips. It was as if the bottle was far too heavy.

Ramu sniffed between words. "I saw him attacking you."

"I was trapped and squashed and he didn't care. I screamed and he didn't care." The water bottle slipped through Oby's fingers and dropped into the bottom of the boat. "The pain in my chest was like fire, but he didn't care." He picked up the fallen bottle. "All he was thinking about was saving his felucca. He wasn't trying to hurt me ... I don't think ..."

"It looked like he was attacking you. He was right on top of you, pushing down ... and you were underneath, completely underneath. I could see your legs kicking out." Distraught, Ramu couldn't stop rolling his head. "How could he be dead so quickly?"

"It wasn't your fault. You didn't kill him. An accident, Ramu, an accident."

They lay in the bottom of the boat for several minutes without a word passing between them.

Oby began speaking so very quietly that Ramu strained to hear. "... seen worse ..."

"Your village?"

"Yeah. The raiders came to kill. The ones that did it liked killing. They wanted to kill. The ones that did it ... that's what they wanted to do."

"Sorry."

Their voices trailed to whispers.

"But I know you're different," said Oby. "You were protecting me. You're my friend."

* * *

The following morning, they climbed out of the felucca, waded through rushes onto drier land and walked away. For two days they walked, hardly speaking. The sun baked. Without their head wraps they could not have kept going as they did, following every twist and turn of the river.

They agreed to bury the memory of the accident, bury the memory of Maktoub. They swore never to speak his name again.

Chapter 29

Songs Of The Ocean

Dark, sinister shapes appeared in the distance. The outlines of hills. Oby and Ramu trudged towards them. They skirted black boulders that were so randomly scattered they might have dropped from the sky. Between boulders, spikey shrubs proliferated and the occasional palm tree shot skywards.

Oby felt he knew this place, although he had never been here before. There was something familiar about it all. After some thought, he suddenly remembered. His grandfather's words were thrown all over these hills. Every single word.

"You know, boy, many years ago the land suffered a terrible stomachache. It was so bad that all the contents of its swollen gut exploded. Missiles of fire, steam and dust shot into the heavens. Red liquid hissed and spat and reached the stars. And when the stars had had enough of this violent visit, they returned it all back to earth on a chariot of ice. The crimson liquid turned grey and black, landing right in the pathway of the Great White River. The river stopped in its tracks.

"A river has as many moods as a donkey. It swaggers like a hunter after his first kill. Sometimes it floods, sometimes dries

almost to a trickle, but it always recovers. You cannot fool a river. It always knows how to find another route. The Great White River turned its nose north.

"For thousands of years it has been battling to get through those hills to the ocean. You can hear its teeth gnashing, biting into those foothills. It will go on forever, nibbling away and one day ... who knows."

Oby sensed a secret lay on the other side of the hills. Breezes occasionally wafted his cheeks in refreshingly cool drifts and a low soothing hum filled his ears. He scrambled up the rocky slope, zig-zagging around vast granite boulders. Some seemed to be embedded with metal dots that twinkled. He could hear Ramu right behind him, occasionally slipping on loose grit. The route was so steep in places that they had to crawl on hands and knees. For two hours they moved steadily towards the secret on the other side of the hills. The further they climbed the louder were the sounds; moans and soft roars.

Grey and chunky like an elephant's back, a slab of rock gave Oby and Ramu a platform with a view they could never have imagined.

Spread out in front of them like a vast sheet of glass, the ocean was breathtakingly huge and beautiful. The ocean rolled in front of them. The Great White River raced behind them. River and ocean were divided only by hills, the two never very far apart. Sun sprinkled glitter over the water.

"My grandad's tale about the volcano that made the Muursa Highlands is from here. I know this is the place he told me about. It is exactly the way he told it. How can it be so big?" breathed Oby in amazement.

"Come on!" said Ramu. "Let's keep going."

They ran and skidded towards the beach, disturbing sand

hoppers and terrifying hermit crabs into the safety of their shells. A salty breeze whispered tunes through the coastal palm trees, in rhythm with the movement of waves.

Their feet sank into freshly washed sand. Mesmerised, they watched waves curl to their highest before splattering along the shoreline in a raggedy white frill.

Dumping Oby's bag safely away from the shoreline, they giggled and shrieked as water cooled their tired legs. They buried their skinny limbs into the sand's cool dampness. They rolled around. Lay on it for ages. Relaxed. Dozed.

Oby stared up at the wide, open sky. Empty.

No Yaki Zakariah.

No marsh.

No desert.

Oby raced back into the water again. "Come on!" He thrashed around in circles and beat the waves with an old palm frond as though he was beating away all his bad memories. He turned his back on Ramu and waded up to his chest into deeper water.

Ramu shouted from the shore. "You can drown."

"Only if you're stupid ..." Then he lost his footing. A wave swept him up and threw him forward. Oby splattered and scrambled onto his feet. A second wave followed, lifting him off his feet, before sucking him down to the ocean bed. He tried to regain his feet, but as the wave receded it pulled him away from the shore.

Ramu's hand grabbed him.

Oby spluttered, his right cheek grazed.

Ramu shook his head. "What did I tell you? You can drown."

Oby stood panting, touching his sore cheek. "Well I didn't, did I?"

* * *

They loved this ocean, its tunes singing in every wave that surged up the shoreline; they loved its frivolous surface with flashing colours and its perfect line of the horizon. They didn't want to leave.

After checking Oby's compass, they decided to walk along the shoreline since it went directly north. They knew that the Great White River was flowing in the same direction on the other side of the Muursa Highlands.

Unwinding his head-wrap, Ramu pulled out some of the provisions given to them by Bill Smith. Oby had a large bottle of water, some beans from the felucca and a lone custard fruit wrapped in his blanket. Their supplies had dwindled since leaving the boat.

They found a few fallen coconuts above the high-water line. Tearing off fibres first, Ramu used his knife to gouge out the two eyes at the top of the coconut and release the sweet liquid. They took it in turns to trickle it down their throats.

Each crescent bay on the beach had its own pattern of pebbles, constantly shifting by the movement of waves. There were struggling grasses. Crusty old skinks and lizards with fat juicy bodies scurried about. Ocean birds wheeled and shrieked before diving into the sparkles for fish. Oby and Ramu paddled through small breakers. Two, thin barracuda with teeth like razors were patrolling the shoreline and chased them from the water.

Walking on sand made their calf muscles work hard. By mid-afternoon, Ramu was lagging behind. His heels were now dry and cracked and his calf muscles so knotted that the length of his stride grew shorter and shorter. Although his legs were heavy, Oby managed to keep a steady pace, but the distance between him and Ramu was slowly increasing.

Continuing north, the Muursa Highlands lessened in height. There were more bare patches of ground as bushes became thornier and thinned out, baked almost white by the sun. Very soon the hills petered out completely and Oby was able to see directly to the west.

Oby stopped to scan the horizon. The Great White River was nowhere to be seen. He wheeled full circle, scanning the land. He cupped his hands over his mouth and yelled back at Ramu, "My river's gone." But Ramu was by now so far behind that Oby knew his call would never reach. He trudged back to Ramu. "My river's gone."

"Your river?" Ramu snapped. "Didn't know you were so important that it was *your* river."

"Why are you snapping at me. My river, your river, who cares? Why are you so mad?"

Ramu snapped again, "Can't you see? It's difficult for me. You're used to it ... all the walking. My legs hurt, my head aches."

"Sorry ..."

"You're not sorry. You couldn't even be bothered to wait for me. I kept calling, but you couldn't have cared less. You're selfish."

"How was I to know your legs were hurting?"

"You raced ahead. All you think about is yourself. All I hear you say is you've got to chase the river. Everything we do is because *you've* got to chase the river. Well, *I've* got things to think about, too. Not once have you asked me if I'm okay."

"Stop blaming me for everything."

"Well, there's no one else to blame. We don't have a river

to follow, we're low on food, we're low on water and we now have to waste time thinking what to do next."

"You agreed. Walk by the ocean, you said."

"Yeah, but I didn't expect you to race ahead. I called and called, but you didn't even look round once. Didn't your stupid head tell you that we might need to check now and again? Maybe climb a hill and get our bearings and check where the river was?"

"You could have checked yourself."

"How could I? You were leaving me behind. I was trying my best to keep up ... keep you in sight."

Oby glowered at Ramu. "Well, it's easy. We go back the way we came."

"Why ... why did I listen to a kid?"

"You're the clever one. You're the grown-up one. And you're blaming me!"

Oby noticed that Ramu had glazed eyes as he pulled his head-wrap off and ran fingers through his hair like a spider – a tell-tale sign that he was upset. He dropped onto the ground and put his face into his hands. Oby had seen Ramu with a sinking heart before. He put a swing into his voice. "It's not that bad. Come on! We can retrace our steps. We haven't lost it. The river is there. I know it is."

"That's a day completely wasted," Ramu muttered into his hands. "I can't walk any further."

"Come on! We *know* how to find the river again," Oby said, pointing back towards the Muursa Highlands they had just left. "Only this time, we can walk on the other side of the hills, not the ocean side, then we can't miss the river."

"Go away!" Ramu refused to get up.

"Are you coming?" Oby walked away a few metres.

Ramu didn't move.

Oby shouted back. "Coming or not?"

Still, Ramu made no reply.

Oby walked back. He tried to take Ramu's arm but Ramu shoved him away angrily. "Don't touch me!"

"Stay here if you want, but I'm going to find my father." Oby walked away. No! He would not look back. No, he would *not*.

But he hadn't gone far when his curiosity beat him and he glanced back hoping that Ramu might be following, but all he could see was a small blob. It could have been a dog.

He forced himself forward. *I'll do it by myself. I don't need that northern quitter. I'll walk this side of the hills until I see the river. Why is he so difficult and moody? He's nothing to me. Why should I care?*

Oby pushed on. When he glanced back a second time Ramu was nowhere to be seen. Oby shielded his eyes from the sun with his hands and scanned the whole area behind him.

He was on his own.

Chapter 30

Night Ghosts

Night settled over the land. No longer able to see very far, Oby crawled under a scrubby bush and made himself as small as he could.

Noises of the night rose around him. His ears took over from his eyes: winds whined, the bush vibrated, cicadas scritch-scritched, seed pods crackled, night-hunting birds whooshed, a couple of small creatures (probably gerbils) ran over his fingers. Oby thought he heard the bark of wild dogs.

The temperature fell and he was alone in a world of strange noises. He hoped the bush he had crawled under would keep him safe.

But he couldn't sleep. He didn't want to sleep.

He pressed his hands over his ears. But still strange noises crept in through his fingers. Beating. Slashing. Screaming. Pleading. Oby's body tightened and twisted and shrank into itself as if he was an old man.

. . .

From out of the black night two lights glowed. Two eyes. Huge. Oby snapped his eyes shut, pressed his hands over his ears and held his breath. And waited. And waited.

When he plucked up enough courage to remove his hands, there was nothing threatening to be seen. He heard a bird trilling.

Birdsong heralded the dawn and he crawled out from the protection of the bush. He stretched out his aching fingers. His knuckles were pink for being clenched so tightly. His night fears did not immediately disappear and he looked around cautiously.

He sipped only two mouthfuls of water, because there wasn't much left and he needed to keep some in reserve.

He had to find the river.

Oby hiked to a viewpoint on the ridge. He thought he could see the river in the distance, or it could have been magic in the haze. However, down below, he spotted a circular mud hut. He headed towards it. Maybe it had been abandoned. Maybe not. Maybe it was a temporary shelter for hunters or nomads. Maybe there would be some food remains. Maybe.

There were enormous spaces in his stomach. He could hear it gurgling and rumbling. His stomach felt as though it was eating itself. With his head turning dizzy, Oby couldn't walk straight. He crashed into the doorway of the hut.

A shadow was moving. It was much taller than him and growing taller. It loomed menacingly. Oby threw all his weight into defending himself and swung a fist. It landed with a thump.

"Ouch! Why did you do that?" cried out Ramu, rubbing

his arm. "It's no good losing your temper with me."

"How was I to know it was you?"

"If you hadn't walked off ..."

"You should've stopped me."

"Why? You're a man now. That's what you said. You said to treat you like a man ... then you decided to walk off. I don't mess with a man's decision."

"Okay! Okay! I'm sorry! What more do you want me to say?"

"I tried to follow you," explained Ramu, in a quieter voice, "but you moved too quickly for me. Then it began to get dark. Then I bumped into the hut. It was a blessing for me. Except ... mmm ... how, how, how could I sleep when ... Honestly, Oby, how did you expect me to sleep when you were out there all alone?" Oby now had his eyes glued to Ramu's face ... big eyes that showed he was listening intently. "You were out there ... somewhere ... somewhere ... alone. I couldn't sleep. I had the knife and so I knew you wouldn't have been able to open coconuts. Well, you might have, but it would have been difficult."

Oby gave a sigh. "Noises kept coming back." His voice dropped to a whisper. "In the dark there were only noises. In the dark you don't know what the noises mean. It's like death sitting beside you ready to pounce." Then he said, "I'm sorry. I'm sorry for yesterday."

"Me, too. I'm sorry." He patted Oby's back, then stepped outside. "Hey, come here! Look at all those palms over there. We've got coconuts."

Oby stepped out of the hut and followed Ramu's gaze.

"Maybe, if anyone lived here recently, there might still be roots in the ground, too," suggested Ramu, hopefully.

Oby kicked and his toes scattered powdery soil. Clouds

of dust flew up, causing Ramu to cough. A sudden gust of wind blew the dust even higher and Ramu's coughing got worse. He gasped for air and his chest crackled like an old goat's weary bleat. Oby pushed Ramu gently back into the hut and fanned him with a palm leaf. Ramu could do nothing but prop against the mud wall and struggle for breath.

"Moussa Khaliffa had a cough like that. It was from all the dust on the Salt Lake," said Oby.

"My ... sister ... too ... born ... with ... this ... crow's ... cough." Ramu rasped and gasped between words. He cleared his chest with a final huge cough. "She died one night. Sometimes she got completely worn out trying to breathe. She couldn't keep going and just gave up. I'm not as bad as her." He put his hand on his chest and blinked back tears.

"Your mum and dad ... you once started to tell me about your mum and dad?" said Oby.

Ramu eyelids flickered. "I can't remember well. They died before my sister. I don't know why. They just did. Then grandmother died. So, my aunt and uncle looked after me, but my uncle didn't really want to be bothered. He made me work in his field and he did nothing, just stood and watched. He sent me out there the same day my grandmother died. As soon as I started hoeing his beans the dust flew up everywhere. Straight away the coughing started. My chest seemed to be stuffed full of goats' hair and I couldn't breathe. So when Ben Sid came to our village looking for workers my uncle told him to take me because I was a 'good boy'."

"Ben Sid!" Oby grunted, his eyes flashing with anger. "I want to kill him! I want to kill him twice! Gold Teeth warned me." Even as he was speaking, Oby knew that for all his teasing Gold Teeth hadn't been so bad after all. Under all the teasing and poking fun at him Gold Teeth had been trying to help. "Stay inside the hut, Ramu. Keep away from the dust and I'll dig." Oby kicked into the ground, using his heel. He hit something knobbly and immediately dropped onto his knees and hooked two fingers under a plump root. He scraped at the ground with his fingers, but the root was stubborn. He called, "I need your knife."

There was no reply.

When he stepped into the hut, he found Ramu sleeping, so he slipped the knife from his head-wrap.

Outside again, Oby plunged the knife into the ground, twisting and heaving around nobbles beneath the surface. Gently, he eased out a sweet potato and peeled it. Next, he opened a coconut and drained the milk into his water bottle. He cut the flesh from the coconut into pieces and did the same with the potato. When Ramu woke up they would eat.

He also decided to open the dried food pack given to them by Bill Smith. The dried peas and chicken looked like nothing more than bits of broken twigs. Oby drummed his fingers on his knees as he tried hard to remember what Bill Smith had said to do with it. He tasted it. "Yuck!"

Ramu stirred. "What's wrong?"

"It's foul. Bill Smith's food is yuck. We should have brought Maktoub's beans with us." Suddenly he was smacked on the back of the head. He picked up Ramu's sandal. "Why did you throw that?"

Ramu hissed, "You said *his* name ... that name."

"Sorry! Sorry!" Oby winced and screwed up his face. "Honestly, Ramu, I didn't mean to."

"Remember, you were the one who suggested it ... never to say *his* name again."

"I know. I won't say it again. Promise."

Chapter 31

Warriors

Dusk crept over the grass-packed roof of the hut. Cicadas sang throughout the night; it was a lullaby for the exhausted pair. With no idea of time, they could have slept for eight or nine or even twelve hours.

A whisk of breeze fluttered through the entrance way and stirred Oby. He rolled over drowsily and slowly his eyes flickered open.

Four large human feet were immediately in his vision just outside the hut.

He scrambled to his feet.

Two bare bodies (apart from small red loincloths) covered in powdered white clay and carrying long spears, towered above him.

One of the men grunted and Ramu awoke.

Oby's heart was jumping in his chest as he rolled onto his stomach. As he did so, he curled his hand over a stone which he had carefully placed at his side the night before.

Four glittering eyes bore down on them.

The two men stepped forward. The shorter of the two

pointed his spear directly at them and grunted. He flicked the spear for them to get up.

Oby and Ramu scuttled out of the hut.

The shorter spear-man indicated for them to turn around. His eyes ran up and down the pair, from head to toe. Then he held his spear out in front of him, as though in defence, as he entered the hut.

Oby gently slid his hand down his side. It was still there. Fud Shifta's bag was still closely attached to him.

With his inspection over, the man withdrew from the hut and his face relaxed. He dropped his spear loosely to his side. So did the second man. They spoke in a language that neither Ramu nor Oby understood. The next moment, they were walking away with fast athletic strides, without a second glance back.

Ramu shouted, "Hey!"

The men stopped and turned.

"Shut up, Ramu," hissed Oby. "Let them go."

"We need help."

"Not their kind of help. Let them go."

"Shh! Right now, we need all the help we can get. They're heading straight into the bush, so they must know this place."

Oby remained tight-lipped and glued to the spot, ready to run, even as Ramu moved forward towards the men.

"River! River!" said Ramu.

The men maintained blank faces.

Ramu squatted, picked up a small, pointed stone and proceeded to draw on the powdery ground. A felucca on a river.

Tilting their heads left and right, the men talked rapidly for a few moments, before laughing and pointing their spears in the very same direction that they had been walking. They strode forward, beckoning.

"Come on. Let's follow," said Ramu.

Oby didn't move.

Ramu gave a sigh. "Don't start being difficult again."

One of the men walked back and pulled at Oby's arm. But Oby dug his heels into the ground.

"Stop making things difficult," snapped Ramu.

"What about your things?" Oby prompted. "You need your head-wrap."

Ramu's face fell. All his life he had owned nothing and now he nearly forgot his head-wrap and his only possession, the knife.

* * *

"It's good we don't have to trek back the way we came." Ramu had had a surge of energy.

The two men's muscular legs rapidly ate up the ground. Gourds containing water hung down from waist strings.

Walking behind, Oby and Ramu were able to study the men in close detail.

"I think they're Buden wrestlers," said Ramu. "They go from place to place for wrestling competitions. I saw them once before."

"So, we wouldn't stand a chance if they turned nasty."

"Yes, any moment now they'll probably use us for practice and tear us to pieces."

Oby muttered, "So, we're stupid to follow them."

"Ha! I was only joking. We're too skinny to practise on."

The track was boring. The distance between the wrestlers and the two followers increased.

One of the wrestlers hung back, falling in with Oby's and Ramu's pace. With one deft movement he untied the gourd from his belt and handed it to Oby.

Oby hesitated.

"Go on," said Ramu impatiently. "Drink."

Oby pulled the leather stopper out of the hole in the top, then hesitated again.

"What's wrong with you now?"

"What if it isn't water?"

"It's water. Why would they carry anything else? They need water."

One of the men tapped the gourd, then pointed to his lips.

Up close, Oby could see the man's enormous arm muscles rippling with every movement; he had seen muscles like this before on Yaki Zakariah's henchmen and it made him jittery. His lips jammed together.

The man snatched back the gourd and took a massive swig.

Ramu held out his hand for the gourd and took a massive swig. "It's good. It's water," he insisted. "See, it's okay." Oby stepped back, still refusing to take the gourd. "Stop being difficult. Why are you being like this?"

Oby saw annoyance mounting on Ramu's face. The two warriors were scowling at him. That made it three against one. Reluctantly, he held out his hand.

The water was incredibly sweet and surprisingly cool, and left Oby wishing he could drink all of it, but having made a fuss about drinking it in the first place he felt that he couldn't now tip the gourd up a second time.

The numerous pathways across the dry scrubland began

to merge into one and widened out as it weaved between thicker clumps of struggling grass.

A village suddenly popped up, seemingly from nowhere.

Two women with clothes as brightly coloured as their chatter were plaiting a girl's hair. A few men were squatting on the ground twisting raffia into small bags. Sniffing dogs wandered about, hens were scratching and a rooster was fussing and preening. Several goats were tethered to poles just outside a circle of huts.

The wrestlers were clearly expected, because three children ran up to them, giggling. They pulled at the wrestlers' arms in an effort to make them dance. The wrestlers put on a display, flexing muscles and leaping high into the air. When they challenged two other villagers to wrestle, everyone laughed and waved them away.

Oby and Ramu were completely ignored.

They had just had enough time to take in the scene, when an old man who had been standing on an oil can and scanning the scrubland to the north, gave a shout.

The wrestlers immediately stood still and stretched themselves up to their fullest height. The remaining villagers congregated quietly in the centre of the village.

Something was about to happen as everyone looked in the direction of the old man. Everyone went silent.

Oby and Ramu kept well back. Should they run? Everyone was distracted so it would be a good time. Except, curiosity kept them fixed.

From the silence grew a hum, then a rumble, as a vehicle lurched from side to side on the one and only vehicle track into the village. It cleverly missed potholes. A cloud of dust gradually settled and an orange bus materialised.

Tourists alighted, most of them wearing sun hats and Bermuda shorts, with heavy cameras around their necks. As the village children rushed forward and ushered the tourists towards low planks propped on rocks, the tourists handed out sweets.

Then a show began.

Ceremonial performances took place: a rooster dance with the children dressed in colourful feathers; a wrestling match so that the men could show off their muscles and best fighting skills. When it was time for a rain dance to encourage large grey clouds to bless the earth with a downpour, the women sprinkled water over the tourists for luck. Through all this, three men with agile fingers kept up a rapid drumming.

But the performance had a twist. The tourists hushed as two little girls led a small goat into the centre of the village. They held the animal tightly. The goat wriggled and shook its head. Its bleating was high-pitched and its little legs stamped up circles of dust.

From out of his hut now stepped the Head Man, his face painted with red clay. Purple feathers were stuck at odd angles into a shocking pink headband. He held aloft a long knife and its blade shone in the bright sunlight. Twice he hopped and whirled around the goat. Three villagers chanted and pulled ridiculous faces. The goat bleated even louder.

The tourists' eyes went wide with fear as they realised they were about to witness a sacrifice.

The knife flew high into the air, then down, then high, then down.

The goat's head was yanked back.

"Noooooooooooooooooooooooooooooo!" A scream rose from a female tourist dressed from head to toe in fuchsia pink.

"No! No! We came here for entertainment. This isn't entertainment! We don't want you to do this." She stood between the goat and the knife. "No, no ... it isn't humane. It isn't ..."

The bus driver was quick to intervene. "Lady, what's the problem?" he asked in broken English (for the tourists were from the United Kingdom).

"We didn't come here to see an animal butchered."

"The chief has a duty to perform. It's his duty."

"Duty!" she squealed. "Killing an innocent sheep?"

"Madam, it's a goat, not a sheep."

The chief strode up and down, swinging his knife over his head, strutting like a cockerel that had just lost his favourite hen to a bigger cockerel.

The bus driver pleaded with the lady. "Lady, please ... either let the chief fulfil his custom, or ... pay the penalty ..."

"What penalty?"

He whispered, "A fee."

"How much?"

"Well, a good goat is two hundred likits."

The woman turned to her husband. "Give me two hundred likits," she demanded.

He hurriedly handed over the money, his face reddening. Fuchsia pink woman handed the money to the bus driver. He handed it to the chief. The chief slung the knife away with a shake of the head and passed the goat over to the bus driver. The bus driver handed the goat to the woman.

"What am I supposed to do with this?" she squealed.

"It's yours," said the bus driver. "You paid for it."

"Don't be ridiculous! Just give it to ... to ... to... those children over there."

The two small children who had brought in the goat in the first place then walked away with it, into the bush.

It seemed to be the end.

The ground was splattered in sweat. Seventeen dancers stood glistening. The performers turned to face the tourists. They neither smiled nor spoke.

"Bravo! Bravo!" The bus driver led the applause. The tourists took the cue and joined in. The oldest man in the tribe shuffled forward, holding out a raffia bag. Suddenly, all the tourists were fumbling in their pockets and bags for cash. Paper bills were thrust into the raffia bag. The old man smiled sweetly at everyone which revealed that half his teeth were missing.

Suddenly, the performers were all smiles, stepping forward and mingling with the tourists, slapping their backs as if they were being reunited with long lost friends. They posed together for photographs.

Oby and Ramu remained almost invisible, standing quietly in the shadows of one of the huts.

Chapter 32

Thieves

Immediately after the yellow bus had swept the tourists away, the entertainers wandered back towards their huts and started to remove jewellery. When they emerged again, they were dressed in jeans and T-shirts splashed with pictures in bright colours with names like Pretty Prue, Ice-Guy, Candy Cute and Z-POP. Two boys wore special-brand trainers with thick purple laces; there were yellow, blue and green plastic flip-flops and one skinny girl had dusky-pink high heels that were far too high and caused her to wobble and walk pigeon-toed.

Oby muttered, "What's going on?"

Ramu shrugged.

They stood quietly in the shadows, confused. They were ignored as if invisible.

A woman collected the jewellery together: cheap plastic neck coils, cheap plastic earrings, cheap plastic bracelets. She placed them all in a well-used straw basket. The chickens were caught by their necks and thrust into a wire crate; the rest of the goats were untied. Every single person turned away from the village and walked into the bush, chattering, with the dogs running in behind. The only things left behind were the huts. And Oby and Ramu.

As the performers disappeared, Oby snapped his fingers. "Oh no! We forgot to ask them how to find the Great White River. Come on. They haven't gone far. We need to know." He started to chase after them.

But Ramu quickly grabbed his shirt sleeve. "Just hang on. Don't chase after them or ask them anything."

Oby tried to pull away.

"Keep still! I've been thinking …" Ramu moved to pick up a knife that lay in the dust. It was the one the chief had flung aside.

"We need to ask them where the river is," repeated Oby.

"No. They might tell us the wrong way."

"What's going on in your head, Ramu? We only want to ask the way to the river. What's wrong with that? We need to know. Anyway, you told me to trust them when they gave us water."

"Well, I've changed my mind. I don't trust them," said Ramu.

"Why should I listen to you? If I listen to you, we'll never find our way. Every time I have a plan you say no. Every time I suggest something you are scared. What's wrong with you?"

"Oby, take a look at this knife."

"What about it?"

"It's plastic. It's blunt. It couldn't cut a mango." Ramu patted the plastic knife on the palm of his hand. "It was a great game for them. Acting. Tourists mean money." Oby could almost read Ramu's thoughts as they flickered across his face. "Think! Think! The river can't be far away. Those tourists won't have travelled far in that rickety old bus.

Remember, we saw plenty of tourists when we were travelling on the river. So, I think they've come from the river ... it's the only place. We just have to follow the direction of the bus. Just keep on the bus track ..."

"... and we'll get to the river." said Oby, his face lighting up.

"Maybe find another boat. We still have all the money Bill Smith gave us, so we can pay for a boat ... unless they want more money than we've got," said Ramu.

"Remember how Bill Smith beat down the price? That's what we have to do."

They left the empty huts behind and continued, taking the same wide track the tourist bus had taken. Drifting from one side of the track to the other to take advantage of shade cast by the occasional acacia tree, it wasn't long before they came across an orange catastrophe.

The tourist bus was not sitting proud on its wheels. It was tilted, with its left front wheel buckled and a headlamp buried in the gnarled trunk of an acacia.

As soon as the woman in fuchsia pink saw Oby she rushed forward, shrieking. "That's one of them! That's one of them!" She was shedding tears and streaks of black eye make-up were smeared over her cheeks.

Oby saw Ramu grabbed from behind. A rhinoceros of a man, wearing a blue shirt covered in sweaty patches, shook Ramu, brandishing a rolled-up parasol. "We've got you now, you conniving thieves. Where are our wallets?" He poked Ramu in the ribs with the parasol. "Give them back. Now!"

Oby understood nothing that was being said. He remained rooted to the spot and watched helplessly.

Ramu yelped. "Let go! Stop it!" He tried to wrench himself free from the grasp he was in. "Stop!"

"Thieves! Our wallets! Our cameras! Where are they?"

"No! *We aren't thieves.*" Ramu held up both hands pleadingly.

The fuschia pink woman started attacking Oby with a fan.

Ramu yelled, "Look! We've got nothing. Can't you see that?" His hands flopped to his side in exasperation.

The Rhinoceros was clearly agitated, moving his weight from one foot to the other. "Search the thieves!" he yelled. "Search them from top to bottom."

Oby tried to duck away as another man rushed forward and held onto him. His shirt was suddenly being lifted. "Get off me!" Hands were patting over his body. "Stop touching me. Get your hands off." Oby screamed and writhed. "Stop! Stop!"

No one had ever intruded on him like this before. He got hotter and hotter. He kicked and kicked. The shame of it. He closed his eyes and kicked and flailed with his arms.

Suddenly, the man pushed him away. He was empty-handed.

The Rhinoceros loosened his grip on Ramu. "Where have you hidden it all, you thieves?"

Oby was almost yanked off his feet as Ramu grabbed his shirt. They ran and ran, backtracking speedily and didn't stop until out of sight of the tourists.

Oby was panting hard. His thoughts were hammering in his head. Nothing? The tourists found nothing under his shirt? Nothing? Frantically, Oby felt around his middle for his money bag, then lifted his shirt, skimmed his hands inside his shorts, then over his chest and right up to his neck. Then searched again.

Then he knew.

Oby exploded with a scream. The small coins that his mother had collected. Gone. The money from Moussa Khaliffa for working on the Salt Lake. Gone. The large gold coin from Gold Teeth. Gone. The photo of his father. Gone.

All gone!

Chapter 33

Hunting Down Trickster Thieves

"It's gone!" Oby howled. "My money bag! It's lost!"

"You haven't lost it, it's been stolen," replied Ramu instantly.

"That's impossible. Nobody's been near me. Nobody would know I had a money bag because it was hidden. Nobody could get anything from under my shirt without my knowing. It was tied with a camel's knot ... impossible for anyone to steal."

"If it was a camel's knot then you could *not* have lost it. It would've been safe, wouldn't it?"

"But who could steal it?"

"The wrestlers. It could only have been them."

"How could they?"

"Thieves are magicians. Quick-handed. Those villagers stole from most of the tourists and they stole from you, too. You didn't even know your money bag was missing. And that village, it wasn't even real, it was a set-up just to get the tourists in. And at the end of the performance, they all crowded round the tourists for photos. That gave them a really good opportunity to slip their fingers into everyone's pockets. I bet that's what they did. It was a great performance they gave, in more ways than one."

Oby groaned and slapped his head. "And after that they changed into T-shirts and shorts. Some even had shoes with high heels. You're right, it was a set-up."

"A gang of professional thieves," Ramu said emphatically.

"It's not fair!" Oby wailed.

Ramu said, "Why should we let them get away with it?" He clicked his long fingernails together. "Suppose we follow the track they took and ..."

"... and take them by surprise."

"No! No surprises."

"Why not?" Oby boxed the air. "Yeah! Let's get them. I want my bag back."

"We have to be careful. Stay calm. We mustn't do anything stupid. They could get angry with us and there were lots of them and only two of us, but we *can't* let them get away with it."

Oby knew Ramu was thinking hard because he was chewing his lip in a way he had seen before.

Suddenly, there was a yell, "Hey! Come back here, you thieves."

Oby swung round.

The Rhinoceros was on their tail. He puffed and panted, red-faced, his fat belly wobbling and performing its own little war dance. "Come back here!"

"He's yelling that he's going to get revenge," cried Ramu.

Oby and Ramu darted for the dirt road leading to the village they had just left. Soon, the Rhinoceros was far behind them. Through the now deserted village they followed the same track that they had seen the performers take. They walked for half an hour, placing stone markers and signs beneath thorn bushes. The track was mostly straight. In the distance was a wide clump of trees. The path led straight there.

As they neared the trees, a voice drifted into the air. They stopped. Ramu put a finger to his lips. Oby knew to stay silent. He heard a deep voice rising and falling as though someone was telling a story, but it must have been a joke, because there was sudden laughter from several people, loud and clear.

"It's definitely them," mouthed Ramu, no sound coming from his mouth.

"What do we do?" Oby whispered. "Beg for our money back? They wouldn't give it, would they? What can we do?"

"There's only one way," Ramu whispered in return. "We'll just have to ... have to ... wait for an opportunity and steal it back."

Oby gulped and swallowed hard. "Do you really think we can?"

"It's the only way. We must be patient and wait for the right moment."

They moved low over the ground, crawling, sliding on their bellies, silent as lizards. Occasionally, Oby noticed Ramu raise his head a little to see what was happening. Keeping a good distance, they circled the whole of the gathering in this way, assessing the target as best possible.

At the very centre of the wood was a clearing. A couple of four-wheel-drive vehicles were parked there, nose to nose. Oby and Ramu shuffled round to get a better view. The wrestlers were lying across the roof of one vehicle. The other entertainers draped and lounged nearby, swigging from bottles. Their children chased each other around the vehicles.

Four of the men moved away from the vehicles and started to stagger in the direction of Oby and Ramu. The sound of cracking twigs was sharp and clear.

Danger was creeping closer and Oby hardly dared to breathe. They kept their foreheads pressed into the ground, terrified that at any moment there would be a shout that they had been spotted.

Unexpectedly, the men disappeared.

Oby got a warning from Ramu with a finger over his lips for a second time. Oby needed to scratch his leg, but bit his lip, instead. Where were the men? How close were they? Occasionally, blurred voices sent a jumble of words in their direction. But where the men were was a mystery.

Having been flat on his stomach for at least half an hour, hearing voices, but not knowing exactly where they were coming from, Oby finally found enough courage to edge forward. His fingers reached the rim of a pit. Down below were the men, chortling and joking. He remained still as Ramu edged forward, too, and gently pushed aside a few leaves that had obviously been blocking his view.

One man was admiring a watch. Stolen goods. Ramu had been right. They were common thieves. The men lovingly handled their haul. Several watches, a pearl necklace, cameras, paper money and, most importantly for Oby, there was his money bag. The strap of the money bag was in two pieces.

Oby made a cutting sign to Ramu. Could the wrestler have used his spear to cut the bag off? Oby hadn't felt anything. It was impossible! The spear was too big. Maybe the wrestler had used a small knife ... he must have. Only a sharp knife could cut so cleanly ... or a razor.

The men were drinking from cans and they had a good stash of them. They were being drained quickly. As they drank the thieves continued picking over their loot and placed it in either one of two canvas sacks. Oby made a very careful note into which sack his money bag was dropped.

For another hour they remained still.

Gradually, the men's frivolous laughter became less raucous. Their tones became softer. Until silence. One by one the thieves slipped into a boozy sleep.

Oby knew that Ramu was being very patient, waiting until there was no movement whatsoever from any of the men. Finally, now on his feet, Ramu edged forward centimetre by centimetre down the slope and into a better position to view the canvas sack. He could not make a mistake. Not a single one.

One of the men rolled over and snorted.

Oby held his breath as Ramu froze. Oby closed his eyes and counted to ten, before nervously peering around again. All was still. Centimetre by centimetre he felt he had to watch every movement Ramu made, ready to help if needed. The gap closed between Ramu and the sack. He stopped at least three times. Oby saw his chest rising and falling rapidly. He guessed Ramu's hands were clammy by the way he was rubbing them against his shirt. As he gently drew the knife out of his head-wrap, Oby was praying, *don't drop it, don't drop it.* He almost let out a gasp as Ramu put the knife down on the ground momentarily to rub his hands against his shirt again, before picking up the knife once more.

Oby watched through shaking fingers as Ramu stepped past the first wrestler and extended his arm. He pushed the knife through the top of the sack and started to lift it, but Oby could see his arm wobbling uncontrollably. Oby snapped his eyes shut. After several seconds, he took a slow, deep breath and peeped. To his surprise, Ramu was lifting the sack over the snoring wrestler's head.

Oby slithered backwards. As soon as Ramu reached him with the sack, he pulled it off the knife.

"Get moving! Go! Go!" Ramu hissed.

Oby swung the sack onto his back. Their feet had never covered ground so fast. They fled back along the track, not once glancing behind.

Chapter 34

Raging Rhinoceros

Oby's arms wheeled into the air. He fought to keep his balance as the fuschia-pink woman pushed him aside, grabbed the sack and tipped out its contents. She cried inconsolably as she clung to small items she reclaimed. He guessed they were travel documents.

Having already retrieved his own bag, Oby took a few steps back as the Rhinoceros began roaring again accompanied by a furious glare, mostly on Ramu. Oby tugged firmly on Ramu's arm in a message that they needed to get away. The man's face was going red and purple, the colour of squashed scrabjuck beetles. He looked as though he was about to explode.

Ramu seemed to be transfixed and muttered, "He isn't grateful that we bothered to return some of their belongings. He hasn't listened to our explanations at all. He thinks we've hidden the rest of his things in the bush and we're plotting to get a reward. He says he's had five thousand dollars of cash stolen. He's furious at his wife, because she was the one who had begged him to come on the excursion. He's furious because he's got an important business meeting tomorrow which he says he mustn't miss under any circumstances."

Oby was relieved that the Rhinoceros was now yelling at his wife and not at them. "Let's get away while they're shouting at each other."

"Now he's cursing the bus driver who ran away after the crash."

Oby hissed, "Come on! Let's run now."

Suddenly, both Oby and Ramu were grabbed by the Rhinoceros' fat hands. "Common thieves! Common thieves! Own up!"

Oby dropped his gaze to the ground, so he didn't have to meet the man's bloodshot eyes. Instead, he saw two very fat stumpy feet with raggedy broken toenails sticking out from thickly strapped sandals.

"Let the boys go, Horace." An elderly man with unruly steel-white hair was now at their side. "These two have explained what happened and I believe them." With a light touch of his hand steering Oby and Ramu away, the old man said, "Why don't you two come and sit in the shade for a while? You both look exhausted. And we have some snack bars."

Oby's skin prickled. Not only did he feel warmth in the smile he was given, but the man was speaking to them in Rubo, his own language.

"I'm Dr Fletcher and this is my wife."

Oby leaned forward, listening in wonder to the sounds. The old man spoke in a slow manner, pronouncing some words a little strangely.

Oby explained his journey to find his father and the doctor listened intently. "I heard about the raid on your village," he said. "A terrible thing. Terrible. This is quite a journey you are undertaking." His eyes brightened. "Well, you will be pleased to know that we aren't far from Kaffassassee and the river."

"Really?" Oby felt a surge of energy.

"Maybe an hour at the most on foot. Wait here with us and when the sun goes down a little more, we can walk. At my age I can't walk very far in full sun." He said he was used to buses breaking down. He had travelled far and wide with his family in search of flora: making sketches, taking photographs, recording sizes and making notes. He told them he was a botanist and most of his lifetime's work had been done in this part of the world. "I love it here. I can sit under an acacia for hours. It's very relaxing."

All through this, Oby had been keeping an eye on the Rhinoceros who occasionally stamped in fury and frequently glared at Ramu intensely. It made Oby feel uneasy.

Suddenly, the Rhinoceros started bellowing again. "It's been three hours! I told you that bus driver wouldn't get help. I knew it."

"Well, it isn't surprising," said Dr Fletcher, "after you threatened him with a fist."

* * *

The shadows from the acacia were now sprawling widely across the ground. The sun was lowering rapidly. Dr Fletcher stood up and stretched. "Yes, I think it is cool enough for us to walk now."

Oby pushed two fingers into his ears as the Rhinoceros bellowed even louder than ever that he wasn't going to walk anywhere. His face was dripping in perspiration. The dampness spreading over his shirt was changing the fabric from pale blue to royal blue even as Oby watched. He kept yelling that this was an emergency and he had to be rescued. Even though Dr Fletcher tried to persuade him it wouldn't be very far to walk, he refused to listen. In the end, Mrs Fletcher offered to remain behind with the other six stranded passengers whilst her husband took Oby and Ramu with him to get help.

Oby felt the Rhinoceros' eyes drilling into his back as they walked away.

They walked steadily north-west, sticking to the track and admiring the changing pinks and reds of the sky. Ramu was the tallest of the three and after thirty minutes he jumped with glee. "I can see the sail of a felucca!" Fifteen minutes later, they could see a radar tower and more sails. And Lake Kaffassassee.

Dr Fletcher said, "Well, you two, what are your plans now?"

Neither knew how to answer. Just what *were* their plans?

Chapter 35

Paddle Steamer Cleo

Kaffassassee stank.

Dr Fletcher laughed and pinched his nose. "Ports can be a bit smelly and noisy."

"Like the Rhinoceros," said Oby.

"The Rhinoceros," laughed Dr Fletcher, "you mean Horace? Yes, that's a good name for him. I like that." He paused to check a street name. "These narrow streets are confusing. Now, what was the other thing you asked me? How will Mrs. Fletcher manage with Horace? Oh, she'll be fine. She's always calm. It's a good quality to have and, to be quite honest, it's helped to get us out of some sticky situations, especially when I was younger ... and quite headstrong. Now, first, we'd better arrange for someone to collect my wife and our stranded friends. It's beginning to get dark."

* * *

Exactly one hour later Mrs. Fletcher was standing beside her husband again, smiling and not at all perturbed about her experience.

"Now ..." began Dr Fletcher.

"... and now I would like a nice cup of tea." Mrs. Fletcher had an insistence in her voice that could not be ignored.

Oby hung back. He gripped Ramu's arm. "Let's go!"

Here they were, at Kaffassassee, exactly where they had wanted to be. They now needed to find the dock and negotiate the price of a felucca to the capital city, Salima.

Dr Fletcher turned round. "Hey! Aren't you two coming? We're going to eat. Come on."

They paused. Then Oby shook his head and raised his hand in farewell as he and Ramu turned away.

"Where're you off to?" Dr Fletcher hurried towards them. "Come on. First, we eat, then we discuss how I can help with your trip. I insist."

Ramu's head began rolling. Oby twisted in his sandals, gazing at the ground, not knowing what to say.

"We are not leaving you here," said Dr Fletcher firmly. "My conscience would not allow it."

Oby's shoulders were aching. Ramu's stomach had never been so empty.

Mrs Fletcher took Oby's arm. "Come on. Food."

Weary with walking, weary with constantly having to look over their shoulders, weary with decision-making, weary with hunger, Oby and Ramu gave in.

In the crowded market the table in front of them was packed with tempting dishes.

"You mentioned that you worked as a house boy. Whose house were you working in, Ramu?" asked Dr Fletcher.

Ramu had difficulty saying the word. "Y... Yaki ... Yaki Zakariah," he said reluctantly.

"Goodness!" replied Dr Fletcher. "He's always in the news, popping up at grand social functions. He's the sort of chap who likes to be at the centre of everything. I've been told that Yaki Zakariah can smell money from miles away. Am I right?"

Oby and Ramu both nodded.

"You must be happy to be away from there."

They nodded again.

"I am under the impression that he is a benefactor, taking from the rich to give to the poor."

Ramu started to choke.

Oby burst out. "No! He takes from the poor and makes himself richer." He leaned towards Dr Fletcher. "I can tell you about Yaki Zakariah," he said. "He nearly killed me." He revealed the long, twisted scar down his thigh.

"Oh! How did that happen?"

"I was beaten up."

"But why?"

"Well, one day I was running around the corner of his house and I saw them unloading ... and they saw me ... and ..."

"Unloading what?"

"Tusks."

"What do you mean 'tusks'?"

"... two huge tusks covered in dried blood."

"What are you telling us?" said Mrs Fletcher.

"Elephants."

She gulped. "He slaughters elephants?"

"Someone does it for him," said Ramu.

"Poaching!" Dr Fletcher closed his eyes and grimaced, as though a massive pain had ripped through him. He groaned and shook his head. "Go on, Oby."

"They grabbed me and said I'd been spying on them." Oby explained about being thrown against the wall, kicked and abandoned in the cellar. He told them everything about that moment.

Mrs Fletcher asked, "So, how did you get away?"

"Awad Sha-Had helped us."

"We worry about him," said Ramu. "In case ..." The words just wouldn't flow. Oby knew that Ramu's heart was bursting with fear for Awad Sha-Had, the only person who had ever been kind and fatherly towards him. The only one *ever*.

"In case what? Who's Awad Sha-Had?"

Ramu fidgeted. He couldn't swallow.

"Please go on. Please try and finish," urged Mrs Fletcher.

"... in case Yaki Zakariah finds out. If he does ... his thugs might kill Awad Sha-Had."

Dr Fletcher put a fatherly hand on Oby's shoulder, "Right! Let's get you and Ramu a comfortable bed for the night and tomorrow morning we shall organise a felucca or a ferry."

* * *

The quayside was slippery with fish scales. The gutting of the fishermen's catch was done right there. Half a dozen old men, working in a slow sweeping rhythm, tried to keep the quayside clear. No sooner had they completed one stretch of quayside than it would be scattered once again with giblets, fish scales and heads with sharp piercing eyes glaring in every direction. Stepping over and around ropes, baskets and plastic buoys, Oby and Ramu followed Dr and Mrs Fletcher as the quay curled to the right and passed in front of some cream-painted buildings. They had beautiful fretwork verandas and sturdy iron columns outside their doors. Dr Fletcher led them into the middle building.

The Kaffassassee Steamship Company had a big fan whirling in its front office. An eager assistant with a crisp, white shirt, pressed black trousers and a massive beam on his face hurried forward with his arm outstretched. He pumped Dr. Fletcher's hand. "Most good to see you again, Dr Fletcher."

"Now, I need your help. These two ..." Dr Fletcher placed himself between Oby and Ramu with hands around their shoulders, "... need to get up to Salima. I want to put them on one of your boats."

"Luxury suite with gold taps and taffeta bed covers, or ..."

"Something simpler, please," laughed the doctor.

They were taken towards an elegant paddle steamer. Painted a sharp white with the name *Cleo* painted on its side, it had many decks that towered above them.

At the foot of the gangway Dr Fletcher said, "I think this is where we say goodbye."

Oby felt his hand being squeezed by Mrs Fletcher. It was the hand of a friend. He thought she had a little tear in her eye. In fact, he knew she had.

On board, a crew member said, "The *Cleo* leaves tomorrow morning, so let's go find your cabin now and you can leave your things there." He glanced round to see what luggage Oby and Ramu might have. "No luggage! No problem. There'll be a meal at seven. After that, no leaving the steamer."

Ramu asked, "If it doesn't leave till the morning, why do we have to stay on board?"

"Well!" The man smiled. "She leaves the quayside very early, at five o'clock. The captain and crew don't want to be hotfooting on the quayside in a stressed state at half past five because half the passengers haven't set their alarm clocks and are missing. We like to start the day calmly."

"Then why can't it leave tonight?" asked Oby, anxious to get going.

"If we travel overnight the tourists can't see the beautiful views. I hope you enjoy your journey."

Lake Kaffassassee was shaped like an aubergine, going thin at the end which flowed through Salima. At the fat end it welcomed four rivers and made them one. It was a great watery wonder surrounded by desert.

The paddle steamer *Cleo* moved north along Lake Kaffassassee at a steady pace, its paddles dipping rhythmically into the water, splashing and humming. Tourists in deckchairs lined three decks of the boat, taking in the view across the lake. Along its banks either side were fields of green. His grandfather's words came back to Oby, *all the greens in the world*. Here they were.

Beyond the irrigated land, towards the west, sand dunes made greyish humps on the horizon, hovering in a menacing sort of way, ready to sweep forward with the next sandstorm.

For most of the time Oby and Ramu remained in their small cabin. Their porthole was just above the waterline and the steamer's massive paddles flashed past, hypnotic and steady, occasionally sending up droplets of water onto the glass.

Sleep came easily, on and off, all that day. Every time Oby and Ramu lay down on their bunks, the droning of the engines lulled them to sleep.

The passengers were divided. First-class tourists ate in a large dining room with white starched cloths on the tables and small pots of hibiscus flowers. The room had plate glass windows which gave wide views of the passing landscape. There were waiters to serve them wearing white gloves.

Standard-grade passengers had no white table linen and sat on fat cushions on the floor of a café, but the food was delicious.

Oby and Ramu chose a spot in the café by a porthole window and sat cross-legged to share a plate of chicken, beans and saffron rice with almonds.

Gradually, a huge shadow passed through the cafe.

"What was that?" said Oby.

Passengers left their food to investigate.

Hurriedly finishing off the rice, Oby and Ramu then ran to the top deck. Hundreds of tourists were already there, cameras clicking.

"What is *that*?"

The towering Temple of Quk stood guard over the lake and faced both east and west. Its dome shone silver in the sunrise and gold in the sunset. Its slim spire was sometimes invisible and sometimes it sparkled. Two hundred granite steps ascended to its four doors. Hundreds of tourists a day traced their fingers over the jade, turquoise and agate stones that were inlaid in intricate patterns over its marble walls. Hundreds of watercraft dropped tourists at the temple's feet every week.

Oby and Ramu had never been tourists. Before departing Kaffassassee, Dr Fletcher had said, "You must enjoy yourselves on this trip. Relax on *Cleo* and marvel at the wonders of Quk."

"This means we're halfway," said Oby, with a new tune in his voice.

Chapter 36

The Temple Of Quk

Oby and Ramu streamed down the gangway with all the other tourists. Surrounding the Temple of Quk was a very tall, chain-link fence. In the fence was a very large gate. From this gate rose a flight of steps to the entrance of the temple.

As Oby and Ramu got nearer they could see a man at a gate selling entrance tickets. Ramu was close enough to learn that each ticket was twenty likits. He said, "We'll have to go back."

They moved back through the queue, retracing their steps.

Suddenly Oby pulled at Ramu's arm, tugging him in the opposite direction and elbowing his way through the queuing tourists. "We must get away from here. It's *him*, the Rhinoceros."

"You sure?"

"Course I am! I'm telling you ..."

"Where? Where?"

"Near the back of the queue."

They hurried away from the temple area.

Ramu said, "You could've made a mistake."

"If you don't believe me, go and look."

Ramu's voice sank. "That means he's travelling on *Cleo*."

Oby said, "He won't see us. He'll be in first class. We can keep out of his way. Come on."

They hugged the fence until they were on the other side of the temple. Here they found a colourful market: a jewellery seller with bracelets and beads dangling from a pole; two women with sewing machines, turning red, green, yellow and purple cottons into long, loose dresses; wood carvings of the Temple of Quk in many sizes; straw weavers making wide-brimmed sun hats; stuffed toy camels made of real camel hair and small pieces of painted pottery. The stallholders waved their wares and called out loudly to attract customers.

Oby smelt the camels before he saw them. Two beasts, one a cream colour and the other brown, were waiting for tourists with their noses thrust high in the air. Miss Proud! Miss Snooty! For Oby, the memory of Mo was still so strong and sweet. Thoughts of her rolling walk and her soft neck and even her stinking breath brought a lump to his throat.

The camels were spaced apart, so that they couldn't bite or annoy each other. Oby marched confidently towards Miss Snooty, but the drover whisked a flail (which he used for keeping flies off his nose and out of his ears) into Oby's face.

"Get away!"

"Just one touch ... it can't hurt."

"She bites."

"It's okay. I'm not scared."

"It's the rules. No touching!"

Obstinately, Oby stood in front of Miss Snooty, not moving.

The drover snorted. "All kids like camels. Think they're cute. Think they can stick their grubby little fingers up their nostrils. Well, you try it."

To his delight, the camel drover suddenly had customers. In one rapid breath of broken English he said, "Once-round-temple-ten-likits. Round-temple-take-along-riverbank-see-green-beans-very-good-crop-you-like-it-twenty-likits. Round-temple-see-green-beans-up-big-sand-dune-fifty-likits. Hey? Which one you like good value cheap?" He extended his nose, almost sniffing the money in the tourist's hand. The man's friends clustered around and they all began to haggle over the price.

With the drover occupied, Oby took the opportunity to stroke Miss Snooty's neck. He spoke softly and the camel continued rolling its jaw from side to side, its eyelashes closing lazily every few seconds.

In the meantime, the drover was not having much luck with trade. "My prices are good," he cried out, looking hurt, as his potential customers walked away. Now he was angry. When he turned to find Oby stroking Miss Snooty, and the camel in blissful contentment, he yelled, "Clear off!" And lashed out with the flail. Oby ducked away, but the flail whipped against the camel's nose.

The young animal began snorting and curling back its lip. The drover yelled, "Shut up!" He yanked hard at the camel's halter, flicking the flail again and again.

"Stop that!" shouted Oby.

"Clear off, brat!"

Miss Snooty flung her head back and spat. She roared, upsetting other camels a short distance away. A great chorus of bellowing started up. She stretched out her hind legs, attempting to stand up. The skirmish between camel and drover caused Miss Snooty to slip. She rolled onto her side, legs peddling. The saddle slipped and dust rose. Tourists hastened to get out of the way.

Almost immediately an official arrived on the scene, jumping over people who had tripped and fallen to the ground. He hastily threw some thorny scrub at the camel in the hope that her favourite munch would keep her quiet.

Waving his arms the official yelled, "Haven't I told you before, these camels are to be kept calm. Angry camels scare tourists away. Would you want to get on an angry camel? No, I don't think so!"

"Not me, official-boss! Not me! See this boy here, this scrawny troublemaker, I told him to get lost ... and see what he does. No sooner do I start to conduct business with rich tourists than he interferes with the camel, causing mayhem."

The official put on his most authoritative voice. "For six months I have listened to your stories and excuses. Let's face it, you don't have much of a way with camels, do you? You don't even like them, do you? I can't understand why you ever applied for this job. And more, I don't know why I bothered to employ you. Well, I'm making a decision here and now; you can work in the ticket office and I'll get myself another drover."

The drover's face turned purple. "Stuff your camels up your nostrils ... and your ticket office with it." He kicked the camel, pushed through the crowd and disappeared.

With a massive snort, Miss Snooty broke free from the tether around her front leg and began parting a route through terrified tourists. As screams rose from the crowd, the jumpy creature began to froth at the mouth, showering strings of spittle everywhere.

The official threw himself at the long rope attached to

the halter. Another of the drovers joined in and they held firm. But the camel was angry; she resisted all efforts to calm her down and was like a kite on the end of a string in a gale.

Oby's face flinched every time the rope was yanked. Suddenly, he ran forward, snatched the rope and with one flick whipped it away from the two men. Valiantly, he slid his hands slowly, one over the other, getting nearer and nearer to Miss Snooty's head. Since the official was secretly scared, he allowed Oby to continue. The boy seemed to know what to do.

Oby held no fear of the frothing camel. Gripping the rope firmly and sidestepping her stamping legs, he gently talked to the anxious beast, at the same time easing himself nearer and nearer until he could feel a blast of warm air on his face every time she bellowed. He took his time, stroking her chest, feeling his way and gently wooing with soft words until she calmed down. He knew that Ramu was watching his every move, so turned and gave him a big grin.

The official stood with his hands on his hips and shook his head in disbelief. "I haven't seen you here before," he said.

"No," replied Oby, "I came on the paddle steamer."

"You a tourist?"

Oby nodded.

"You're a tourist and you know about camels? How's that?"

"I ..."

Oby got no further because he could see that Ramu had moved behind the official, and Ramu was mouthing for Oby to be c-a-r-e-f-u-l.

"Well," continued Oby, thinking very quickly, "my grandfather had a few camels and he always expected me to sit with them when he was busy. He always said to me, 'give them respect, but be firm,' that's what he said."

"Is that so?" The man grinned. "Your grandfather trusted you?"

"Yeah."

"Some people have a way with camels. I guess your grandfather trusted you because you have a certain way ... I can see it. You make it look easy," the official said.

Oby rolled his head and chewed his lower lip, embarrassed at the praise.

Two other drovers came and led Miss Snooty away.

"Thanks," said the official, and he slipped two likits into Oby's hand. "By the way, where's your family? Have you lost them, or did they lose you?"

Ramu stepped forward. "Oh, don't worry, I'm here." He put an arm out to steer Oby away.

"And I suppose," said the boss, "that you are an even better camel handler than your brother!"

"Oh no, not me, camels ignore me," Ramu rapidly responded. "Oby's the gifted one."

As they walked away Oby said, "Do you really think so?"

"Yes, of course."

"Thanks ... Brother."

People drifted about, some towards the Temple of Quk and the café; some took camel rides or explored the lakeside. Oby and Ramu drifted too, grinning at each other and repeating the word 'brother' over and over, as though they had discovered a new joke.

"What time do you think we should go back to the *Cleo*?" asked Oby.

"Maybe a couple of hours. The ship blows a horn."

"How'd you know that?"

"It says so."

"Where?

"In the cabin."

"You didn't tell me that."

"You didn't ask."

Behind the Temple of Quk, patients queued for cures. Pinky-toned desert sand, hot and dry, was turned over regularly by white-coated sand healers. The Temple of Quk Healing Centre attracted visitors from all over the world. They came to be buried in hot sand and be relieved from aches in their joints.

Oby and Ramu watched, amused. An old man with stiff joints was gently stretched out across the hot sand and, as every shovel of even more hot sand was gently spread across his legs and arms, he groaned and repeated a prayer. After he was covered, the sand-healer fixed an umbrella to protect his head from the sun.

Oby's and Ramu's curiosity led them along the line of patients. Several seemed to have fallen asleep. A woman, whose face had turned almost crimson, was being fanned by her sand-healer with a large palm leaf.

"It looks weird," said Oby.

"It *is* weird," responded Ramu.

Oby was walking slightly ahead of Ramu when suddenly he froze. The bloated face sticking out of the sand was as red as cherries. The puffy eyelids were as baggy as a thick-lidded lizard. The nose looked as though it had been stolen from a walnut.

Oby hissed, "Get back, Ramu! Get back! It's the Rhinoceros."

In his haste, Ramu stepped back onto someone's foot. The woman was wearing open-toed sandals and as her toes crunched she gave enough of a shriek to startle all the heads sticking out of the sand. Eyes flashed open.

Oby and Ramu were immediately in the Rhinoceros' sights. His eyes almost popped out of their sockets.

"Stop them!" he bellowed.

Oby and Ramu dodged through the crowd.

"Dig me out of here at once!" The thunderous voice exploded with rage. "Catch those thieves! Come back here!"

Ramu grabbed Oby's arm and they dived under a drinks stall and out the other side, straight towards the Temple of Quk. A party of tourists was leaving from an exit door at the side of the building. Oby and Ramu pushed past them, then dashed through the exit and disappeared into the temple. The marble floor was slippery and Oby found himself skidding several metres before stopping at the foot of an immense golden statue. Having caught his breath, Oby glanced around for somewhere to hide.

Hot on their heels, the Rhinoceros stormed into the temple.

Ramu pressed himself flat behind the statue, Oby crouched at its feet.

The Rhinoceros rumbled past.

The Rhinoceros rumbled back again.

He stopped.

Both Oby and Ramu could hear him panting and knew he was directly in front of the statue.

They dared not move. Not even a finger.

Oby's mind wasn't still, though. Why had the Rhinoceros stopped? Oby ran his eyes up and down the statue. He saw nothing but gold. Gold. A charging bull made of gold, flared nostrils of gold and horns of gold and hooves of gold. The Temple was bathed in a golden light that radiated from the statue. Why was the Rhinoceros standing in front of it? Did he know that they were hiding behind it? Did he?

Click! Click! Click! Click! Click! At least twenty clicks followed. Then nothing. Then click, click, click, click. Then footsteps fading. Footsteps moving away.

Ramu peered cautiously around the statue. He was just in time to see the Rhinoceros putting away his camera as he left the temple.

Oby and Ramu slid out of the Temple of Quk and hurried away in the opposite direction. They went straight to the *Cleo*, locked themselves into their cabin and decided to stay there until they reached Salima.

"There's something about the Rhinoceros," Ramu muttered. "The way he kept pushing his head into my face the day before yesterday ... threatening ... as though he still believes we have his stuff. He *knows* we don't."

"Why do you think he suddenly stopped chasing us to take all those photos of the statue?"

"Maybe he liked it."

"Maybe he wants to steal it."

"He's weird."

"At least we're safe here," said Oby.

Chapter 37

Salima

In his bunk, Oby stretched his legs. For once, every muscle felt rested. For once, his head felt clear. Although midday, he had only just awoken.

Ramu held his cheek against the porthole. Buildings of all shapes, from chunky blocks to skinny towers, rose to the sky. This was Salima, the capital. Fretted verandas and decorated gables dangled over the Great White River.

"Let me see!" Oby jumped off his bunk.

"I'm starving," said Ramu. "But we shall have to keep a watch out for the Rhinoceros."

"I think he wants to kill us," said Oby.

"Kill us? You think so? Why would he want to kill us?"

"Don't know," said Oby, "but I can see it in his eyes, especially when he looks at you. I dreamt he had a huge horn and came charging straight at me."

Ramu flicked Oby's ear. "You're crazy!"

Sliding out of the cabin and into the dimly lit corridor, they glanced left and right before moving along to the cafe at the end. There was a gentle buzz inside. Spread out in front of them were soups, chunks of meat swimming in large bowls of broth, tomatoes, green beans, brown beans, white beans, flat bread, cucumber with garlic and yoghurt, vine leaves stuffed with ground lamb, roasted chicken and platters heaped with rice. It was easy to fill their plates and even easier to empty them.

As the *Cleo* cruised towards the centre of Salima, the amount of water traffic increased. Either side of them feluccas were almost prow to prow, stern to stern. Oby and Ramu took it in turns to gaze through the porthole. Occasionally, footfalls echoed in the corridor outside the cabin. Occasionally, voices burred in the corridor.

There was a sudden sharp knock at the door. "Are you boys in there?" called a gravelly voice.

Oby and Ramu stiffened and shot knowing glances at each other.

The voice demanded, "Open the door."

They remained silent.

The door handle rattled. Eventually, the footfalls moved away, back along the corridor.

"The Rhinoceros!" Oby hissed.

Ramu groaned and flung himself onto his bunk. "How has he found us? Why does he want us? Why is he chasing us?"

Oby said, "I keep telling you, he wants to kill us."

"That's nonsense! But he *does* want us for something, that's for sure, and I wish I knew what it was."

More footfalls moved along the corridor, halting outside the cabin door.

Ramu moved from his bunk and pressed his ear to the door.

"I want to know if there are two boys in this cabin," said the first voice.

"Yes, sir," said the second voice.

"One tall skinny one and one short skinny one."

"Yes, sir."

"I need to speak to them. It's important."

There was a sharp knock at the cabin door. Inside, Oby and Ramu remained motionless.

"Excuse me," called out the second voice, tapping at the door. "Excuse me, there's a gentleman to see you." There was silence from the corridor for a moment or two. Then, "I'm sorry sir, but there's no one in the cabin."

"Huh!" grunted the first voice. "They're in there hiding. I know it. I want you to open the door for me."

"I'm very sorry, sir, I'm not permitted to do that."

The first voice was lower now and Ramu had to strain hard to hear what was said. ".... see .... how much money I shall give you to open the door."

"No, sir. I'm very sorry."

Footfalls moved along the corridor away from the cabin. Ramu told Oby what had been said. They were both shaken that the Rhinoceros was prepared to pay a crew member to open the door.

"I don't get it," said Ramu, with a slight tremble to his voice. "He knows we don't have his money or any of his other belongings. He knows that. Which means he wants us for another reason." Ramu scratched his ear. "Anyway, what can he do to us with so many people around?"

"I keep telling you, Ramu, I can feel it ... he wants to kill us. His eyes change when he sees ..."

Oby didn't finish. There were more footfalls along the

outside corridor. Again, they stopped outside the cabin door. Keys rattled. A key was tried in the cabin door. Another key was tried. The third key rattled into the keyhole ... and it clicked.

"Thank you," growled the Rhinoceros. "Your young cabin boy refused to open the door for me ... something about rules."

"Here you are, sir." The door slammed back against the cabin wall. "Oh! It seems to be empty, sir. Your young nephews must be somewhere else," said the chief steward.

"Slippery as eels, those two. I must have missed them somehow. They keep playing tricks on me and hiding." The Rhinoceros stomped out of the cabin.

The chief steward closed the door and locked it.

Slowly, the drawer under the bottom bunk-bed slid out. Ramu's arm reached out from the drawer and took hold of the upright post of the bunk bed. He hauled his body from the drawer, then pulled out the drawer completely allowing Oby to slide out from the back of it. There was a red streak on Oby's face where the drawer had pinned him against the wall.

"His nephews?"

"Did you hear that? Do we look like his nephews?"

Oby stamped his foot several times to get rid of pins and needles. "Thank goodness we're skinny."

"He's up to something evil, otherwise why would he lie like that?" Ramu was more furious than scared.

The *Cleo* was now dawdling. It jerked a few times. The rhythm of the paddles changed and the vessel began to swing round into its berth. From the porthole the Great White River could hardly be seen, since its surface was jam-packed with boats of all sizes that were sidling along with the *Cleo*.

Clank! Clank! The paddles roared in reverse and the

Cleo came to a standstill. Clank! Oby could feel a final vibration running through his feet and up his legs.

Ramu checked that his knife was tied securely in his head-wrap and Oby knotted together the two straps that had been cut when his money bag had been stolen. He fixed it around his middle and secured his other belongings in his sleeping rug which he pitched onto his back.

"Are you ready? Let's go ..." Ramu took a deep breath and tentatively opened the cabin door.

They moved silently along the corridor, alert to every door click. Checking the backs of heads before taking the open stairway to the exit deck, they slipped behind a supporting pillar, then slid from pillar to pillar, gradually getting nearer the gangway which stretched across to the quay.

"Stay!" Ramu reached across with his arm, holding Oby back.

At the top of the gangway, scanning passengers' faces as they departed, was the Rhinoceros.

"I want to push him in the river," hissed Oby.

"Ssh! We need to think and act carefully."

They made themselves as slim as possible behind the pillar, taking turns to occasionally peep out.

"Here's the best plan," said Ramu. "If we wait long enough, he'll think he's missed us. We'll wait 'til he goes, however long that takes. We'll wait."

So they stood behind the pillar until the last person departed, dragging a huge suitcase.

A finger tapped Oby's shoulder. He jumped and bumped his head against the pillar.

The cabin boy grinned. "You have to leave now."

Ramu opened his mouth, but at first couldn't speak. Finally, he caught his breath. "We can't, we really can't."

"You have to ..."

"Look down there, by the gangway," indicated Oby. "He wants to kill us. We don't know why, but he does."

"That's the man who told the chief steward you were his nephews."

Ramu snapped, "Well, do we look like we are?"

"Of course not. I knew you weren't. I could see that. I'm not stupid. That's why I wouldn't open the cabin door." He took a quick glance around. "Listen! Just wait here. I finish work in ten minutes. I can get you off another way. Stay right here."

Another wave of panic crept over Oby. "Can we trust ..."

"We have to trust him ... there's no other way."

Chapter 38

Boat Hopping

Ramu peered over the side of *Cleo*. "It's vertical. I can't climb down there!"

"It's easy. Follow me." The cabin boy scrambled over the safety railing of the first deck and down a rope ladder that ended about two metres above the water.

Ramu's hands clutched the rail as though they were stuck there with glue. "I can't swim," he yelled down.

The cabin boy looked up from his position on the last rung of the ladder. "Neither can I," he laughed.

Feluccas were moored together in a long line, but drifted and bobbed as water currents beneath them played. The cabin boy waited. When one drifted until it was directly beneath him, he dropped straight into it. "Come on, now you."

Oby clambered over the safety rail, wobbled down the rope ladder and collapsed into the bottom of the boat.

Ramu closed his eyes and felt his way down. He felt safer that way. "Tell me when to drop." He landed quicker than expected, because the cabin boy reached up and yanked his leg. Ramu found himself on top of a pile of foul-smelling fishing nets.

Expecting the boy to untie the craft from the next one and sail it to shore, Oby and Ramu were even more taken aback when he beckoned them to follow him as he scrambled over the side and tumbled into the next one. Then the next one and the next one, over an obstacle course of ropes, fishing nets, boxes and barrels.

"Come on," he yelled.

"It's all right for you!" cried Ramu.

The obstacle course was constantly moving and more than once both Oby and Ramu found themselves in tricky positions, with a leg in one felucca and the other reaching out to the next one, just as they started bobbing apart. Oby could feel the flesh in his groin being stretched as though his leg was about to be ripped off. Noticing Oby's predicament, the cabin boy grabbed his shirt and yanked him hard. He crash-landed, flat on his face with a piece of wood jammed hard into his chest. He winced and grimaced with the wind knocked out of him.

A passing motorboat stirred the river even more and Oby felt himself being lifted high, then dropping: up, down, up, down. His stomach couldn't keep up. He curled forward as his mouth filled with liquid that spurted all over a pile of fishing tackle. Just in time, he noticed the next felucca was about to ram into the one he was in. "Whoooah!" He snatched back his hands before the two smacked together with a resounding crack. Oby stared at his fingers. They could have been smashed to pulp. He momentarily thought of Maktoub. He blew through his teeth; that was a close.

The feluccas were slippery and by the time they reached the quayside both Oby and Ramu had crashed onto their backsides so many times that they had to accept that pain was a fair price to pay for getting to safety.

As they finally scrambled onto the quay, the cabin boy grinned. "Well, what did you think of that?"

"I don't want to do it every day." Oby gave a tortured smile.

"You'd get used to it. Bye." The cabin boy disappeared into the quayside crowd.

Oby and Ramu were left with the dry, pungent smells and cacophony of Salima.

Chapter 39

The Alley Girl

Salima was vast. There were no single-storey buildings. Brick and stone rose skywards, creating great shadows. In places the city was almost as dark as night.

The noises of the city never stopped. It was a twenty-four hour, high-decibel machine, with people moving shoulder to shoulder and vehicles blasting their horns for no good reason. Donkeys and bicycles raced to keep pace with each other; small kids clung onto vehicles for free rides; sandaled feet got grubby; shopkeepers flicked small flails to keep flies away from their heads.

The Sunshine Souk sat on the banks of the Great White River. It was a marketplace with a hundred alleyways. Some were wide enough for a small car, others so narrow that people could hardly pass. They were lined with stalls and boutiques, selling everything a person could ever need: cushions, beans, lamps, tools, scarves, fish.

Using likits from Oby's moneybag, they bought sweet tea and two bags of small pastries filled with gooey cheese. They rapidly drank the tea, then strolled casually along, stopping only once to cast an eye over weird gadgets.

Their pastries were in small brown bags. Oby pushed his nose in: almond or pistachio, pistachio or almond? *Ouch!* That was his toe against something hard. Oby kicked the stone aside. His hand returned to the bag again, then to his mouth, then to the bag, then to his mouth. Last one. He took one bite, grinned at Ramu, glanced ahead.

"*Nooo ...*" Oby's pastry sat like a pebble on his tongue. His throat zipped shut.

"Hey, what's wrong?"

Oby couldn't reply. Not even the flicker of an eyelid Ramu nudged him. "Hey, Oby!"

But his lips were twitching in fear. His hands shook.

Ramu swung around to see what was hypnotizing him.

Coming towards them, eyes flashing left and right, were Yaki Zakariah's thug bodyguards.

Ramu grabbed Oby's arm and hauled him roughly in the direction they had just come from. "*Run! Run for your life! Use your legs!*"

The market bubbled in sounds, but rising above it all came a sudden massive roar.

"*Faster! Move! They've seen us!*" But already Oby was faltering. So Ramu grabbed his shirt and half hauled him to keep up the pace. "Come on! Faster!" A second bellow spanked their ears. "Just keep going," Ramu panted. "Don't stop."

An old man lashed at them with his stick as they jumped over his buckets and coffee pots and streaked through his store – in at the front and out the back.

They kept weaving and dodging through throngs of shoppers with several advantages over their pursuers: youthfulness, skinny and nimble. They had put a good distance between themselves and Yaki Zakariah's thugs, but Oby didn't feel they were safe. They stopped momentarily behind a black weave curtain at the entrance to a house, listening. Although there were no longer any sounds of running feet, they both knew they had to keep going.

Along narrow alleys, dark alleys, twisting alleys, Oby noticed Ramu glancing over his shoulder every few moments to make sure he was keeping up. Suddenly, they found themselves on a quayside.

The quayside was busy with people queuing for water taxis. And ... a striding figure with a face the colour of ripe cherries ... a walnut nose ... the Rhinoceros.

Oby froze to the spot. His tongue would not move in his mouth. His thoughts came to a standstill. He felt Ramu grab his arm roughly. Oby was dazed and clung to Ramu's arm as he was pulled back into an alley.

"It's okay, he hasn't seen us," said Ramu. "Let's go this way." Oby didn't protest as he was pulled towards a slim, low passageway, half hidden by a display of fabrics. "In here!" Ramu released Oby's arm and peeled the layers of rainbow fabrics aside, twenty, thirty, fifty and more. It was gloomy inside the passageway. "Let's stay here a bit ..."

He received no reply.

Ramu moved his hand out sideways to nudge Oby. His hand swept up and down. "Hey, Oby, answer." Still no reply.

He moved back into the array of hanging fabrics. He peered cautiously through gaps in the drapes, searching for his companion's familiar face amongst the sea of shoppers.

But there was no sign of Oby.

Ramu began chewing his nails. He was unsure what to do. Backing through the fabric and into the depths of the passageway again, he attempted to think sensibly and logically. He chewed and spat out a second bit of fingernail. What if Oby had been caught? What if they made him talk? What would he tell them?

He flattened himself once more against the cold wall. He wiped his sleeve across his face. What if Yaki Zakariah's thugs had caught Oby? As he stepped further back into the passageway his hand brushed something warm. Ramu grabbed the hand. "Thank God! Thank God! I thought I'd lost ..."

His words faded away. Beside him, two large eyes glistened through the gloom. He froze to the alley wall.

"Why are you shaking?"

Ramu shook even more.

Her voice was silvery.

He snatched back his hand. Words stumbled out of his mouth. "Sorry! Didn't mean to ... to ... bother you. Sorry." Apart from her eyes, the only thing he could make out was a light scarf flung loosely over her hair. Ramu clasped his hands over his head in anguish and slid down the wall. His head dropped onto his knees. He groaned, "Oby, where are you?"

"Who's Oby?" she asked, airily.

"My ... my little brother."

"He'll be okay."

"I've got to find him."

"Why were you running away?"

"Who said I was running away?"

"No one ... it just looked that way. I saw you."

"I've got to find him."

"Why are you so scared? Why are you shaking? Who was chasing you?"

Ramu could tell he wasn't fooling her. "Some …"

"Bullies?"

"Yes, yes, bullies."

She squatted down next to him.

Ramu glanced sideways. Her large eyes were level with his.

"What does he look like?

"The bully?"

"No … your little brother, silly."

"He's about thirteen."

"About thirteen? So, he could be eleven or fifteen?"

"Yeah, could be … I can't remember …" Ramu straightened his legs and stood up. She did the same. Her glistening eyes were still level with his.

"Is he skinny, like you?"

"Yeah."

"Okay! Stay here. Don't move from here," she ordered. Her sandals grew wings under her billowing skirt.

He couldn't think. A girl. He couldn't stop shaking. His nose started running again. A girl.

Ramu waited … and he waited. It could have been seconds. Or minutes. He should have known. Another flash of panic came swooping over him. She was going to betray him, he felt. Those crafty, menacing, flashing eyes of hers. He had to get out of there.

Ramu edged to the entrance of the passageway. He inched sideways so that he was once again enveloped in the hanging fabrics of the stall. Holding a length of fabric aside with the back of his hand, he was able to observe the alley. There was no sign of Oby, nor of the Rhinoceros, nor of the girl.

He clung to the fabric, trying to think what to do next.

All of a sudden, he heard footsteps approaching from the other end of the alley. He shuffled further into the fabric stall, concealing himself.

"This is where I left him," a silvery voice piped up. "Told him not to move ..."

It was her. And the other figure by her side?

Ramu flung aside the fabric and rushed forward. "Oby, thank God."

* * *

Oby clutched his hands to his chest and let out a long sigh of relief as Ramu grabbed his hand and held onto it.

"What happened? I thought they'd got you. Tell me!" said Ramu. "What happened to you?"

Oby gulped. "I ... I ... my feet just wouldn't move. As soon as you let go of my arm ... my feet ... well, it was like they were tied together. That's when I tripped. Went flat. Nose first. When I got up you weren't there. Then I got kicked by a woman and her kid even stepped on top of me as though I was invisible. I wriggled him off and he started screaming, so I crawled away on my belly to the back of one of the shops and lay behind some sacks. I was too scared to move."

"Honest! I thought I'd never see you again."

"I knew *I* could find him." The girl was very sure of herself.

Ramu said snappily, "Thanks!"

Oby wondered why Ramu was so abrupt. He didn't seem thankful for her help. Instead, he started to steer Oby away from the passageway towards the alley.

"Where are you going?" she called after them. Neither replied and kept walking. "Hey, you two!"

Oby turned round to her. "Railway station." He had suddenly remembered what Gold Teeth had said; there were trains from Salima up to the delta. This girl might be able to help them. "We have to get to the railway station."

"Know the way?"

Oby shook his head.

Ramu pulled Oby roughly. "Come on, we have to go."

"You haven't answered me," she called.

Oby and Ramu walked a few more paces.

"Are you deaf?" she cried.

Oby turned round. She stood in the middle of the alley with arms folded, not a flicker on her face. "Okay! Tell me. Where is the railway station?"

She glided forward. "Follow me."

Chapter 40

Salima Railway Station

Boxes covered in different coloured labels were piled high. There were crates of squawking chickens, battered suitcases, rusty metal trunks, shiny new trunks, trays of freshly picked beans: the railway station was alive. Oby, Ramu and the girl had walked for an hour to get there.

"Which train?" she asked.

Oby replied, "To El Malla."

"Wait here," she said, "and don't move."

Moments later she came running back, her pale blue scarf trailing behind her, hair wisping across her face, eyes big. She pointed. "Quickly! Over there!" She ducked behind a trolley piled with boxes. "Who were the bullies chasing you? Were they boys or men?"

Both Oby and Ramu knitted their eyebrows. One waited for the other to speak.

"Answer. It's a simple question."

"Men," said Ramu, finally.

"Did one have a dog tattoo on his arm?"

Oby's eyes exploded with fear.

"Come on!" she said. "Keep close behind me."

They dodged behind platform three.

She peered around the corner. "Over there. See?"

Ramu gasped. His eyes grew as big as hers.

"He's here?" Oby's teeth juddered.

"Yaki Zakariah! His thugs were chasing you, weren't they?"

"How do you know that?" Ramu's eyes widened in fear.

"How do *you* know *him*?" Oby's voice rose in alarm.

"There's no time now ... Yaki Zakariah's here and that means he's up to something ... I can tell. We can't stay here." She kept glancing over Ramu's head. "Come! Follow me!" Her legs took off again.

Oby and Ramu sprinted behind her and they quickly left congested Railway Station Street behind.

The streets became narrower and narrower. Buildings juggled with each other; the ancient ones sandwiched between chunky modern blocks. On and on they ran, past houses that were crumbling, past doorways with peeling paint and clogged with rubbish.

Beggars were scattered like pebbles on a beach, some claiming archways and doorways, calling out for likits as their fingers reached out to passers-by.

Not one of the beggars approached the girl, though. They allowed her to pass unbothered, except one, who sat in the middle of the road like a lump of rock. Draped in a quivering black tent, with just one hole for an eye to see through, a voice cried and held out a hand.

The girl replied gently. "Not now, Hussa, not now. I'll be back, I promise."

Taytour Street had tall, elegant buildings. Midway along

was an open square with palm trees and a fountain. Beside the fountain sat a man. The girl ran straight to him and dropped at his side. She put her hand on his. He continued to stare straight ahead, not looking at her, nor Ramu, nor Oby. His eyes shuttled back and forth in their sockets.

"Yaki Zakariah's here again, Father. He's been chasing these two, and now he's at the railway station."

Her father stiffened. "Help me up, Sarah, help me up."

"Come with us," she said to Oby and Ramu.

She led the way to the front of a buildings that looked onto the square. A slope led up to an entrance door. As her father shuffled to the top of the slope the door opened.

A woman with her hair tied back into a fat knot came forward and took the man's arm.

The girl beckoned Oby and Ramu to follow.

The house smelt of vanilla and lavender; it smelt of soap and coffee.

"Don't fuss, Nina, don't fuss. I can find my chair." The woman stepped back looking hurt, whilst he felt his way to a chair at the end of the table. The girl went to the woman's side and put her arms around her and smiled and the woman kissed her forehead.

"So," said Sarah's father. "Tell me who you have found this time."

"They were in the Sunshine Souk and they were scared. I saw them chasing all over the place like frightened rabbits, so I followed them."

"And their names?"

She turned to Oby and Ramu. "You didn't tell me your names."

"You didn't ask," said Ramu, his anxious face now covered in beads of damp.

Oby noticed Ramu glancing at the girl – again and again. Oby's fingers were clutched tightly together into a fist which lifted now and again before dropping onto his thigh in a little punch. He observed Ramu's throat moving in an exaggerated way as though he was having difficulty swallowing. Something was bothering him.

"I'm Sarah," the girl said. "This is my father, my mother." She turned to Ramu. "And you?"

"This is Oby and I'm Ramu," he said, his mouth dry, wringing his fingers.

Sarah's mother pulled out chairs from under the dining table. She nodded and gave them a warm smile. "Sit down. Eat with us." Then she called out to someone who was out of sight. "Amin, we're ready."

A man strode in, placed a huge platter of rice and chicken on the table, then sat down. Two maids came from the kitchen and joined them.

Sarah's mother smiled gently. "Come on, eat. Don't be afraid."

"Now," said Sarah's father, having eaten in silence, "why do you think Yaki Zakariah is after you? Tell me."

Oby's heart began drumming. Was Yaki Zakariah a friend of Sarah's father? No, he couldn't be, because this house was different, because the servants were eating with the family ... and they were smiling. Not only that, Sarah had helped them to escape from Yaki Zakariah at the railway station. Or maybe it was a trick. Oby felt a huge sadness creeping over him. A huge tiredness, too. His legs ached. His head was banging. A murky blur swam in front of his eyes. He looked towards Ramu for support, but he was staring down at his hands with lips pressed tightly together. Oby stuttered and stopped.

"Take your time," said Sarah's father.

Rebels were chasing his little sister. Her screams were bigger than her small body. His little brother was howling. His mother was begging and pleading to not hurt them. The rebels wanted her husband. Where was she hiding him? She said he wasn't there. She said he'd gone up north to the delta to work, but they didn't believe her. They said she was a witch to lie. Only witches told lies. Witch! Witch! Witch! And the beating started ...

Oby faltered. Tears trickled down his cheeks. Sarah's mother reached across and patted his hand.

Sarah's father continued with questions that were difficult for him to answer; not that he didn't have the answers, but because of the painful memories. The blind man wanted information. Oby struggled on, kept finding words ... unlocking more and more ... more words about what happened that night than he ever knew he had.

"What an ordeal! You brave, brave boy. Thank you for telling me."

Ramu tried to give an outline of his ordeal at the hands of Yaki Zakariah, but Nina interrupted. "That's enough for one day." She added, "Yaki Zakariah has little respect for others. He has lost his way in life."

"He's obsessed by greed," retorted Sarah's father. "But he has a weakness." He asked, "Does he still wear strings of gems around his neck?"

Ramu answered, "Too many to count. All different colours."

"Do you know why he wears them?"

"Because ... to show everyone he's a rich man ... an important man."

"That's what everyone thinks. But no. That's not the real reason why." Both Ramu and Oby looked at Sarah's father in surprise, guessing that they were about to learn something completely new. "His father was an old-style healer who passed down some of his knowledge to his son. Yaki Zakariah still believes that rubies will protect his liver when he drinks too much alcohol, and that sapphires will prevent him from ever needing glasses, and that emeralds will keep the devil from his door. Yaki Zakariah is scared."

Oby suddenly asked, "So why must he have a black stone in the bottom of his teacup? Gulum ... she's his personal maid ... was terrified of losing it."

"Huh! He probably believes it will bring him many children. I heard that he wants to build a statue of himself in Tembo Dolo with blue diamonds for eyes. It's to scare people. They'll believe he's watching them all the time." Sarah's father grunted. "The man is mad."

"That's enough," Nina said. "I think you all need to be quiet now." She got up. "Sarah, can you ...?"

"No, Mama, please, I promised Hussa ..." and Sarah bolted, letting the door slam behind her.

Nina sighed, then took Oby and Ramu up two flights of stone stairs. She led them into a large bedroom with windows framed by heavy brocade curtains that looked out over the city. She pulled back the covers of the beds, revealing crisp, white sheets. "There are plenty of clothes in that chest. I'm sure you'd like to change. The bathroom is through that door and there's plenty of warm water. Make yourselves comfortable." She stood in the doorway for a few seconds and smiled at them. "My husband will help you. You are quite safe here, I promise." And she closed the door quietly behind her.

Oby flopped onto the bed. As he immediately began drifting into sleep, he could see the outline of Ramu perched on the edge of the bed, confused and exhausted.

Chapter 41

Who Can We Trust?

Oby lay as limply as a newly fallen leaf. The room's huge whiteness stung his eyes. He gazed across at Ramu in the adjacent bed staring up at the ceiling. Little did he know that every time Ramu lowered his eyelids two glistening eyes fixed on him and wouldn't leave. Little did he know that the girl with the wispy curls trickling over her forehead and long dark tresses tumbling down her back was dancing in front of Ramu like a fly he couldn't swat away. Oby heard Ramu sigh and pull a pillow over his eyes.

Over breakfast a few days later, Sarah told Oby and Ramu that her father would arrange their travel by train to El Malla.

Later, when she had left the house and they were on the veranda alone, Oby swatted a few flies and said, "She said the same yesterday and the day before. She keeps telling us her father will get us away safely. Why is it taking so long?"

Ramu didn't reply. Oby knew that he was struggling with something. He couldn't even put a short sentence together without stumbling over the words. They had been told to rest, but Oby knew that resting wasn't easy for Ramu, because he had never been allowed to rest in his life before. Oby had muddled thoughts, too, as he stared across the rooftops, chewing his lip. He thought of Ben Sid and the lies he had told while smiling like a hyena. So many adults pretended to care. It was hard to know which ones were genuine. He wondered how to tell the difference between someone who was honest and someone who pretended to be honest.

* * *

Late afternoon, Sarah came bouncing home. Oby and Ramu were still on the veranda. As she approached, Ramu turned his head away.

She said, "What's wrong, Ramu?"

He didn't answer.

She placed herself in front of him and pulled a funny face to try and make him laugh, but Ramu's face remained carved in stone.

She scowled. "I don't understand you. You are so secretive." With a noisy, exasperated sigh Sarah flounced away.

"Why don't you talk to her?" said Oby.

Silence.

He observed Ramu: chin pushed out, stubborn, perched on the edge of a wicker veranda chair, back straight, fingers twisted together, staring across the city in a trance.

Oby stepped away from the veranda and into the room. With its carved and chunky furniture, it was restful. He took a book from the bookcase illustrated with hundreds of photos of bridges: tall, metal structures that carried traffic, swinging rope bridges, hump-backed stone bridges just wide enough for a pack animal or a few sheep, bridges of all kinds. He returned the book to its slot on the shelf.

Even though the room was peaceful, Oby was fidgety. His life was at a standstill. He needed to move; needed to keep chasing the river. Find his father. He became decisive. Very suddenly. He stood in the doorway of the veranda. "Let's go. We haven't been locked in. We can walk out. Anyway, why did she bring us here in the first place?"

Ramu finally found his tongue. "For safety. She said we'd be safe here."

"How do we know that? We hardly know them and we're supposed to trust everything they say. 'Wait a few more days!' they say. Why? Another thing, they ask too many questions. Questions! Questions!"

Ramu moved to lean against the veranda railing, mesmerized by the spread of flat roof tops as far as the eye could see. The maze of narrow streets between buildings led out to the rest of the city, to the rest of the world. One of them was their route and it was a powerful magnet. "You're right. Let's walk out of here," he finally said. "We can find our own way." He slipped his feet into his sandals. "Come on. Let's go ..."

"Go where?" Sarah stood in the doorway, holding a large bowl of oranges and dates.

"Nowhere!" they chorused, fidgeting awkwardly.

"What's wrong? Have I done anything wrong?"

"No," muttered Ramu.

Sarah drew in a deep breath. "I know it's difficult ..."

"Nothing's difficult." Ramu gave the chair leg a kick.

"I'm sorry if ..."

"Are you?" All day long dark clouds had been gathering in Ramu's head. Now, they piled into a thunderstorm. He snapped, *"You're not sorry. You don't know how to be sorry. This is just a game for you."*

Sarah took a step back and opened her mouth, but no words came out. She dumped the bowl on the small table and ran out the door.

"Why are you suddenly so mad at her?" said Oby. Ramu turned his back. "It's her, isn't it? You like her."

"Shut up!" Ramu snatched up an orange and threw it. Oby ducked. It hit the railing, burst open and splattered juice across the veranda.

Oby dodged and ducked, but the orange missiles still came. "Hey! Stop it! I'm only telling the truth. You're scared of the truth."

"Shut up! Always telling me what I'm thinking."

"Stop throwing things at me!"

"Get moving. We're leaving now." Ramu pushed Oby through the doorway.

Chapter 42

My Eyes My Beautiful Spies

A door slammed. The voice of Sarah's father boomed up from the hallway below.

"That's done it!" Ramu hissed. "Now we can't get away."

Moments later Sarah's father stood in the doorway to their room. He felt his way to an armchair on the veranda and sank into it. "What's been going on here? Smells like a juice market." Then, in the next breath, "I must have some tea. Then we shall take you …"

"Take us?" Oby's grey mood lightened. "You mean, to the railway station?"

"Not just yet. I'm still getting reports of problems there."

"Where, then?"

"I suppose you are scowling at me, Oby. I know you probably don't trust me … and why should you? But just hear me out, please. Yaki Zakariah has an army of thugs at the railway station who are trying to recruit boys. At this very moment they are waving golden promises under those boys' noses."

"What are golden promises?" asked Oby.

"If you're a boy begging for scraps on the street and

someone promises you a fantastic job, a comfortable bed and as much food as you can eat, it isn't something that you can turn down easily, is it? It's the chance of a lifetime."

Ramu began to take an interest. He said dryly, "Well, if the boys are skinny, they'll be forced down a mine. He wanted Oby to dig in a place he called pink seam because he believed there were unique pink diamonds to be found. Yaki Zakariah wants skinny boys because they're the only ones that can squeeze into those narrow spaces. If they were to use dynamite to blow open the rocks, the noise would attract attention. It's wet and slippery down there and the rocks are jagged, but Yaki Zakariah doesn't care."

Sarah's father reached out to find Ramu's arm and patted it gently. "But *you* don't need to worry, he wouldn't want you."

"You're wrong. He definitely wants me, but for a *different* reason ... well, a reason I don't exactly know, but I'm beginning to *think* I know."

"Well, what are you thinking? Explain."

Ramu didn't know where to start, but finally got his words out. He explained that one day a foreign businessman came to Yaki Zakariah's office. Ramu made them tea. The man spoke to him in English and so he replied in English. When Yaki Zakariah heard, he jumped out of his chair and ordered Ramu out of the room. After that, Yaki Zakariah questioned him at length, to find out if he could read English words. But he pretended he couldn't.

"And *can* you read English?" asked Sarah's father.

"A little."

"And why do you think Yaki Zakariah was concerned about that?"

"Well, there were papers everywhere, mostly in English.

I used to tidy them up. Yaki Zakariah is very untidy, you know. What I think is, he became worried in case I could read them and that's why he never paid me ... so I couldn't leave ... so I couldn't tell."

"Yaki Zakariah always looks so elegant, he's always so charming, but actually, he's a wolf in sheep's clothing," said Sarah's father. "You know, Ramu, the information that you have given us is invaluable. It helps us to understand the situation more clearly." Sarah's father tapped his stick. "We citizens of this country must do everything possible to stop this villain from bleeding our country dry. There's little money for nurses and teachers. Our hospitals are crumbling to dust and for every diamond he steals we could build a school. Our children need an education. They must not fall into the hands of Yaki Zakariah."

"How can you stop him?" asked Ramu.

"His luck will run out, because he's getting too greedy." Sarah's father sighed, but Oby was sure he heard more of a sob than a sigh. "We have many good citizens here. A group of volunteers give hours of their time to help tackle the problem. Right now, some of them are at the railway station, carefully observing. When Yaki Zakariah's men start talking to beggar children our volunteers intervene."

"How?"

"Oh, they march straight up to them, grab the child and yell something like, 'Where've you been? I've been looking for you', pretending to be the parent. The thugs slink off because they don't want a public drama. It's difficult to keep track of the problem, but we don't give up." He paused for a few moments. "You were lucky that Sarah was with you when you went to the railway station, otherwise you might have been caught. Sarah knows exactly what to look out for;

she's good at judging situations. On top of that, she also knows which policemen are being paid to turn a blind eye. Yes, the railway station is a hotbed of trickery."

"So, when can we get to El Malla?" asked Oby anxiously.

"Don't worry, we'll get you there ... and it will be from the railway station, too. Please be patient. In a couple of days Yaki Zakariah's men will have departed ... that is, until probably next year when they need more workers." Sarah's father paused, rubbing his chin, scratching his ear. "Another thing you should know, he's always one step ahead of the authorities because there's always a market-stall trader or boatman who tips him off and gets rewarded."

"How do you know all this?" asked Ramu.

"The beggars," said Sarah's father. "They are my eyes, my beautiful spies."

Nina came in with a large tray of lemonade, flatbread, ewe cheese and tomatoes. "What a mess in here! What have you boys been doing?"

"Before you eat anything, please clear up the mess you have made," said Sarah's father to Oby and Ramu. "After that I'm going to show you something so you understand exactly what we do."

Chapter 43

Haven In A Houseboat

They squashed into a taxi. It rattled along with windows wide open, its occupants forced to squeeze eyelids together because of all the dust thrown up by traffic. The taxi swerved from one side of the road to the other, trying to gain an advantage by overtaking with horn blaring, as though it was a matter of life or death.

Finally, the dusty machine dipped down onto the quayside of the Great White River and slammed to a halt near moored houseboats. They were secured one to the other, stretching as far as the eye could see.

Sarah took her father's arm and led him across a gangway and into the hold of a faded-blue houseboat. As he moved away from her protecting hand, two other hands reached out from the gloom to draw him to a seat. Sarah followed. She beckoned Oby and Ramu and ushered them to a bench covered with orange and red cushions.

Oby suddenly found several children staring at him.

"Let me sit near you." A small girl shuffled across the cushions on her hands to sit at Sarah's side.

"Comfortable, Hussa?" asked Sarah.

"New boys, eh?" Hussa flashed her eyes over them. "Are you good actors?" She shook her shoulders in a little dance. "Can you perform for a crowd?" She grunted. "No, I think not. Let me guess. Singers ... you're out-of-tune singers."

Oby shrank into himself and Ramu clenched his teeth. He looked uncomfortable with such forthright manners.

"I'm an actress. What shall I perform for you?" Hussa waved her arms in the air. She pointed at Oby. "You look scared. How are you going to survive begging on the streets? You'll have to go to the orphanage."

"I'm not an orphan."

"Ah, he has a tongue!"

The light coming through the doorway of the hold was suddenly blocked out. A huge man with a bushy beard filled the space. He wore a flamboyant red kaftan and had twinkling eyes. Immediately, he addressed Sarah's father. "Ah, Professor, you are here already. Good. Good." The man dropped into the only space left, almost squashing the two girls on either side. He asked, "These are the two boys?"

"Yes, Oby and Ramu."

"I'm Fred. You call me Fred." He then pointed a chubby finger at Ramu. "Stand up." He frisked Ramu so quickly that it was over before he realised what was happening. "Professor, I thought you said he had a knife."

"Yes, he's got a knife, but he left it behind at the house."

Ramu scowled at no one in particular.

Fred laughed. "It's okay, we don't want your knife."

"Or your money bag," laughed Sarah's father.

"How do you know about my money bag?" cried Oby.

Sarah's father chuckled. "You've been in my house for a few days now. I may be blind, but I have learnt to read with my ears and nose. Like the orange fight you had this morning. You must have been angry, Ramu." Ramu remained silent. "I am very sensitive to what is happening around me. All your movements are like a gale of wind."

Fred tapped Oby's shoulder, making him jump. "Come here, tiny! We search everyone. You might be enemies and secretly working for Yaki Zakariah. We don't take chances with anyone who comes here."

Oby jumped off his seat and pulled up his trouser leg. "Do you think I would choose to work for a man who did that to me?" He revealed the scar that slouched down his leg.

"It looks like a cheetah did that," said Hussa.

Fred said, "That's nasty. Why did they do that to you?"

Oby explained about witnessing the cart with the two elephant tusks and his punishment.

"Thank goodness you escaped." Fred went on to tell them that poor families, especially those that had children with a disability, had difficulties making ends meet, so did not have the money to send them to school. Instead, they went out on the streets and begged. It was a harsh life. He encouraged shopkeepers and tea houses to employ older children, but often there wasn't enough work for their own families. Life was hard. His charity provided food, clothes and shelter, and tried to protect children from people like Yaki Zakariah. The houseboats were a haven. There was always a volunteer on board, cooking rice and chicken, washing and mending clothes.

The sound of bells on a donkey cart drifted into the houseboat.

"Time to go," said Fred, slapping his thigh.

The children wriggled off their seats and headed to the donkey cart. Fred lifted the ones that couldn't climb in themselves. He stepped up behind them, leaving Oby and Ramu behind with Sarah and her father.

"There are so many street children that need help," said Sarah's father. "We do our best."

"What if they're sick?" asked Ramu.

"My mother looks after them at home," said Sarah. "She used to be a nurse in the hospital in Qusena."

"Qusena? She lived there?" Ramu said, suddenly alert. "That's where the president's palace was."

"Yes," said Sarah. "My mother used to live in the palace."

Ramu scowled as though this information was nonsense. Even Oby wondered why she was showing off with such a far-fetched story. Such a show-off!

"My grandfather – that's my mother's father – *was* the president."

What was coming next? Oby glanced at Sarah's father, but the expression on his face hadn't changed. It suddenly dawned on him that Sarah was telling the truth. Even Ramu looked her in the eye when Oby asked, "The president was your grandfather?"

She nodded. "My parents escaped from Qusena. When the fighting started my grandfather was assassinated."

Unbeknown to Oby, Ramu's head was kicking. He was hearing things that brought back his childhood. He was hearing things that he began to understand. Events he once heard his parents and grandparents talking about were being repeated here. "Go on," he said, almost reluctantly.

"It was roughly at the time when Grandfather became president that Yaki Zakariah first became known. He used to wait around schools, telling kids not to go in. He told them not to listen to their parents. He was a hot head at nineteen and told them he was going to start an army and they should join. They listened and loved him. They wanted to be like him." Sarah lowered her voice. "Sadly, many were killed when he attacked the presidential palace. Their training couldn't match up to the presidential guard."

"Go on! Go on!"

"Eventually, Yaki Zakariah became more powerful. Everyone could see he was getting rich very fast. And no one knew how."

"Diamonds!" hissed Ramu.

Chapter 44

Quiet Enemy

There was quietness in the houseboat cabin when Sarah finished speaking. It was as if everyone needed time to absorb what had been said.

"Tell us, Ramu. Tell us what happened when you were first taken to Yaki Zakariah's house," said Sarah's father. "Sometimes it helps to share pain. Memories that are sweet are easy to share with friends. Not so with pain. However, in sharing it with others it is distributed a little. Its heavy burden is broken down. It is less heavy to carry around."

Oby saw Ramu fidget before suddenly lifting his head and straightening his back. Oby was very surprised that Ramu seemed to be preparing to speak.

"Boy, come out of there! Now!" A booming voice echoed down the mine shaft.

Ramu wriggled, pushing his bare feet into the rough rock, scratching his arms, bumping his head. "Ouch!" A pain in his side made him yell as a jagged rock sliced into his hip. He could feel blood trickling down his leg. He pushed down with his hands; one last push. And finally, Ramu squinted in the sharp sunlight.

"Boy! You're no use to us. You're too big to work down that shaft any longer. We'll find someone smaller. Yaki Zakariah wants a boy in his office. I told him you were obedient. Go!"

The office was cool, better than the mine.

Although Ramu's cuts and bruises were healing, since working underground his eyesight had deteriorated. He found some old glasses stuffed into a drawer alongside leaky pens. When he tried them on out of curiosity, all the fuzziness around the huge photo that hung above Yaki Zakariah's desk disappeared.

Yaki Zakariah laughed at him. "Why are you wearing those old things? Fashion or something?"

"Yes, Yaki Zakariah." Ramu always agreed.

The glasses gave Ramu a new life: seeing clearly; reading; a life of learning about things that Yaki Zakariah didn't want him to know about.

Oby winced as Ramu jumped up suddenly, bumping his head on the low houseboat ceiling. "That's it! I know!" His face shone. "I know!" He kneeled in front of Sarah's father, grabbing both hands. "I think I know the person who does business with Yaki Zakariah."

"Tell me, then."

"It's the Rhinoceros!"

Oby grabbed Ramu's arm, pulling him back to the bench seat. "What? What are you saying?"

Sarah chortled. "Rhinoceros? Who's got a daft name like that?"

. . .

He stared at all the photographs of a big man with a walnut nose shaking hands with Yaki Zakariah. And all around the man's feet the earth was stained red with blood. Ramu studied the first photograph more closely, then the next photo. Where were they exactly? Yes, out in the bush ... and piled up in front of them, curved and smooth ... two elephant tusks. The men were grinning from ear to ear.

Sarah's father gave a soft whistle. "Are you sure?"

"Well, he was not as red-faced, and not as fat, but it was *definitely* him. I'm sure. That's who I saw in the photo."

The Professor snapped. "We *have* to stop him. Our wildlife is precious. We cannot tolerate the bodies of beautiful tuskers being littered over our grasslands, leaving their young to perish."

Ramu jumped up again, bumping his head for a second time. He spoke fast. "The Rhinoceros told lies to the chief steward on the paddle steamer, pretending that we were his nephews. He was desperate to find us. So, what I think is ... he's no longer after us because of his stolen possessions, but because he has been in contact with Yaki Zakariah who told him about us running away."

Sarah's father said, "It seems to me that whilst you remained working at Yaki Zakariah's house you were safe. You always agreed with him, you were polite and obliging. But he was manipulative, always promising to pay you ... keeping you waiting. He never imagined you had the courage to escape."

"And now I suppose he guesses that I might know too much about him."

"He doesn't guess. He definitely knows," said Sarah's father. "He has realized that you are the quiet enemy. You have accidentally learned too much about him and have enough information about his secret activities to destroy him. You are a key witness."

Oby grabbed Ramu's hand as his lips began trembling.

"And that is why," said Sarah's father, stony-faced, "there is no doubt in my mind that he would make you disappear at the first opportunity."

Chapter 45

New Beggars

The dressmaker, Madame Shaffili, stood back and admired the scruffy clothes. "You two look as though you belong to the streets of this city now. Much better." Oby squirmed as she stitched a button onto his shirt. "Just keep still." She tweaked his ear. "That's it!" She rubbed some bronze powder into Ramu's hair. "Now you look like an alley boy. You blend in better with these old buildings and all the muck. We're a city of greys and browns." She pushed them towards a mirror. "Take a good look."

Oby rubbed the striped cloth between his fingers, unused to its rough woven texture. "I look stupid," he complained.

"Stop making a fuss." She pushed them through the doorway. "Get going!"

* * *

Sarah hurried them along narrow alleys; they skirted quiet courtyards. She stopped momentarily where some children were selling sweets. "You must tell Hussa if you see anything today, anything suspicious. Be extra careful! Yaki Zakariah and his men are at the railway station looking for boys. Tell Jacob. Tell Elodie. Tell Sami." She turned to Oby and Ramu. "This is a safe route. Stay close." Her eyes suddenly twinkled. "Come! There's something I want to show you first."

She jogged along a derelict wharf of the old city. Here, a tributary of the Great White River was nothing but a dumping ground for wires and metal cans, for plastic chairs and worn carpets. It struggled to flow in places and dredgers regularly hauled out plastic bags, corpses of animals and bicycles. It stank.

A couple of drunken men lay on the narrow quayside, sweating and swearing. One lunged at Sarah. She skipped aside, then tugged at Oby's sleeve. "Keep up!"

They ran for another few minutes. Ahead of them was a huddle of people who all turned at once and whose eyes lit up at the sight of them. Sarah immediately changed path because she suspected they might be robbers.

They snaked in and out of dusty shrubs and jumped over two walls before moving down onto the wharf again. Sarah sprang onto moored feluccas and jumped from one to the other. Oby and Ramu leapt and landed, over and over: slipping, sliding, chasing over obstacles, grabbing ropes, oars and masts for balance. Then up metal rungs and onto the quayside again.

Sarah led them into an alley where tiny window frames hung by a thread. It darkened into a tunnel. The bleak route led through the bowels of an ancient building before coming to a dead end. A blockade of crisscrossed wooden struts forced them to stop. Sarah yanked at one of the wooden planks in the blockade. It slid away easily and she squeezed through the space. She beckoned them to follow.

The other side opened into a garden. This was another world.

Oby gazed up into the frothy blossoms of a jacaranda tree. It was festooned with bluey-purple flowers and was a scented umbrella of cool shade. He flopped onto a stone bench, rubbing his tight calf muscles. Sarah wasn't even out of breath. She replaced the plank across the blockade.

Oby gazed around. Flowers everywhere. He had never seen anything so vivid. Bougainvillea seemed to hang from the sky, clambering along hidden wires: electric pink, fluorescent purple and neon orange.

Sarah spoke at last. "What are you thinking? Isn't it beautiful?"

"Yes ... and it smells a lot better than the river," said Oby, lifting his nose.

"The perfume is coming from over there." She pointed to a circular rose garden filled with red and pink blooms. "You should walk around it. The perfume will fill your head with beautiful dreams and carry your troubles away." She gave a faint smile. "This used to be my grandmother's garden. When they escaped Qusena, she came here. She never really recovered from Grandfather's assassination, but the garden gave her a purpose."

"Whose garden is it now?" asked Oby.

"It still belongs to our family, but we no longer keep it to ourselves. My grandmother lived in that cream building facing us. Now, it is the headquarters of the organisation my father founded."

Oby noticed Sarah's scarf slip. He also noticed the Kamu could hardly take his eyes off her. With hair that curled over her shoulders and cascaded down her back, she had energy. She had fire. And fight. More frequently Oby observed

Ramu settling his eyes on her face. He wondered what was going on in his mind.

Ramu found his voice. "When we were at the houseboat you said the word *organisation*. You have just repeated it. Does it have a name?"

"It doesn't." Sarah made herself comfortable on the garden seat next to Ramu. "It is safer if it doesn't have a name."

"All right, no name, but tell me more about it."

She said, "Well, apart from supporting beggars and keeping as many orphaned kids off the street as possible, my father is a freedom fighter. Before he lost his eyesight, he was politically active. He says it's important to stand up to thieves and thugs that want to overthrow our elected government."

"And Yaki Zakariah is one of them," said Ramu.

"Yes. He's become powerful. Clearly, those diamonds have made him a lot of money and he can buy himself into an even greater position. And that's dangerous for all of us." She paused. "It takes time to collect evidence, but my father is determined. He said that the information you have given is vital. With all the things you have seen, Ramu, you're a key witness, especially connecting the photograph with the Rhinoceros."

"A witness?" Ramu scratched his chin a little nervously.

"Yes, you are." She looked at him with wise eyes.

Ramu's head rolled. He pulled at his ears. "I never thought my life would be in danger. Never!"

Gently, she placed a hand on his arm. "Ramu, we'll protect you."

He gazed down at the slender hand.

Oby said, "I think we should leave now, escape Salima now, whilst we have the chance. Are you listening to me,

Ramu? If your life's in danger, we shouldn't stay here any longer. Anyway, I need to find my father. I can't wait around."

"No! No!" begged Sarah. "It isn't safe for you to move at the moment. Stay and help us just a short while ... please."

Oby had been lying flat on his back under the shade of the jacaranda when he suddenly jumped up. Standing immediately in front of Sarah with his hands on his hips, he barked, "That's it, isn't it? You've been killing time, taking us to the houseboat, bringing us here. You're pretending to help us, telling us it's too dangerous at the railway station, and all the time what you really want is for us to stay around and supply you with information to help *your* cause. Well, I've got a cause too ... and it's my father. I don't think you're helping us at all. I need to find my father and I'm leaving now."

"No, no, please, Oby, you can't go to the railway station alone. It isn't safe. You've got to believe me."

But Oby turned and walked towards the alley.

Sarah shouted at Oby's back, "Okay. Okay. You win. I'll take you to the station now, if that's what you really want, but you are taking a huge risk." There was awkward silence for a few moments before Sarah put in a final plea. "Please, please, I'm begging you to stay for just a few days. We need you. Both of you. You are eyewitnesses. We need you to help us discover who this Rhinoceros man is. You're the only ones who know what he looks like. Your help could be the start of changing everything for our country forever." A teardrop fell and she hurriedly brushed it aside. "Pleeeease. I'm begging you."

Oby felt confused. Ramu was looking at him in a strange way and Oby couldn't read what it meant. Was he saying yes or no? Sarah was talking right into Oby's face and pleading. She was now gripping both his arms. Oby pulled away and covered his ears with his hands. He didn't want to hear. No, he mustn't listen to Sarah. He couldn't waste any more time. He had to get to his father. He looked up with the intention of being very firm in his decision, but her begging eyes were now producing more tears. Oby swallowed hard and bit his lip. "Okay! Two days. If Ramu agrees, we'll help for two days, but only if Ramu agrees."

Her huge begging eyes turned. "Ramu, please?" She spoke as though the request was as fragile as a petal.

Oby had a hunch that Ramu was completely defenseless against her pleading. Little did he know how right he was. For at that moment it wasn't the *staying* for two days that filled Ramu's head, it was the *leaving* afterwards. "Just two days then," said Ramu quietly.

* * *

Sarah's father said, "I know I have asked you lots of difficult questions already. I know this is painful, but I just want to be clear in my mind. Ramu, I don't suppose you ever saw the Englishman's passport, did you?"

"No, no, never."

"You see, it would be helpful to know what kind of visa the Rhinoceros has; whether he always gets into this country on a tourist visa or a business visa."

"What's a visa?" asked Oby.

"It's permission to travel into a country; it's stamped into one's passport. If you have a tourist visa it means you cannot work." Sarah's father tapped his fingers on the arms of his chair. "This photo that you saw several years ago, Ramu, is most disturbing. Whether this Rhinoceros person came in as a tourist or a businessman, shooting elephants is illegal. So what is he really doing here? I wonder if his connection with Yaki Zakariah is deeper than we know."

All Oby could hear at that moment was the steady rhythm of tapping fingers.

Sarah's father added something else. "I wonder ... I wonder ... if there is a connection with trading in diamonds."

As they sat on the veranda sipping sweet lemonade, Ramu said, "Even though Dr and Mrs Fletcher and the other tourists had some of their belongings stolen they were calm. But not the Rhinoceros. He was really stressed and furious ... and in a hurry."

"Yes, he was furious," added Oby. "He was bellowing at his wife."

"His wife! I'd almost forgotten her," Ramu added. "She got really cross with him. The Rhinoceros didn't want to go on an excursion to Kaffassassee or the Temple of Quk, but I remember his wife insisted. He exploded with fury because he was going to be late for a very important *business* meeting. Definitely! That's what he said."

Sarah's father pursed his lips. "You keep remembering more and more information, Ramu. Good! Good!" He paused before asking, "Are you absolutely sure it was him in the photograph?"

Ramu gave a small scowl. "Definitely!"

Chapter 46

Feather Hawkers

The railway station had at least half a dozen child hawkers. Day after day the movements of Salima railway station were watched by them. Travellers, luggage, camels, trucks, rusting cars, wobbly carts, tea trolleys and donkeys all wove their own pattern. Hawkers were part of the scenery, part of the cacophony. They knew how their city operated.

"Right," said Sarah. "Try to remember everything you've been told. You must not show your faces."

Three new hawkers squatted near the entrance to platform seven, half hidden by a clutch of long feather dusters. The three peered through the feathers, each pair of eyes closely observing a different part of the railway station.

Four heavily built men in army fatigues were idling around the station forecourt, glancing about as though seeking entertainment, seemingly in competition by taking turns to flick cigarette butts high into the air. The ground at their feet was littered with them.

Sarah whispered, "They are part of Yaki Zakariah's mob,

but they want everyone to think they're government soldiers. Those old-style military uniforms don't fool anyone." She continued a running commentary from behind her feather dusters. "They're showing off. See how most people walk around them and steer clear. I want to get nearer. I want to hear what they're saying."

"Be careful," warned Oby.

Ramu put out a hand to stop her, but she was already out of reach. He and Oby started waving pink feather dusters at passers-by. Ramu muttered, "I feel stupid." In the next breath, they both starting calling, "Please buy. Please buy."

Sarah shuffled back to them. "Listen, if I suddenly disappear and you hear lots of shouting, it's a sign for you both to move back, move right away. You can't risk being caught. Get back to the villa garden where you'll be safe. There are many others to help me if I need it."

Pulling down her scarf so it cast a shadow over her face, Sarah sidled slowly past the men in army fatigues, waving her dusters, looking sad and frail. The men's cigarette smoke wafted across her path. She didn't speak to them, but waved her wares. One of the men grabbed hold of a duster and tried to yank it out of her hand, but she held on and was flung to the ground. The men leered at her, laughed, pointed at her torn skirt and cheap shoes. One kicked her dusters away from her grasp.

Oby saw Ramu stiffen in anger. He gripped his arm, "Stay still. She said to stay still."

Oby glanced to his right. There was Hussa, dragging over the ground towards Sarah. She helped her up and swore at the men, letting out a volley of words. One of the men raised his arm, clearly itching to strike, but his colleague prevented him. Oby noticed that other beggars remained perfectly still and silent but were watching with piercing eyes. Through his feather dusters he could see Sarah and Hussa whispering together, then settling on the ground beside the men.

"They're as near as they can get," said Ramu.

Two policemen patrolling the railway station used the toes of their boots to nudge Oby and Ramu onto their feet. Without warning, the policemen's short canes came raining down on their shoulders, sending sharp cracks into the air.

With watering eyes from the sting of the canes, they leapt aside, still clutching their goods.

Suddenly, Ramu grabbed Oby's arm.

"What's wrong?"

"HIM! Rhinoceros!" hissed Ramu.

"Where?"

"Left of your yellow feathers."

"Got it." In front of them was a large bulbous head with bullfrog eyes.

"We've got to tell Sarah."

"Wave the green feathers signal."

"She never looks this way."

"Do it anyway."

Ramu held out a green feather duster in pretense of selling it. He waved it high in the air.

Oby spotted a boy on the far side of the station looking their way with his green duster waving in return. "See! It's working."

As they shot glances in all directions, green dusters were being raised around the railway station forecourt.

Sarah turned her head slowly and looked directly at them.

Ramu pointed his green duster in the direction of the Rhinoceros.

She fixed her eyes on the target. Then gathered her goods and began to move. Ramu's outstretched arm was visibly shaking, so Oby patted him on the shoulder for reassurance. They both knew that Sarah would shadow the Rhinoceros for as long as she could to find out where he was going.

The four men wearing old army uniforms suddenly seemed to have a good reason to walk rapidly away from the railway station forecourt.

Although Oby and Ramu kept their faces concealed behind feathers, they continued scanning the area. Oby said, "See that man over there? What do you think?" The man stepped a few paces back into the grey of an archway. "Just look at his shape. Can you see it?"

"Where?"

"There! Look right! Doesn't it look a little like Yaki Zakariah?"

"Where? I can't see anyone."

"Your glasses need cleaning." Ramu spat on the lenses and wiped them on his shirt. "There, at the entrance to the archway," repeated Oby.

"You mean the one wearing huge black glasses?"

"Yes. I'd recognise those glasses anywhere. He's preventing people from going through the archway. What's he up to? We need to find out. We need to get closer," said Oby. "I'm going to try. Watch me, Ramu. Don't let me out of your sight."

"Be careful! Be careful! Keep your face covered."

Oby wiggled the bouquet of feathers in front of his face as he pretended to look for customers. He stopped momentarily to talk to a passer-by. With the sun glaring, he was forced to shade his eyes with one hand. He almost bumped into a bread boy carrying circular loaves covered in sesame seeds and strung onto a long pole lodged over his shoulder. After a brief chat, they both approached the area in front of the archway. The shadowy figure remained there.

Oby fanned out his clutch of feather dusters to hide his face better.

"Push off, you filthy pair! Move!"

Oby shuddered as he recognized the unmistakable booming of Yaki Zakariah. He took a deep, deep breath to gain courage. He and the bread boy pretended that they hadn't heard the warning and proceeded to hover in front of the archway, holding out bread and feather dusters. "Freshly baked! Freshly baked!" cried the bread boy.

"Are you two deaf? Push off!" The voice roared. "Get out of my sight, filthy street trash!" Yaki Zakariah strode towards them.

The two scuttled away, pretending to be scared, then hid behind a parked lorry. Peeping from behind it, they saw Yaki Zakariah move forward to talk to two men.

With the men wrapped up in conversation, this was an opportunity for Oby and the bread boy. They slipped from behind the lorry and sidled into the gloomy archway, without taking their eyes off Yaki Zakariah's back.

Oby's jitters were making his lips tremble. *Please don't turn round. Don't turn.*

The archway extended into a short tunnel. Above it, was a railway track and the tunnel shook and echoed to the sound of a train passing overhead. Just a few more steps and they would be out at the other end. The tunnel was completely empty, so Oby was puzzled as to why Yaki Zakariah was preventing anyone from coming down it. What were he and the bread boy about to discover at the end of it? Just a couple of steps more ...

"Run! Now!" Oby hissed.

He and the bread boy sprinted.

"GRAB THEM!"

Chapter 47

Muscleheads

Oby twisted to get free. "Let me go, let me go, let me go!"

The muscle-head had his fat arm around Oby's neck in a tight head lock. "Shut up, mouthy."

He spluttered; he could hardly breathe.

A second muscle-head appeared and grabbed Oby's legs. He was hoisted off his feet. He tried to wriggle. He held his breath and pushed with all his might, but the two muscle-heads kept walking, carting him like a tree trunk, face down.

Where were they taking him? A river of dread shot through him; a feeling that he might soon be dead. Where had the bread boy gone?

"*So!*" Two polished black shoes were planted beneath his nose. Oby knew who they belonged to. One shoe was tapping the ground ... tapping in triumph. "So, we meet again!"

A hand slashed across Oby's face. All of a sudden, his right cheek was stinging and swelling and he swallowed blood. His nose began dripping blood.

They tossed him upright, onto his feet.

Yaki Zakariah had a grin on his face. "Here's my plan."

He spoke deliberately slowly. "Firstly, you're going to tell me everything you've learnt about me; then, where you've been hiding, who you've been talking to ... in fact, everything you know."

Oby muttered, "Telling you nothing ..."

A hand slashed across his cheek once more. He felt a tooth sitting on his tongue.

"Oh, but you will. Now tell me."

Oby gritted his teeth. He could smell Yaki Zakariah's fishy breath. Although blood trickled from the corner of his mouth, Oby was stubborn. What a time to start being stubborn! Another shot of lightening ripped through his stomach and he suddenly didn't care what he said. What did it matter now? "I'll win ... I'm smarter than you think."

Yaki Zakariah guffawed and paced up and down. "Clearly I underestimated you."

The two muscle-heads began whispering to each other. Yaki Zakariah turned around and snapped at them, "Shut up!"

Oby jerked and sprang away.

CRUNCH! Too late. They had him again. They were tearing his arms out of the sockets, each pulling like a tug-of-war.

"So! So! So! You have fast legs, right? In five minutes you will have nothing to run on." Yaki Zakariah bellowed. "Make sure he never runs again. Get it? Never runs again."

The muscle-heads' grins grew wider and wider. "Yes, boss."

Oby started to choke and spat out more blood and a tooth. His breaths got shorter and shorter. He kicked out as they dragged him into a dimly lit warehouse. There were tools: wrenches, chainsaws and a sledgehammer that was so enormous it would be capable of pulverizing a leg with one blow.

The bread boy was nowhere to be seen. Oby wondered how he had got away, then realized that Yaki Zakariah wasn't after the bread boy. Then another thought flashed through his mind. Maybe the bread boy was in it too. He was part of the trap. How stupid to trust him.

"Talk," snapped Yaki Zakariah. "Talk."

Oby remained silent, his jaw and cheek throbbing.

The massive doors of the warehouse slowly closed.

"No one will hear your screams ..."

Oby sensed that one of the muscle-heads was slowly moving up behind him. Any moment the sledgehammer would fly down ...

... it slammed into the ground. Dust and debris flew. The noise echoed all around the vast warehouse.

Oby felt no pain. He peered through slitted eyes. His feet were intact. He stared at them. There was no blood. His chest thump-thump-thump-thump-thump-thumped.

Yaki Zakariah yelled, "Talk."

If he spoke, they'd kill him; if he didn't speak, they'd kill him. Oby hung his head.

"*Okay, do it!*" Yaki Zakariah's furious screech hit the walls of warehouse and bounced back.

Oby closed his eyes. Shuffling, scuffling noises filled the warehouse. Nothing happened. Were they waiting for him to open his eyes so that he could see his own torture? He was lousy at balancing with his eyes closed. He was swaying to the right. He tried to stay upright, but could feel himself beginning to sway, to topple over, but a hand was pulling him ... a small hand. Oby's eyelids flipped up.

Yaki Zakariah and his two muscle-heads were on the

ground with enormous sacks over their heads that came down to their knees, and spewing from the bottom of the sacks were clouds of white flour. White flour puffed everywhere. Scrambling over the rafters of the warehouse, just above Oby's head, were six agile kids.

* * *

"Keep going," the bread boy hissed. "Faster. You're lucky we got to you in time."

Oby and the bread boy ran on and on, in and out, weaving through baggage, boxes and carts. Metal cages on trolleys crammed with mail were waiting to be loaded onto trains. Oby shot looks left and right, then he saw exactly what Yaki Zakariah had not wanted anyone else to see.

A group of children about the same age as Oby were huddled together. Standing beside them were two minders with upper arm muscles the size of footballs.

"Get back!" Oby pulled the bread boy behind one of the railway station's massive support pillars. He leaned back against it, panting heavily. "Y'know, when those muscleheads got me ... I thought ... yeah, I began to think you were one of them."

The bread boy glowered. "Y'idiot!"

Oby smiled. "I owe you ..."

"Come on," urged the bread boy, "we need to get out of here."

"No!" Oby put out a hand to hold him back. "These kids need to be saved. We can't leave them. These are the ones that've been made promises by Yaki Zakariah." He talked faster and faster. "They think they're going to be rich. I bet he's promised them a new hut, a field and a couple of donkeys."

"*Get those two!*"

The shout came from behind. The voice was unmistakable.

Two figures doused in white flour with the third lumbering up the rear were on their tail again.

"Lead the way. Go!" yelled Oby. "Run! I'll follow!"

They sprinted. And when the bread boy squeezed between two mail cages, Oby did the same. The bread boy twisted immediately to the left and leapt across the rail line. Oby kept up.

"This way," the bread boy pulled him behind a passenger carriage. "Now, crawl under and quickly."

The underbelly of the carriage was a maze of steel shafts.

"Pull yourself up, onto that bar."

"You joking?" Oby stared in horror at the thin metal shaft.

"Do it ... or you're dead!"

Thank God he was thin! He kept wobbling. The shaft dug into his stomach and chest. For balance, he clutched two metal rods at either side. From his precarious position Oby could see feet running up and down the platforms, on both sides of the carriage. From all directions voices babbled. He hardly dared to blink an eye in case the movement made him lose balance. It seemed there might be hundreds of them out there, all after him.

"He went this way."

"No, slow down."

"He can't have got far."

"He's sure to be close by."

Oby knew that Yaki Zakariah had raised the alarm and

that he and the bread boy were now surrounded. He was perspiring rivers, making his hands slippery against the metal. He began to wobble.

Then the moment he had been praying would happen actually did. The noises began to fade away.

Oby cautiously turned his head to look at the bread boy, but he wasn't there. Oh well! Taking a deep breath of railway-station-under-carriage air, he slithered from beneath the carriage. He stretched warily. Peering through empty carriage windows to try and see what was happening on the other side, he stepped silently, on the alert for any sounds and movements.

When he reached the last carriage, Oby flattened against it and peered round the end. What should he do? What could he do? Where were the children now? His instincts told him he should not give up but keep searching until he found them again. Then find Sarah.

Just as he was slowly working his way around the end of the last carriage, his heart skipped.

There they were.

Chapter 48

Saved By A Mail Cage

They had been moved but were now right here in front of him. There were seven of them in a tight cluster, leaning against mail cages, looking neither scared nor unhappy. There was no sign of Yaki Zakariah or his muscle-heads.

Oby took a couple of gulps to help stay calm. He wiped his sweaty palms against the carriage window, which was a stupid thing to do because his hands were now filthier than before. He knew his next move would be difficult but he had to take a chance.

He dodged from mail cage to mail cage, ducking down behind each one, checking that the coast was clear, until he was within earshot of the children. He took a very deep breath. "Don't look round." he hissed. "Just listen!" Another deep breath. "Answer quickly. Have you been promised jobs with good pay?"

"What's it to you?" came the retort.

"Are they going to give you a brand-new bicycle? Did they promise you that?"

"Clear off!"

"Whatever they told you, they're liars. You'll be sent down a diamond mine. You'll be crawling underground in the dark, working at night, covered in sludge. Your feet will get cut to pieces. There are rock falls. You'll barely be able to breathe. When you get injured so you can't work, they'll just dump you in the desert and you'll be left to die. Think about it. You'll probably die. When that happens, they'll just come back here again next year looking for another supply of kids. They don't care ..."

"Just shut up, stupid! We ain't going to work in no diamond mine. They said some of us would make good strong hunters, but Sami and me, we're going to be soldiers and we're going to have real guns."

Oby closed his eyes. It was worse than he expected. Guns! Boy soldiers. The guns would be bigger than them. He kept glancing round. Moisture was forming on his top lip and he began to feel faint from heat and the anxiety of being caught. It was exhausting trying to persuade the children to run.

Despite that, Oby kept talking. "I know about Yaki Zakariah. His thug bodyguards beat me up for no reason. He forced my friend to work in a diamond mine, but he never paid him anything. One day my friend and I got lucky. We had help to escape." Then Oby noticed there were two girls in the group. Girls! His chest thumped even more. "How old are you girls?"

"Old enough!"

"Tell me, how old are you?"

"Twelve."

"Do you know what they'll do to you? Do you? It'll be worse for you. Some soldiers don't care how they treat girls ... and you'll end up with babies. Do you want to have babies out in the desert? Do you want to be carrying a baby on your back and a gun in your hand? Do you? Do you want to have babies that are going to be brought up to carry guns as soon as they can walk? Do you? There won't be anyone there to help you when you're hurt, when you cry ..."

One of the girls had already started to cry. Oby felt he couldn't take her away to safety and leave all the others. He had to keep trying, but how much time did he have?

Then he hit on an idea. He said to her. "Climb into those mail cages, crawl under those parcels and stay there."

She obeyed immediately and, to Oby's surprise and relief, three more followed.

He was soaking in sweat. He stank. But he had to continue. "Come on, don't be stupid. I will help you, I *promise*." As soon as he said it, he wondered how he was going to keep such a big promise. But he had to.

Two more kids started to move. There was one boy left. He turned his back on Oby.

"Don't be stupid ... guns are for killing ... it isn't a game ... and you might be the first to die. Do you want to die? It might be next week."

The boy swung round and stared at Oby. There was confusion all over his face. There was fear. Then he ran towards Oby and jumped. Then dropped into the mail cage.

"Hurry! Tunnel yourselves under all those papers and parcels. Stay down until I tell you it's safe to move." Oby clambered into the mail cage with them. He hissed, "We may need to stay here an hour ... or a day ..."

They hid just in time. Feet rushed along the railway platform stopping and starting, up and down.

"Where are those kids?" stormed Yaki Zakariah. "You were meant to be minding those kids! Where are they?"

"Don't know, boss. We did our best, boss. There were military policemen coming our way, boss. We had to hide until they'd gone, boss," yelled back one of the muscle-heads.

Yaki Zakariah screamed even louder. "They were on our side, you stupid dumbheads. Our men. I paid them."

Yaki Zakariah was standing on the platform so near to the mail cage that Oby could almost touch him. He heard every word of the orders that he was barking out. That meant the children could hear.

"You, get to the front of the station. You two, find those kids and when you do lock them in the storehouse at the back of the station. You, find Horace Dingle. He should have been here half an hour ago."

Oby's thoughts were racing. Horace Dingle. Horace Dingle. Yes, Horace was the name Dr and Mrs Fletcher had used. Horace was the Rhinoceros. Oby kept repeating the name to himself: *Horace Dingle, Horace Dingle.* He knew he mustn't forget it.

Suddenly, a police whistle shrilled. Then another ... and another close by. It was so highly pitched that Oby had to put his hands over his ears. He heard more thuds of feet. The railway station seemed to have been thrown into pandemonium once more with many boots and shoes slapping at speed up and down the platform. He heard screams.

Oby would later learn that those screams were passengers in fear, trying to get out of the way of men with guns who were elbowing their way through.

And through all this he and the children remained still, buried deep in mail, tucked away snugly like mice in a straw stack.

Police dogs started up, then faded away.

A train departed.

Another arrived.

Another departed.

The mail cages stood silent on the platform.

The noises faded and there was silence for half an hour.

Oby was about to signal that he thought it was safe to move when he heard more footsteps. They stopped in front of the mail cages. The cage rattled as though someone had just leaned heavily or fallen against it.

Oby held his head between both hands. He prayed that the children wouldn't move and give themselves away. Next, he heard a breathless voice.

"You told me he would be around here somewhere. He isn't."

Then a reply. "Yes, he's here *somewhere!* I know it."

Oby hurriedly pushed aside some parcels and rose from his mail-hole. He leaned over the top of the mail cage. "Sarah! Ramu! Quick! Get in here!"

She swung around towards him. "You scared us. We thought Yaki Zakariah had got you. It's okay now. The Chief of Police and a bus load of armed officers have arrived."

"Thank God you're okay." Ramu reached up and grabbed Oby's arm as though he would never let it go.

"How did you know where to find me?"

"Didn't you tell me to track you?" said Ramu. "So I did. Well, I tried to. You disappeared a couple of times, then I spotted you again. Then you disappeared again. You were a nightmare to follow." Ramu ruffled Oby's dusty hair.

"Unfortunately, we think Yaki Zakariah's managed to get away with some children," said Sarah. "Come on, it isn't over yet. We've got to try and find them."

With a sudden burst of energy and a triumphant smile, Oby jumped cleanly out of the mail cage. "He may have got away, but *not* with any children." He rattled the mail cage and called out, "It's safe, you can get out."

A few boxes moved and two heads appeared. The other children stirred, until all of them were huddled together, sitting on a pile of mail, looking bewildered.

"Who are these kids?" asked the Chief of Police, striding up. He studied the frightened faces that were staring at him through the mail cage.

"These are the ones that Yaki Zakariah recruited," said Sarah. "Oby has saved them."

"I had a choice," said Oby. "Try and save these children or try to trap Yaki Zakariah. I couldn't do both."

"You've done well," said the Chief of Police. "Yaki Zakariah may have given us the slip for now but the net is closing in." He turned to the children. "You're safe, but don't listen to strangers again … and before you go anywhere, we need a lot of information from you."

"Well," said Oby, "the situation is worse than you think. He's training kids to use guns to form a private army and the training involves hunting wildlife … any wildlife." The Chief of Police scowled. "Not only that, I think Yaki Zakariah has been paying for weapons with diamonds."

The Chief Inspector scowled even more deeply. "Diamonds! What makes you think that? What makes you think he can get his hands on diamonds?" He had the tone of voice that showed he was not convinced.

"From the mine."

"There's only one diamond mine in this country and it belongs to the government," said the Chief of Police, "and it is closed because of flooding."

"Well, he was *definitely* going to send me there," piped Oby.

"Nonsense! What bird-brained ideas you kids have! What nonsense! What a rich imagination you have."

Ramu said, "He hasn't got bird-brained ideas and he isn't telling lies. I know, because I was sent there myself. I was made to scratch for diamonds for Yaki ..."

The Chief of Police roared with laughter. "Stop wasting my time."

Oby could feel every part of his body stiffen. He suddenly had a horrible thought. Maybe the Chief of Police was in league with ... all his thoughts fluttered around his head in a disorderly way.

From under his shirt, Oby rummaged in his money bag. He pulled out a very wrinkled letter. It was the one written by Ben Sid to Yaki Zakariah; the one that mentioned pink diamonds, the biggest, rarest, most valuable in the world. "Here ... read it ..."

When Oby noticed Ramu staring wide-eyed in disbelief at the letter, he said, "Well, you dropped it in the gazelle shed. I snatched it up."

The Chief of Police gasped. "This is appalling. A lot of the water was pumped out of that mine, but there were so many flashfloods it made working conditions too dangerous. The government had no choice but to close it. I don't understand, because there are permanent security guards patrolling to stop thieves."

Ramu and Oby both shook their heads and Ramu said, "The guards are paid by Yaki Zakariah to turn a blind eye."

"What!" The Chief of Police looked from Oby to Ramu and back again. Neither of them wavered, both looked very certain of the information they had given him.

"So, Yaki Zakariah is sending kids down that mine!"

"Yes, he is."

"There! Do you finally believe what I've been trying to tell you all this time?" said Sarah's father, coming up from behind, being led by Hussa. "You thought I was just a dotty old professor."

The Chief of Police looked shaken. "What he's doing is illegal … he is stealing our country's wealth." He made lots of notes, then looked up. "What was the other important thing you had to tell me?"

"Yaki Zakariah's accomplice is the Rhinoceros," said Oby. "He's English. His real name is Horace Dingle."

"Thank you. Excellent! I shall give his name to Immigration. We'll be patient and not go looking for him. We'll wait for him to come to us. When he tries to leave the country, he will be arrested."

"That won't be necessary," said Sarah. "When Oby and Ramu pointed out the Rhinoceros to me on the station forecourt, I followed him. He is now trapped in a disused office at the back of Railway Repair Yard and guarded."

"Who's guarding him?"

"A few beggars with very effective feather duster weapons."

Chapter 49

El Malla

A hand came out towards Oby. The Professor squeezed Oby's fingers gently, as though they were precious. It felt like something had ended. It felt strangely comforting. It felt sad.

They settled into the rail carriage. Oby had noticed even earlier that morning that Ramu was distant. Now he stared blankly ahead as though lost.

Suddenly, there was an unexpected and impatient rapping at the window.

Oby glanced sideways. "Look!"

Ramu immediately leapt from his seat. "Sarah!"

Oby knew that Ramu had been hurt and disappointed when Sarah told him she couldn't come to the station to see them off. Now, here she was, looking anxious. Ramu sprang to the door. Through the glass Oby could see that Sarah had a hand on the door handle, gripping hard, as though she wanted to get on the train. Ramu pressed hard against the handle, too, but it was too late. The handle had automatically locked ... the train started to pull away. She raced along the platform, keeping up with the carriage. Ramu continued fighting with the handle, but still it wouldn't move. The train gathered pace. It was clear to Oby that Sarah was tearful as she ran to keep up with their carriage.

Ramu tried the window catch; it released so suddenly that it flung him backwards. He scrambled back to the window and leaned out.

She was shouting and running.

"What?" He leaned out as far as possible.

Her scarf fell to the ground and her hair streamed out behind her. It was impossible for them to hear each other. The train's speed increased and it began to curve on the track. Sarah was suddenly out of sight. Ramu slumped onto his seat and closed his eyes. Oby knew that if Ramu had been able to open the door, he would have jumped out. Or would she have jumped onto the train? He wasn't sure. The moment had gone. He would never know. Ramu looked beaten.

The train rocked on its rails. It clickety-clacked like two metal knitting needles. It lurched noisily on skinny bridges across the delta of the Great White River; the carriages swayed like skittles.

They gazed out at green fields filled with beans, coriander, parsley, potatoes and fruit. Irrigation channels linked all the fields and workers were bending low, cutting and collecting crops. Donkey carts full of carrots trundled towards feluccas on the Great White River.

* * *

Only a dozen people left the train when it stopped at the village of El Malla. The platform ... well, there wasn't a platform, so it was a huge step down from the carriage. The ticket office was a small shed. An earth road led away from the station and into the village.

A small girl wearing an oversized pink dress stood a little way along the road. She was clutching the ropes of two goats, and the trinkets dangling from her ears were identical to the ones worn by her goats.

"Do you know the house of Madame Betcha?" called out Oby.

She stood scowling at them.

"Madame Betcha?" Ramu repeated more slowly.

She pointed.

Isolated and surrounded by green fields and trees, stood a large and elegant white house. The little girl moved off the road and onto a brick track that obviously led straight to the house. Oby and Ramu followed. Now and again she turned round, seemingly to check that they were following. The goats kept up their bleating.

Oby began to feel nervous.

The house of Madame Betcha had palm branches tickling its walls. The little girl continued her slow walk: through large decorative gates, along a gravel path, round the side of the house and into a courtyard. It was a courtyard with both sun and shade.

A woman wearing a straw hat sat in the shade. On the table in front of her were empty teacups, several books, writing paper, pens and pencils.

As the little girl led Oby and Ramu nearer, the woman looked up and removed her glasses.

"Yes, Evellie?"

"These two are looking for you."

"For me?"

"They said they were looking for Madame Betcha."

"Yes?" Madame Betcha waited for one of them to speak.

Oby drew in a deep breath. His voice was cracked and his words came out in little shots. "My father. I came to find my father. He works for you."

"And who is your father?"

"Boudi Malassa."

Madame Betcha had a few moments of confusion, when her eyes flashed like fireworks. "Come here. Sit down. We must look after you." She hustled off, her bottom rolling.

An assortment of plates was brought out into the courtyard by two maids: glasses of cool lemonade, plates of fat round breads and puffy cheeses, olives and mangoes. All were placed in front of Oby and Ramu.

"Now, I would like to know your names and how you found your way here, exactly," she said kindly.

As they began talking and eating, Madame Betcha dashed back into the house. She returned moments later with an old man. He remained standing just behind her chair.

"No, no, no, not there, Yusuf, come and sit down here."

The old man fidgeted a little and coughed. Madame Betcha coughed too, and glanced at the old man. His eyes had dropped into his lap. She wriggled on her chair.

"Yes, your father…"

"Where is he?"

"Well …" Madame Betcha turned to the old man. She spoke softly. "Yusuf, please … help …"

Oby sat bolt upright. Little did he know that Ramu was already beginning to realise that something was wrong. One of the girls hovering in the background began chewing a finger. Madame Betcha's right hand was shaking as she adjusted her pearl necklace.

"Where's my father?" asked Oby again.

"Your father," said Madame Betcha, fiddling even more with her necklace, "was very worried about you. He was very upset ... at the news of your village."

There was a long, long silence.

"I don't know where my mother is," Oby whispered.

Mme Betcha's voice was quiet. "I'm so very sorry ..."

"... or my brother and sister ... don't know what happened to them ..."

Her voice grew even softer. "I'm so sorry, my boy, so very sorry. God keep you." Although Madame Betcha's voice had dropped so low it could barely be heard, everyone knew exactly what she was saying. She suddenly pulled herself together. "We are so pleased you are here. We are so pleased to welcome you. We thought you were ..."

"Dead?" Oby lifted his head to her, waiting.

Madame Betcha nodded, her eyes were moist. She hastily wiped them. "Yusuf ... please ..."

Yusuf gripped the arms of his chair. "Your father, my boy, had such a broken heart when ..."

"Yes?"

"He thought ... he thought you were all dead," explained Yusuf, his voice a little shaky.

"That's why I had to come and find him," said Oby, now perched on the very edge of his chair. "I want to surprise him." He threw a timid smile at Yusuf.

Yusuf returned the smile, then leaned forward. "Oby, my son ..."

There was yet another long pause as if time was standing still. Nevertheless, Oby knew that all the answers to his questions were waiting in Yusuf's wise eyes.

"Your father was very proud of his family. He was a very good man and loved you all very much."

Oby wondered why Ramu was looking at him so strangely. Little did he know the struggle that Ramu was going through as he listened to Yusuf speaking about his father in the *past*. Little did he know that the reason Ramu was gritting his teeth was in preparation for the moment a terrible pain would drop on him. Never having met Madame Betcha before, Oby didn't know that the sag of her chubby cheeks down to her jaw line was a sign of deep sadness.

Yusuf was gentle. "Your father was heartbroken, Oby. After he learned about the raid ... the massacre ... not hearing any good news ... for days he sat on the riverbank just gazing into the water."

Oby leaned a little closer to Yusuf, urging him to get quicker to whatever he was trying to tell him.

Yusuf's words seemed to be sticking to his teeth. "The river it was ... it was the river that helped to take his pain away." Yusuf's head dropped onto his chest.

Madame Betcha rose silently to her feet. "Come, Oby," she said gently. "I have a very nice room where you and Ramu can rest after your long journey." She waved an arm to the hovering maid to get moving.

Ramu took Oby's arm.

"No!" Oby pushed Ramu away. "Yusuf hasn't told me where my father is yet." He was beginning to get cross and impatient. Why were they having difficulty answering his question?

"I know what happened," piped Evelli. "He fell into the river ..." Oby jumped up from his chair to look at her. Immediately, great thunderstorms began gathering in his head. "Everyone knows." Her goats began nosing into Oby's hand.

Oby began to rock on his feet and Ramu caught him as he slumped forward.

Chapter 50

A Quiet Time

He was given an airy, cool room. Dr Ali said that he needed rest and quiet.

But Oby was too quiet. For days he remained silent. He was shrinking. All around him the world was getting bigger and bigger. It was too big for him. He was too small and he was entirely alone. He hid under white sheets, motionless, wrapped in his old sleeping rug.

...his mother's red dress hoisted above her knees so that she could run faster, clutching his little sister to her chest. And his little brother's bare feet scampering into the bush behind her...

Ramu sat day after day beside Oby's bed, reading. Every time Oby opened his eyes there he was, with a smile. Through his fuzziness and numbness, Oby didn't know of Ramu's own struggles; that Sarah's face kept appearing and when that happened his stomach tied in knots. Oby had no idea that a hundred times a day Ramu pushed her face away, feeling guilty about his thoughts, feeling embarrassed.

Ramu picked out a selection of books from Madame Betcha's library. The pile that he had read was getting taller, and a pile of books that he hadn't read was getting shorter. Very soon there was only one pile and he had read them all.

The doctor visited Oby regularly. He prescribed medicines that dulled Oby's mind and allowed him to sleep.

It was on one occasion when Madame Betcha was taking a turn to sit with Oby that Ramu had a serious chat with Yusuf who told him the full story about Oby's father. "It was the kupti, you know." Yusuf was quite explicit. "The pain was too much for the man. He was drunk for five days and just wandered around in a daze. No one noticed that he had gone towards the river. It was Evelli who saw him fall in. We all rushed down there, of course, but it was too late. Not a sign of him anywhere and his body hasn't been found."

Ramu said, "Maybe I have to be responsible for Oby now. There's no other way. I mean, there's no one else for him."

"He's all right here for now," reassured Yusuf. "Madame Betcha would never throw him out to the wolves. She's very good that way. We can look after him here."

Ramu sighed. Here he was, free at last ... free ... but ... he didn't feel free. "D'you think Madame Betcha will let me stay for a while, until Oby's better?" He needed time to think and plan. "Just a short stay?"

"Stay here? She's already hinted to me she thinks you're the ideal person to take my place."

"Take your place?"

"Why not? I'm over eighty and should have finished working years ago. She's very impressed that you speak English so well and read widely. Madame Betcha used to teach at the university, and she still has a lot of friends that come to visit from the capital and from all over the world. She always speaks to them in English. Once, you know, two of her old students came all the way from South Korea to see her. She was very pleased."

Ramu mused about being in the big modern house. He imagined gliding through rooms, looking after guests, speaking English. He imagined living in Yusuf's little bungalow that overlooked green fields, watching herons fish near water channels. He imagined so many things. But even though it was all more than he could ever possibly have dreamt of, it was not completely perfect.

His heart still held the dream of being a teacher; he wanted to be in the city, so that he could study and go to university. The dream was closer than it had ever been, so close he could almost touch it. Should he want so much, though? Should he?

* * *

Oby gazed out of the bedroom window. It was quiet. Tall palms lifted and fell just outside his window, moving as steadily as pickers in the fields. He looked round at Ramu who was buried in yet another book.

"What are you reading?" asked Oby weakly.

Ramu smiled. "It's the *Medieval History of the World* with lots of maps."

"I want to see it?"

"Come here." Ramu made a space on the sofa. Oby was now so thin that there was hardly an indentation in the cushion when he sat down. Ramu turned the pages, gently talking, explaining, making it into a beautiful story.

"Yes, he would make a very good teacher," came the voice of Madame Betcha from the doorway. "What do you think, Oby?"

A small smile forced itself through Oby's sunken eyes and cheeks.

Madame Betcha remained in the doorway and Ramu continued turning pages.

Oby asked, "What will happen to me?"

"I will look after you." Ramu and Madame Betcha both spoke at once, before raising their eyebrows at each other in surprise, before starting to laugh.

Oby managed a small giggle.

"This room is so much sunnier when you smile," said Madame Betcha.

* * *

Gradually, Oby began to eat a little better, to take short walks and join in a few conversations. There was always someone with him, always someone to understand his tears when that enormous, empty loneliness dropped in.

Madame Betcha said to him, "Would you like to do something different today?"

"S'pose so."

"We could drive to the sea. Have you ever seen the sea?" she asked.

"Once I did," he replied.

"Did you like it?"

"I don't know."

Ramu said, "Don't you remember, it was because we liked it so much that we lost the river ... can't you remember that?"

He sighed. "S'pose so."

* * *

The coast was different from the first time they had seen it. This coast was alive. This coastline was a shipping highway and Ramu started counting vessels on the horizon, hoping that Oby would join in.

He didn't.

Ramu made small sandcastles, hoping that Oby would join in.

He didn't.

Ramu lobbed stones at a rusty can that twanged and jumped helplessly. He messed at the water's edge.

Oby did neither.

Ramu said, "Let's go along the beach and explore."

Oby sighed. "I don't really feel like it."

Madame Betcha sat on the beach observing. She nodded to Yusuf to get the picnic out. She even produced a little radio. It blared out over the sand and Ramu played air guitar as accompaniment, but he had no audience.

Oby heard no music.

When a boy came down to the sand with two camels, Oby pushed his picnic aside and stood up. The others simply observed as Oby walked towards the boy, but before he could get close, the boy moved his camels away, along the beach.

"That is the first time I've seen him show an interest in

anything," said Madame Betcha to Ramu. "He seems to like those creatures."

"He can handle them very well," said Ramu. "He has a way with them ... he even loves their stink."

Madame Betcha grimaced.

"I know his biggest dream is to be a camel drover. His grandfather had a few. When we were at the Temple of Quk he dealt with a young bull that was getting out of control. Everyone was scared except him."

"Pity I don't have any camels," said Madame Betcha, sighing.

Dr Ali had to be called again. Madame Betcha was constantly worried about Oby. Dr Ali explained that some-times pain and grief took many years to overcome and could not be hurried. "I've told you, be patient."

Madame Betcha was generous with her time. She sat with Oby and Ramu most evenings, willing to talk about literature, art, camels and on one occasion she spoke about Sarah's father.

At the mention of Sarah's name, Oby saw Ramu's eyes light up.

"He is a wonderful man. He used to be a professor at the university and that's where he met Sarah's mother. One weekend he went to visit his father-in-law in the south, and that's when the rebels attacked. It had been very carefully planned. There was a massive explosion that killed Sarah's grandfather and Sarah's father was blinded in the explosion."

"So that's how it happened!" exclaimed Ramu, shocked.

Chapter 51

Surprise Guest

Months passed and one morning events took a different turn.

"Look! Look!" Madame Betcha came rushing into the courtyard to find Oby and Ramu. She showed them the headline on her smart phone. YAKI ZAKARIAH AND ACCOMPLICE GIVEN LIFE SENTENCES. Ramu read out the article slowly.

"You two should be very proud of yourselves. You have done a great service for this country," praised Madame Betcha.

"Read that bit again," said Oby, "about catching the Rhinoceros."

"Horace Dingle has been found guilty of trading in ivory, stealing gold statues and other artefacts from the Temple of Quk, attempting to smuggle state diamonds out of the country and supplying illegal weapons to Yaki Zakariah. He now faces a long prison sentence, followed by deportation.

"Yaki Zakariah has been given a life sentence for illegally trading in ivory, enslaving children, forcing children to work

in dangerous conditions, stealing state diamonds, trading in illegal weapons and inciting war. He will never be released.

"*Two major witnesses ...*"

"That means us," said Oby.

"*...were able to positively identify Horace Dingle and expose Zakariah's activities. They will remain anonymous. Had it not been for the courage of these two young men the criminals may never have been caught.*"

Later, on that same perfect morning while the sun was sneaking through the palm fronds, Evelli scampered along behind her goats on the way to the water trough and Oby and Ramu wandered not far behind her, towards the garden.

"Doesn't it feel strange?" said Oby. "There's no one to run away from anymore." He looked at Ramu. "You've changed."

"Have I?"

"You used to be like a frightened rabbit."

"I did?"

Their attentions were suddenly diverted.

A taxi was heading up the driveway. They watched it all the way to the front of the house. A man got out and walked up the steps to the front door. He was wearing a long, loose white torb-shirt ... a torb-shirt of the desert ... and his hair was tied back into a scrappy ponytail.

Oby started.

No!

Yes!

His heart leapt.

He jumped over a low, ornamental hedge, ran across the grass and flew up the steps to the front door, straight into the arms of Moussa Khaliffa. The arms were strong and held him tightly. Oby wiped away tears and a drippy nose, half choked and laughed, all at the same time.

Madame Betcha came bustling out.

"Moussa Khaliffa, Madame," growled Moussa Khaliffa, giving a slight bow, trying to disguise a tear.

Ramu dashed up. "Moussa Khaliffa from the Salt Lake?"

Moussa Khaliffa nodded.

Although bewildered, Madame Betcha quickly invited him around the side of the house to the courtyard.

"I came to have an operation on my eye ..."

"It was bad ..." joined in Oby, with more life in those three words than in all the words he had spoken since he arrived at Madame Betcha's house. "It was full of pus."

"So, after the operation, I took the train to El Malla to see if the boy Oby was here ... was safe." Moussa Khaliffa cleared his throat loudly and spat into the flower bed.

Madame Betcha muttered to herself, "My word, that's an unhealthy cough."

"My apologies, Madame, it's all the muck from the Salt Lake." Moussa Khalifa held Oby's shoulders with both hands and studied his face. He tutted as though reprimanding himself. "From the moment you left I knew I should never have let you go. My wife and I have been worried ever since. Gold Teeth has been hearing all kinds of rumours about what had happened to you."

"Gold Teeth? Who on earth has a name like that?" asked Madame Betcha.

"He's got a camel caravan," said Oby.

"More camels!" exclaimed Madame Betcha.

"Where I live," explained Moussa Kaliffa, "the camel is our way of life."

Oby added, "And the salt business. That's the way of life too."

"And that's the most important thing," laughed Moussa Khaliffa. He patted Oby's head. "You're looking even more skinny. Did your father know who you were when you arrived?"

For a moment there was no reply. The sound of distant dog barking was loud and clear.

Oby quietly said, "My father's dead."

Moussa Khaliffa didn't bat an eyelid. "Is that so! I'm sorry. Sorry."

He was studying Oby and looking for the right words when Madame Betcha quickly blurted, "He can stay here. Both of them can. I've already told them."

"Both?"

"Oby and Ramu," said Madame Betcha.

Seeing Moussa Khaliffa's raised brow, Oby rapidly explained how he and Ramu had met; their team-work journey chasing the river; the good days, bad days; all the funny bits and the sad.

"He's from the north," explained Oby, "from where the raiders came. But he's not a raider, he's my new brother."

"So, you're going to stay here! Very lovely." Moussa Khaliffa gazed around.

Oby's face dropped slightly.

Moussa Khaliffa noticed and scratched his stubbly chin, and when Moussa Khaliffa scratched his chin, it meant he was thinking ... and thinking. "I've got more than one hundred camels now. Things have changed a bit at the Salt Lake ... and ... am thinking of getting a few more ... there's plenty of work." He looked steadily at Oby and growled, "Do you know what I'm saying?"

Oby was paying close attention and his eyes never left Moussa Khaliffa, not for a second.

"Camels need drovers."

Oby swallowed, his eyes still riveted on Moussa Khaliffa.

"I mean, there's plenty of work for a good drover."

Madame Betcha was watching intently, too. She said to Oby, "You have to choose what's best for you."

Oby's eyes flashed from Madame Betcha to Moussa Khaliffa. He was sparking inside. They were telling him he could choose.

"Salt Lake ... can I ... can I go back to the Salt Lake?"

Ramu leaned forward, "What about going to school? This is a good chance for you, Oby. Think carefully ... please."

"Yes," piped up Evelli, "I'm going to start school soon. You can come with me."

"I want to go back to the Salt Lake," said Oby quite firmly.

"But you can't." Her little face peered up into his.

"Why not?"

" 'Cos you have to wait for your father to come back."

Madame Betcha gasped. She scolded, "Evelli, you know that Oby's father fell into the river and we couldn't find him."

"That's because the man in the felucca with the green patch on its sail pulled him out of the river and took him away. I saw him."

Chapter 52

Searching The Brickworks

Ramu dropped onto his knees in front of Evelli, so his face was level with hers. He held her little hands. "The boat ... Evelli, tell me about the boat with the green patch on its sail."

"On the river."

"What did you see?"

"Boudi tumbled in and made a big splash."

"And next ..."

"The man got him in."

"In? You mean, the man pulled him into his boat?" Evelli nodded. "What happened after that? Did you see?"

"The boat went away."

Yusuf blurted, "Why didn't you tell us all this before, Evelli?"

Lots of eyes were on the little girl. She didn't know what they wanted. Tears strayed down her cheeks, then her mouth opened wide and an enormous howl came out.

Madame Betcha hastily reached forward and wrapped her arms around Evelli. "It's all right. It's all right."

Yusuf was impatient, though, and blurted again. "Why didn't you tell us about the boatman?"

Evelli sniffed and between her sniffs she squeaked, "I did. I did ... but you ran away to the river and didn't want to listen to me."

Madame Betcha's mind flew back to the day of the accident. She went over what had happened. Yes, Evelli had told them that Boudi Mallassa had fallen into the river, but no sooner had the first words come spilling from her mouth than they had run towards the river.

"Oh, clever girl, Evelli, clever girl for remembering." Madame Betcha gave Oby a hopeful smile.

Yusuf burst out yet again, "You should have told us ..."

"Stop it, Yusuf," snapped Madame Betcha. "Enough."

But the howling had already started again.

Oby stood rigid, unable to move in case it spoilt the words that he was hearing; in case it wasn't true; in case there was no boat with a green patch on its sail. His head began to throb.

Moussa Khaliffa squatted on the ground next to Evelli. He growled softly, "Well, clever girl, was it a small boat or a big one?"

"Big."

"A felucca, then," said Yusuf. "It must have been."

Moussa Khaliffa said, "Which way do you think it was sailing ... that way," and he spread an arm out to the west, "... or that way?" and the other arm he extended to the north. "Can you show me?"

Evelli pointed.

"That's north," Moussa Khaliffa said. "What's north from here? Where would it have been sailing to?"

"It's hard to say, but there's a village, Aalay, about two

miles along the banks. There's a brickworks and boats travel between there and Salima, transporting building materials. I'm sure someone in Aalay will be able to help. Someone will know something." As an afterthought she muttered, "Let's pray Evelli has got it right!"

It was as though a firecracker had gone off. Oby started to run. He had to get to Aalay. Just follow the Great White River as he had been doing since leaving the Salt Lake. He had gone no more than fifty metres when he toppled over on the dirt road. His sudden new hope didn't mix well with the ordeal of the last few weeks; his legs would not hold him and weakness left him curled on the ground.

"Just look at you! You're in no fit state to go searching." Madame Betcha crouched down beside him. "Bring a damp cloth, Yusuf. Mop up this blood. Let's get him cleaned up. You cannot chase after that river anymore. It's enough for now. We'll send out a search party."

Moussa Khalifa pleaded, "Let him go, Madame, you have to let him go. He's a man now. And he won't be alone."

Madame Betcha sighed, "But just look at him ..."

"Sick or not sick, he's been through worse than this. Just let him go."

She sighed again. "I suppose you're right ... but he can't walk. Go with them Yusuf. Take the jeep and plenty of water."

* * *

In spite of his age and suffering from arthritis, Yusuf strode off quickly to get the jeep keys. He returned with bottles of water and a bunch of bananas. Hardly had the doors banged shut than the machine roared away, dust flying.

Behind them Madame Betcha had her arms wrapped around Evelli, who was now howling like a wild dog because she had been left behind.

The road hugged the weave of the Great White River, a copy-cat of gentle curves. Yusuf hunched over the wheel, his foot down hard. The jeep rattled like a string of empty cans. Ducks and geese that seemed to like hanging about on the road flew into the air like massive snowballs. Up ahead, Aalay's houses lined the road.

Ramu leapt out as they came to the first house. He thumped on its sun-bleached door. "Hey, answer the door!"

A high shutter swung open. A grey-scarfed head popped out. "What d'you want?"

"The man with the felucca with the green patch ... do you know him?"

"No!"

The shutter slammed.

He thumped at the next house.

"The man with the felucca with the green patch ... do you know him?"

"Tobias Marl. He's the one. He's got a patch."

"Which way?"

"Next house. Next house."

True, Tobias Marl's sail was patched but it wasn't green, it was cream. "There aren't any green patches," he informed them. "They're all cream."

They asked every person. The reply was always *no, no, no.*

Oby sank to the ground. He felt sick again. Then he yelled at the three. "Did Evellie say green or cream? You were all listening. You heard. What did she say?"

The adults looked quizzically at each other. Had they all misheard? Had she said cream?

"She said green ... green." Yusuf was quite sure.

And Moussa Khalifa nodded in agreement.

Then there was only the brickworks left.

The brickworks road was not inviting because of all the ruts in it. Yusuf paid little attention to that and the vehicle lurched and jolted along at the same reckless speed, so that they hadn't gone half a mile before the front left wheel collapsed causing the jeep to jolt to a standstill.

Yusuf stood in the middle of the road waving his arms and shouting. "I told her to buy a new one ... I told her!"

Since the vehicle was not drivable, Oby and Ramu went on ahead, leaving Moussa Khaliffa and Yusuf to deal with the jeep.

Just inside the entrance of the brickworks was a scattering of wheelbarrows and hods. A guard appeared wearing an oversized outfit covered in cigarette burns and tied at the waist with string. "No work here. Not a chance in heaven," he chirruped. "We've got fifty people like you calling here every day and there's nothing for none of them." He stood legs astride with his arms folded.

"We're not looking for jobs," snapped back Ramu.

"Then why are you standing in front of my gate?"

Oby had had enough encounters with danger and dangerous men in the last few weeks to know that this guard was probably all mouth and nothing much else. He walked forward and stood right under the guard's nose. "I want to know if you know a man with a felucca with a green patch on its sail."

The guard smirked. "And if I know ...?"

"Tell me."

"If I give you the answer to that and I tell you slowly it will cost you a lot less than if I tell you quickly. Telling is a job around here so I'd have to charge you a telling fee. I'll be reasonable because I'm a reasonable man." He puffed out his chest. Then without warning gave a huge sneeze.

Oby suddenly saw his chance, hopped sideways and slipped past the guard and into the maze of brick piles that were rising in front of every brickmaker. From brick-maker to brick-maker Oby dashed, repeating the same question. "A felucca with a green patch on its sail, have you seen it?"

No one had. No one knew about it.

By now the guard had caught up with Oby. He grabbed him by his hair. Oby squirmed and kicked out.

"Shut up, ratbag!" The guard held on tightly and marched Oby towards a scruffy brick building. He flung open the door and pushed him inside. "I caught a trespasser. What do you want me to do with him?"

However, Ramu was already inside and talking to a man at a desk.

"No," said the desk-man to Ramu, "we don't have such a felucca like the one you have described. Sorry." He turned to the guard. "Leave the boy with me and get back to your post."

The thumping in Oby's chest was now hit-a-beat miss-a-beat. He felt nauseous yet again.

"What's wrong, boy? You look tired. Take some sweets."

* * *

Before leaving, they drank from a cold-water fountain that gurgled in the corner of the office. In their disappointment, Oby and Ramu turned in the wrong direction and couldn't find the exit gate. They only realised their mistake upon arriving at the very edge of the brickworks, to a massive storage area piled high with bricks of all shapes and colour. Behind the storage area was the boundary of the brickworks, a very narrow stream which flowed into the Great White River.

They looked around for direction.

Just a solitary felucca drifted on the stream.

It was barely moving.

It almost filled the stream from bank to bank, but there was something else. Something that made Oby's heart leap.

A green patch! The felucca had a small green patch on its sail.

Chapter 53

The Monk In The Cave

For a few seconds Oby and Ramu were rooted to the spot. However, the felucca was gliding away from them, having already passed the spot where they were standing.

Suddenly, there was no question of tiredness. Tiredness didn't stop Oby's legs from eating up the ground along the riverbank.

He ran and ran ...

Behind him, Ramu ran and ran ...

... slowly making headway ...

... breath snatching ...

... gaining ground ...

... jumping over plants ...

... panting heavily ...

... catching up ...

...... within ear shot of the felucca.

Oby yelled, "Stop! Stop!"

The man turned his head slowly.

Ramu called out, "We need to speak to you."

On his head the man wore a small bonnet made of brown

coarse-weave fabric. He gave a gentle smile and stood up as the felucca slowed. Oby noticed he was dressed in a strange robe.

"Did you pull a man out of the river at El Malla awhile back?" called Ramu. The man nodded *yes.* "Where is he, then?"

He pointed along the course of the river towards the hills. "At St Anthony's Monastery."

"My father. He's my father." Oby's face quivered; he could barely speak for all the saliva that was filling his mouth. Fear. Hope. His tongue and teeth were locking horns like a disgruntled yak.

The man gestured to climb into his felucca as he edged to the riverbank. He patted a sack of rice for them to be seated. The journey was as quiet as the man himself. The felucca made no sound. He looked straight ahead; eyes steady on his route.

"He's a monk," Ramu whispered to Oby.

The felucca had an atmosphere of peace about it, a calmness which spread its effect on the two. With this gentle pace, Oby's stomach quietened. His mind went from racing to walking.

Around a loop of the river appeared a pageant of white buildings surrounded by tall white walls and cosseted by hundreds of umbrella palms. The felucca approached a small jetty where two monks were waiting to help with mooring.

"These two are looking for Boudi Malassa."

Oby stood up. "He's my father."

One of the monks on the jetty raised his eyebrows. "You say he is your father?"

Oby nodded ferociously. "I have to find him, because he thinks that I am dead after the raid on our village."

"Yes, he thinks you're dead."

"Where is he?"

"He took to those hills," replied the monk, pointing. "After a few days, he took to the hills. Your father was searching for peace. That's what he needed, peace and quiet. He has found a place for himself and we don't disturb him."

"Where in the hills?"

Ramu placed a reassuring hand on Oby's shoulder.

Oby was fidgeting. "Which direction should we walk?"

"You can't walk up there without a head-wrap." He waggled a finger at Oby and Ramu. "Where are your head-wraps?"

"We were in a hurry," said Oby.

"I'll find you a couple. Now! First, water and food. Come! I shall help you."

He glided along a pathway that ran through a plentiful vegetable garden, then stepped into a long breezy corridor, decorated in wall paintings of holy knights and hermits. There were candle holders in the walls and below each one was a thick mass of candle grease that had accumulated from constant dripping over the years.

"You must eat first," said the monk. "I insist."

In a dining room of rough-wood tables and benches, they were offered vegetable soup and chunks of brown bread.

Oby's stomach was sore and almost empty. He swallowed a few times even before putting anything into his mouth. Would it stay down?

The Abbot joined them. "My dear boys, your father is safe ..."

"He isn't Ramu's father."

Because he was a great observer, the Abbot noticed an emptiness sweep across the tightened lines on Ramu's forehead. As Oby fidgeted and twisted his fingers, the Abbot saw flashes of both pain and hope written in his eyes. But he asked no questions. "I see true courage on your faces. It is a gift from God. It warms my heart," he said.

For Oby, the warm food was comforting. His father was alive, alive, alive! Alive! The word sprinted around is head. He continued sipping soup and with every mouthful the taste improved.

The Abbot said, "He is living in a cave."

Oby's voice squeaked in disbelief, "A cave?"

Ramu said, "Alone?"

"Yes, quite alone. It's what he wanted."

Oby could not imagine this. He became suspicious. His father liked playing with the gambling stones. He liked laughing and joking with his friends and playing football. And drinking kupti. Alone? Oby couldn't believe it. In a cave? No, this was not his father; it couldn't be his father.

"He went to search for peace." The Abbot smiled. "He had so much pain to bear, but I expect you already imagined that to be so."

* * *

With water bottles and fruit, Oby and Ramu started up the hill slope, picking their way over broken rocks and stones and every now and then staring into the hills looking for dark patches which might indicate the entrance to a cave.

"My father would never go off alone ... to a cave ... he just wouldn't ... I know ..." Oby was fearful, because deep in his heart he felt that the chances of this man being his father were very small. He began convincing himself that this man could not be his father; he was preparing himself for disappointment. Yet, this was the man that had fallen in the river and they had said his name. Oby had to find out.

Dry heat bounced off enormous slabs of rock and created mirages. Distorted rocks became drifting smoke. Tiny grey plants might once have been green. Intermittently, there was relief when a breeze picked up.

Every so often they looked around for signs of a cave entrance, but as the Abbot had told them, when you move round behind the first hill, then you will see.

And they did see.

Not one, nor two, but several gaping entrances. Every cave entrance was high in the rock face. Every entrance was a climb. To get up there you had to really want to be up there.

"How can we …?"

"We'll do it," Ramu assured, "even if it takes all day and the next. We're not going to give up now."

Two caves were empty. Could they climb sideways to the next? No! A chasm, blacker than a moonless night with jagged teeth for jaws, sat between them and the next cave.

They climbed down and flopped onto flatter ground, exhausted. Both lay there in the shade of a large boulder with eyes closed. Their breaths began to even out. Then Oby heard Ramu snoring.

Oby felt fidgety, though, and stood up, surveying the cave entrances in turn. Against the blue sky he suddenly spotted a small figure standing high on a rock that protruded from the hillside. The figure was motionless.

His heart pounded in his chest. He moved up the slope a short distance, trying to make out the features of the face, but it was impossible. The person on the hillside seemed to be clothed in brown with a small bonnet on his head. Just another monk.

Oby's heart sank ... and rose again ... at least he could ask this man if he had seen Boudi Malassa. He continued walking, but he didn't get far. Weakness swept over him. Stars twinkled in front of his eyes. He tried crawling.

... he saw the flash of his mother's red dress...

"Stop! Stop!" Oby looked back to see Ramu stumbling towards him, rubbing his eyes, flapping an arm. "Don't move!" he yelled. He grabbed Oby's wrist so he couldn't move any further. Panting heavily, he blurted, "Look! You're drifting towards a cliff edge. Just look at you! You can't even stay upright."

Oby rolled onto his back. He waved an arm in the direction of the protruding rock. "Look up there."

Ramu studied the still figure on the hillside for a moment. "Listen, Oby, you're exhausted. Stay here. Whoever it is seems to be watching us, so I'll climb and ask him. He might know something. Just stay where you are and don't move."

With aching legs and a stiff neck, Oby gently maneuvered to a sitting position and watched as Ramu climbed. The figure on the rock was still completely motionless.

* * *

Ramu clambered the final few metres to the foot of the protruding rock. Above it was a cave. There were ropes dangling down the rock face for climbing assistance. He leaned against a boulder and called up breathlessly. "I'm looking for Boudi Malassa. Do you know where I can find Boudi Malassa?"

The man remained nothing but a statue.

"Boudi Malassa," Ramu repeated. "Have you seen him?" With still no reply, Ramu decided to speak anyway. "Well, see that boy down there, that's Boudi Malassa's son. He's exhausted. He's chased the length of the Great White River to find his father. If you have seen his father, the boy needs to know. So ... please ... if you know ... for the boy's sake if you know, please tell me."

The person still didn't move, as though what Ramu had said was unimportant to him.

Ramu shielded his eyes from the sun, trying to see the man's face clearly, wondering if he had fully understood what he had been saying. It was beginning to feel pointless. He began to turn away.

Suddenly, the hermit jumped at the rope. In a flash he had slithered down it and landed at Ramu's side. His face was patterned with sunburnt wrinkles, his lips were cracked, the hair protruding from his bonnet was matted and dusted with terracotta sand and his eyes looked as though they had died long ago.

There was something about the way this man was looking at him that told Ramu he was waiting for more information. "His name's Oby and he's thirteen ... no, I think he might now be fourteen ... or fifteen years old ..."

The hermit hoisted his brown tunic up around his waist and flew down the hillside.

Ramu raised his hands to heaven. *Please don't hurt him ...*

don't hurt him. He watched as the hermit dropped to Oby's side. Ramu swallowed hard, gulping back tears. Right now, he felt an outsider.

Madame Betcha shrieked when Yusuf and Moussa Khaliffa arrived back at the house at El Malla. They were covered in muck and engine oil. The jeep looked as though it had been dragged up from the river.

"I told you to get a new one," Yusuf said. "It's not reliable. Finished! Kaput!"

From out the back of the jeep stepped Ramu, Oby and his father.

Madame Betcha gave another little shriek. "We thought you had drowned."

Yusuf poked Boudi Malassa and joked, "I hope you're not a ghost!"

But Boudi Malassa didn't seem to understand the joke. He clutched at Oby's arm as though he would never let go.

A while later, Madame Betcha had the chance to speak to Oby alone. "You and your father can both remain here, if you wish. There's plenty of work and it's peaceful. It might be easier for you, with things the way they are."

Oby knew what she meant. His father's mental health seemed to be frail. He kept weeping. He kept picking flowers and tearing off their petals. And he never spoke. Not a single word.

Oby had to deal with his own nightmares, too.

. . .

... his mother's red dress was disappearing into the bush, with his little sister clutched to her chest, crying in fear ... and his brother screaming in terror as his legs could hardly keep up ...

Where was his mother now? Were his brother and sister safe ... or dead? Oby had to know. If he stayed here he would never know. He had to take his father back to the Salt Lake.

* * *

"It doesn't seem right for you to leave ... not after all this time ... not after all we've been through," said Ramu, sadly. "After all, we're brothers. You said so yourself."

"You could come back to the Salt Lake with us," said Oby.

Ramu shook his head and laughed. "And bake in that oven? No, thank you!"

Oby grinned, "I know exactly what you'll do."

"Okay, clever, tell me, then."

"You'll go back to Salima."

"Yes ... maybe ... then I can study."

"You could study the same here."

"Maybe."

"But I know you won't."

"You seem to know a lot about plans that I haven't even made."

"Well, it's pretty obvious."

"What is?"

"Within a week you'll be back in Salima!" Oby danced

around Ramu singing, "Sarah! Sarah! Sarah!"

Ramu rolled his head and grabbed Oby in a wrestling tackle.

"Sarah! Sarah!"

Ramu released his hold. "Seriously, Oby, I want to study ... I want to ..."

"You want to ... *be near her.*" Oby got up close and peered up into Ramu's nostrils. "Admit it."

Ramu pushed Oby aside and rolled his head in embarrassment. "I have to try ... don't I?"

"She likes you a lot."

"How do you know?"

"She asked me what you thought about her."

Ramu's mouth opened but no words came out.

"I told her you liked her from the moment you first saw her big brown eyes."

Chapter 54

Flash Of Red

The soaring silver-bird followed the Great White River. For the three-hour flight Oby's head remained in the same position, gazing down at the vast river as it glistened and glided like a giant snake.

Patchworks of green farmland, villages and small towns clung greedily to its banks. Oby recalled his grandfather's words. *'This river rules with a mighty power over all the people along its course. It gives life. If it dies, people die.'*

The plane rose higher, over mountains. Below it, with the power of a giant machete, the river sliced through rocks; like a too eager sculptor, it didn't know what shapes it carved.

"Look at it! Strong as steel," said Moussa Khaliffa.

"It's sometimes huge and scary when you're close to it, but from up here it looks like ... like ..."

"... liquid silver," finished off Moussa Khaliffa.

"Look over there. It's gone a bit crazy, squirming everywhere. There. Look!"

"Yes, that's the Junka Marsh," said Moussa Khaliffa. "Many men have lost their lives there."

"I believe you." Oby scratched his knees as he remembered all the insect bites he and Ramu suffered.

Moussa Khaliffa asked, "Would you want to chase the river again?"

"No way! This time I was lucky, because I had Ramu. No one could do it alone."

"You're going to miss him."

"I know."

"Down on the Salt Lake much has changed. Since the war things have moved rapidly. Now that we have mobile phone reception you can talk to Ramu anytime. It's easy to stay in touch these days. And now that we have an airport, Ramu could visit easily."

"He doesn't like the stinking heat," Oby said.

"He'll come. You'll see."

* * *

The periphery of the little airport was still under construction, but a terminal building, which was nothing more than a very large shed strengthened by reinforced concrete, stood beside the runway.

The airport had only been open for four months and already it was like a termite mound: people dashing for flights, people hauling bulging suitcases, pots and pans rattling on people's shoulders, people greeting and bidding farewell, children hanging around the perimeter fence in curiosity. These were signs of better times.

In the airport car park Oby's eyes popped wide. "*What is that?*"

Moussa Khaliffa held open the passenger door of a brand-new truck.

"Like it?"

"Can it go fast?"

"As fast as you like."

Oby held onto his father's hand as the truck sped on the newly patched road to the Salt Lake. The distant tops of the Chagat Hills rose slowly out of the sky, bathed in bright sunlight.

Brrrrrrrrrrrrr, then louder, BRRRRRRRR! A buzzing filled the truck.

"Now what?" Moussa Khalifa jammed on the brakes.

This wasn't an old truck like Madame Betcha's. Oby couldn't believe a brand-new truck could break down so quickly.

Moussa Khaliffa rummaged in the dashboard pocket and pulled out a mobile phone. It buzzed with impatience.

"What?" he shouted. "I answered as soon as I heard it ... okay ... what? Well, I left it in the truck ... well, I forgot ... I'm listening now ..." His voice quietened. "Okay ... okay ... I heard what you said. Okay. Okay ... Bye."

Moussa Khalifa slowly closed the phone. Momentarily, he gripped the steering wheel with both hands and stared out through the windscreen and into the distance.

Oby watched with eyes that said *hurry up and tell me what that was about.*

Moussa Khaliffa said very quietly, "Let's get out and talk for a minute." He indicated for Oby to move out of earshot of his father.

The heat came wrapping around them. Moussa Khaliffa strode into the bush a short distance and surveyed its expanse.

Oby surveyed Moussa Khaliffa.

The man with a thousand wrinkles on his face cleared

his throat, turned and rested his hands on Oby's shoulders. He spoke tenderly and with a smile. "Your mum is safe. She and some other people were found wandering in the scrub and taken to a village ten miles away."

"True?" Oby mouthed the word, but no sound came out.

"True! The UN have provided some cabins and placed them at the oasis near the Salt Lake. And your mum is there. My wife has been helping out, because there are some kids there without family. She's cooking ... mending clothes ... that sort of thing. She's been talking to a woman who told her story about the massacre. That woman is your mother. She's there. Your mother is safe."

Not a word left Oby's tongue.

Moussa Khaliffa patted his head. A few seconds later, he was back to his noisy growling self. "My wife can get mad sometimes. Phew! What a din she can make! She's been trying to phone me for more than a week ... real mad at me for leaving the phone in the truck. She didn't even ask how I was."

Oby felt wobbly. He had stood at a spot not far from here and felt weak once before. This time it was for a different reason. He sat down on the hard earth ... dizzy and blank. The weight of his biggest fear had been lifted, but it left him exhausted.

"You okay?"

"I'm okay."

"I'm gonna leave it up to you to tell your father. Tell him gently. You know what I mean?" He paused. "I'm going to take a five-minute walk around and stretch my legs."

A smile spread across Oby's face and a tear trickled down it.

* * *

The hut of Moussa Khaliffa on its black rock looked shabby and a little lopsided. It was now dwarfed by a much larger stone building.

"What's that?" asked Oby as the truck drew nearer.

"My new house ... it needs a few finishing touches."

"It's enormous."

The truck halted.

Oby took his father's hand and pulled hard, making him walk fast. "Come on, I know they're this way. Come on! Run! Come on, Dad, faster! Faster!"

Boudi Malassa had always been fast. When he was a boy they called him *Gazelle*, because of the way he sprang over the ground. With a huge smile on his face, he kept pace with Oby.

"Look!" called out Oby. "Look! Look over there."

To their right was the oasis and on the far side of it some new cabins had been constructed under palms. As they approached, Oby noticed a girl sitting in the doorway of one of the cabins. She was plaiting a palm leaf. He thought he could see bright yellow bangles on both wrists. Yellow bangles! Oby pulled his father even faster.

Then a woman wearing a red dress stepped out of the cabin.

"*Mum!*" Oby screamed.

She looked up. Shaded her eyes momentarily. Then screamed back, "Oby, Oby boy, come here boy." She grabbed him. Clutching tightly, his mother planted kisses all over his curls. "Where've you been? You disappeared. You didn't follow. Where've you been?" She pulled his ears and patted his cheeks and planted even more kisses over his curls.

"You're taller than me now." She clutched him as though she would never let go.

Then she stopped short, staring over Oby's shoulder. "Boudi? Boudi Malassa, is it you?" She took his face between her hands. She studied him carefully and tenderly and nodded ... as though she understood he was not the same. "Oh, my husband, what a time we've all had."

Reeta jumped to her feet and launched herself at Oby. He picked her up and swung her around, calling out, "Ouch" Ouch!" as the yellow bangles knocked against his ears.

As he released Reeta, his mother was drawing her husband into the quietness of the cabin. But where was Bendo?

"Oby! Here!" Moussa Khaliffa strode towards him, beckoning. "Come! I have been longing to show you this." They walked for fifteen minutes, then strode up the pitch of black rock that looked over the Salt Lake with Reeta clutching Oby's hand tightly. The warm wind brushed Oby's face in a familiar way.

"Who's working on the salt now?" asked Oby.

"My same reliable team, plus some of those gold panners from Mokolee. They didn't find any gold and they had families to feed. They can earn more from me."

"Salt is good business," said Oby.

"Not as good as my new business." Moussa Khaliffa grinned at Oby.

Oby cocked his head, raised his eyebrows.

Moussa Khaliffa chuckled. "Follow me."

He led Oby around the edge of the black rock, then picked up a shard of loose stone and held it up. "This stuff ..."

"Stone," said Oby, not very impressed.

Moussa Khaliffa gave a triumphant smile. "This is

special. It's top-quality beautiful stone and everyone wants it. It's the fashion."

Oby couldn't understand it at all. He followed as Moussa Khaliffa strode along the seam of black rock until it reached a point where it suddenly dipped under the Salt Lake. He stared down into a large, excavated pit. Here, two men were chiselling and cutting out stone.

"What do they want it for?" asked Oby.

"For kitchens and bathrooms. People love the way it shines."

"Shines! It's dull and dirty."

"After a good polish you can see your face in it. Beautiful! It's good business. That's why I had to buy more camels. Until they finish making a road for vehicles through those mountains, we need camels."

"Who did you buy them from?"

"Abdul Sid."

The mention of the name brought a scowl to Oby's face. "I hate his brother, Ben Sid. He gave me to Yaki Zakariah as a gift."

"I'm sorry! I'm sorry I let you go ..." Moussa Khaliffa studied Oby momentarily, before nodding. "Yes, yes. You had to go." Then he said, "Poor old Abdul Sid! He had lazy sons and he never realised how corrupt his brother was. By the way, Abdul Sid's dead. He collapsed a week after he left you at Tembo Dolo. His sons didn't want to continue, sold me their camels and went to the city. They say that Ben Sid has disappeared since the arrest of Yaki Zakariah. He'd better stay hidden because he'll be hunted until the day he dies."

Oby's chest puffed out. "I want to join the hunt."

Moussa Khaliffa gave one of his wise rumbles. "No, Oby!

Never waste your good time in getting revenge. Don't get bitter. You're safe now ... you're safe."

"I want to kill him."

"No, you don't, boy ... killing gets you nowhere."

Oby asked, "How can we tell who's good and who's bad?"

Moussa Khaliffa just shook his head. "Life teaches us."

Two dogs came racing in from the bush. Oby expected to see Bendo racing in behind them. The dogs whirled around them, barking and sniffing. They played a mischievous game, attempting to nip at Oby's feet. The brown pup – no longer a pup – was strikingly handsome, immediately recognizable by the white streak over his right eye and down his nose.

"Lovely dog, that!" said Moussa Khaliffa.

Oby sank to the ground and the dogs leapt all over him, tails propelling.

"Is he still mine?"

"Why not?"

A cloud of dust and a noisy speck of blue moved towards them. It flew straight past and came to a juddering stop right outside Moussa Khaliffa's new house. Swathed in a billowing flowery dress, the wife of Moussa Khaliffa scrambled out of the vehicle.

Moussa Khaliffa tutted. "Got her own truck ... drives too fast ... always in a hurry."

His wife waddled from truck to house and back again, carting enormous bags of rice. Then climbed into the car again, reversed, sent up more dust, accelerated rapidly and drove at top speed the fifty metres to where Oby and Moussa Khaliffa were standing at the foot of black rock. She hauled herself out of the vehicle and stood in front of Oby with an enormous smile on her face. She raised her hands to the sky.

"Praise God! Praise God you are back. How tall you are!" Her dress batted against her fat belly in the wind. "Are you our new camel drover?"

Oby nodded. He leapt down from his lofty position on the black rock.

"Good." She rubbed Oby's cheeks with her chubby fingers. "Where's that old sleeping rug?"

"I've still got it."

"Good!" She gave a deep throaty laugh. "It was blue, wasn't it?"

Oby laughed and scratched his head. "I can't remember, it's so faded and grubby."

"Well, I suppose it's travelled a long way."

"Hey! Am I invisible? See how my wife welcomes you and ignores me," complained Moussa Khaliffa. "She hasn't even asked about my eye treatment. She hasn't even looked at me. I want to know if I am still handsome."

"Where's Bendo?"

But his mother had already stepped outside with a bucket to collect water. For two days, Bendo hadn't been seen or mentioned and Oby was scared of digging for information. He had already guessed the answer.

Moussa Khaliffa, his wife and children arrived at the Malassa family cabin in the big truck. "Get in! Get in!" ordered the wife of Moussa Khaliffa. "Hurry up!"

Holding onto her husband with one hand, Oby's mother

carried a small basket of acacia petals in the other. Oby, his parents and Reeta piled into the back of the truck. Everyone seemed to know what was happening except Oby. The dogs leapt in behind them and they drove north, in the direction of their destroyed village.

Oby took a long time to pluck up courage, but finally quietly asked, "Mum, what happened to Bendo?"

With the dogs barking excitedly, she either didn't hear, or ignored it, because the truck had stopped and there was such a clatter and chatter as everyone jumped off.

Oby shivered when he saw the flattened earth. The ground lay bare except for black and grey stones laid out in straight lines. So many dead. His mother held out the basket for everyone to take a few petals as they walked slowly between rows. So many stones – so many dead. His mother dipped into the basket. As petals fluttered from her fingers, tears trickled down her cheeks. His father copied, but Oby didn't know if he fully understood; there was no point in trying to explain anything to him. Boudi Malassa smiled and threw petals.

Oby crouched on the stony ground. He figured this spot was where their hut had stood. His stomach tightened and he whispered, "Where are you, Bendo?"

The wife of Moussa Khaliffa was right behind him, holding a toddler in each hand. She whispered, "What did you say?"

He whispered back, "Which stone is for Bendo?"

"Bendo doesn't need a stone. He isn't dead," she said gently. "Haven't they told you?"

"Told me what?"

"He's sick. Just sick."

"Where is he then?"

"In Tembo Dolo." She kept her voice low. "We took him there. He's being looked after by my sister who's a nurse."

"What sort of sick?"

"Malaria."

"He'll die!" Oby remembered that his friend's little sister, his aunt, his mother's cousin, his other friend's brother, his friend Sudu, all had gone with malaria because there wasn't any medicine.

"No. He's recovering well. We've got good medicine now. Life's getting better for us."

"Good medicine?"

"The best."

He said, "Why didn't anyone tell me?"

"Your poor, poor mother! Such an ordeal she's been through. She didn't think. She's exhausted. There's been so much going on … she probably thought you knew … or she just forgot … she just forgot … such difficult times."

Oby reached into the basket and clutched another handful of petals and scattered them over the ground. They scattered petals until the basket was empty.

So much fighting. So many dead.

No one could quite remember why.

* * *

"Are you going to start working those camels tomorrow?" asked Moussa Khaliffa.

"As soon as it's light."

"Good! And very soon I'm going to teach you to drive that truck."

About the Author

At age fourteen, Sidney Edgar Giraud filled three school exercise books with his first story! As a teacher, he has lived and travelled in three continents. *Chasing the River* was shortlisted in the prestigious *The Times* (*London*)/Chicken House Children's Writing Competition and is his first published novel. He lives near the sea in North Norfolk, UK, and enjoys writing poetry and stories outside in all kinds of weather.

To contact the author or for any other enquiries please send an email to jbpublishercontact@gmail.com

Printed in Great Britain
by Amazon